CUT THROAT DOG

Joshua Sobol

CUT THROAT DOG

Joshua Sobol

Translated from the Hebrew by Dalya Bilu

MELVILLE INTERNATIONAL CRIME

MELVILLEHOUSE
BROOKLYN, NEW YORK

Cut Throat Dog

Originally published as Whiskey Ze Be-Seder by Hakibbutz Hameuchad/
Siman Kriah, Tel-Aviv, 2004

© 2001, 2010 Joshua Sobol
Translated from the Hebrew by Dalya Bilu
Worldwide translation copyright © 2010 by The Institute for the Trans-
lation of Hebrew Literature
English translation copyright © 2010 by The Institute for the Transla-
tion of Hebrew Literature

Melville House Publishing
145 Plymouth Street
Brooklyn, NY 11201
www.mhpbooks.com

ISBN: 978-1-935554-21-9

First Melville House Printing: September 2010

Printed in the United States of America

Library of Congress Cataloging-in-Publication Data

Sobol, Yehoshu'a.
  [Viski zeh be-seder. English]
  Cut throat dog / by Joshua Sobol ; translated from the Hebrew by
Dalya Bilu.
    p. cm.
  ISBN 978-1-935554-21-9
  I. Bilu, Dalya. II. Title.
  PJ5054.S627V5713 2010
  892.4'36—dc22   2010025924

1

He stands on top of a high tower and looks around. At first sight he sees the sea to the west, the mountains to the north and east, and the desert to the south. Then the tower starts to grow rapidly higher, like a bamboo cane in a nature movie. Now he can see the marina with the yachts in the Famagusta harbor, the minarets of the Damascus mosques, the dams on the Tigris and the Euphrates, and the lights of Cairo and Alexandria. The tower goes on shooting upwards and his head breaks through the clouds and the strata of air above them, which become colder and colder, until the endless icebergs of Greenland are revealed in the distance, and beyond them the frozen lakes of Canada, and here's Lake Michigan, and the lacy lights of Chicago on a clear night, and the broad cornfields of Illinois, and the glass and metal forest of Manhattan, and the palmetto jungle of Florida, and the train of reefs stretching to Key West, and Cuba and Haiti, and further on Santo Domingo and the ring of the Caribbean islands, and what have they to do with you, those raised voices, that exhausting argument going on down there, in the office under your feet? The man hears his name thrown like a stone. The shouts are aimed at him. No doubt about it. They're trying to reach him, to hit him. To intercept him and force him to come down to them.

Air, air, air!

He takes a step forward, and he's gliding through the air. He draws in his arms spread out like wings and thrusts them out ahead, like an arrow, like a swimmer diving head first from a high diving board, his legs stretched out behind him, his head aimed at the ground, and his body gathering speed in a crazy dive. With a loud bang he breaks through the sound barrier and dives towards the newspapers announcing his mysterious death: 'On the eve of signing the deal of the century, for no apparent reason, the advertising tycoon Hanina Regev dives to his death'—'Was the burden of international success too much for the country boy Hanan Rogev?' screams the headlines of the rival paper. 'Was Hen Avihen, self-styled poet of lost identity, nothing but a versifier whose life had grown empty of content?' ponders a think piece in the culture supplement, while in the big city's local paper they wonder about his sexual identity as a motive for the deed: 'Was the indefatigable swinger, celebrity and womanizer, Nino Honan, simply gay preferring to get out of the world to come out of the closet?'

2

It all began when he wandered the frozen streets of Manhattan in order to kill time until his meeting with Sol Lewis, director of public relations for the pharmaceutical company, and before he realized what was happening he found himself following a man in a black suit, who walked past him while he was standing in front of the display window of the big bookstore opposite Lincoln Center. It had all begun many years before, in the most bleak and terrible chase of his life, when after running for two hours over the broad plains, as he was closing in on Jonas's murderer, he suddenly discovered, as in a nightmare, that he had set out empty-handed, and in that fraction of a second, as he bent down to pick up a stone from the hard ground of the Libyan desert which was strewn with rough pebbles, his prey slipped from sight in the dim light and disappeared behind a fold in the land, and darkness descended on the earth.

This fraction of a second comes back to haunt him now, as the back of the man in the black suit is almost swallowed up in the dank mist creeping over the streets of Manhattan between the Christmas trees decorating the buildings with their drops of sparkling light. Before disappearing into the doorway of the Irish pub, the man turns his head, as if he senses that someone is following him, and immediately the green door closes behind him. A quick glance at his watch shows that he has half an hour before his meeting with the director of public relations. Whether he's Jonas's murderer or not—a shot of whiskey is exactly what he needs now, his inner voice tells him, at the same time commanding him to wait outside for a while, in order to remove any shadow of suspicion from the heart of the man in the black suit, and to enter the pub three minutes later with a limp, and not to take off the dark sunglasses he had put on to protect his eyes from the snow which had begun to fall.

In the dim light of the pub, which is fitfully illuminated by the flickering flames of gas lamps suspended from a ceiling covered with imitation cooper tiles, he makes out the man in the black suit, who is now standing at the bar, next to a New Zealand kaka parrot in a cage, and trying to get it to join him in singing 'Jingle Bells', which he sings in a lyrical tenor, punctuated by the parrot's exhortations to fuck off.

A double shot of Bushmills, he requests in a Southern Italian accent.

A double shot of Bush what? asks the barman in the kind of Israeli accent you can only get rid of with the help of laborious exercises, such as he himself performed when learning to speak Arabic, English, Italian, French and German in a variety of strong regional accents.

Bushmills, Bushmills he told you, the man in the black suit, who was already seated at the bar, rebuked the barman. It's the bottle standing exactly underneath the muscatel.

I'm new to the business, the barman apologizes and looks for the metal double shot measuring cup.

You can see that from two miles away, the man in the black suit crushes him, and explains to the stranger in his unique velvety tenor: I had to show him the muscatel bottle too. If somebody asked for a 'Rusty Nail' he'd probably give him a rusty nail, and I don't want to even imagine what would happen if anyone ordered a 'Scotch Horse's Neck'.

What's a 'Scotch Horse's Neck'? inquires the apprentice barman with Israeli naivete.

It isn't a steak from a horse's neck, the man in the black suit says nastily. It's whiskey with vermouth, so you'll know next time.

Far from accurate, the stranger with the melodious Southern Italian accent corrects him, channeling his desire to smash the guy's face to a pulp into a series of precise instructions which he conveys to the barman with great sweetness:

Take a twist of lemon peel, stretch it from the rim to the bottom of the glass, add ice. Now take two measures of Scotch, two measures of French vermouth, two measures of

Italian vermouth, two drops of angostura, mix, pour it into the glass, and fill it up with ginger ale.

You're wasting your time, says the man in the black suit contemptuously. This guy comes from a place where they boil sweet fish balls minced with white bread in water and serve it up as food fit for human beings.

What do you say, marvels the man with the Italian accent, there are human beings who actually eat the stuff?

There are, says the man in the black suit, if you can call creatures who eat this dog food human. As long as they're over there it's no skin off my nose. But lately there are too many of them in this city.

What's your profession? The man with the Italian accent asks the barman.

I studied film, says the barman. I write scripts.

Great, says the Italian, here's the beginning of a movie script for you. Two strangers and a novice barman, who is a beginning scriptwriter, meet by chance in an Irish pub.

And what happens next? asks the barman.

Ah! The Italian smiles, that's your problem.

Beginnings are always easy, says the barman.

Right, beginnings are easy and endings are hard, agrees the man with the Italian accent, but the beginning-script-writer-barman sees that he is not the object of the speaker's interest, but the man in the black suit. And indeed, the Italian removes his dark glasses, and his eyes wander in a strange, unfocused way round the dimly lit pub, and the barman-scriptwriter notes to himself that the man is apparently almost blind. Now the blind man's eyes grope over the man in the black suit's face and fasten onto it like two laser beams reaching far into space and time. To the barman it looks as if the almost blind man is examining the man in the black suit like an entomologist contemplating an insect whose name he is straining to bring up from the recesses of his memory, as if he has already seen it once upon a time, as if he is making an effort to remember when and where he met this man before, if indeed he ever did. And while he is busy going through the archives of the mug-shots of his memory, the other addresses him in a hostile tone, and his velvety tenor is jagged as a knife:

Do you know me from somewhere?

No, the Italian makes haste to reassure the man in the black suit, whose message of suppressed violence is very clear under the velvet glove of his voice.

You're staring at me! whispers the man in the black suit in the voice of an Indian cobra a split second before it strikes.

My eyesight is very poor, the Italian apologizes. I only see patches of light, I can't make out facial features.

The man's blind, the barman hurries to relieve the tension.

A blind and bleeding soldier, the blind Italian introduces himself with an exaggerated smile.

Now you have to put on an act of searching for the glass, he says to himself, and imagines darkness and sends a groping hand cautiously in search of the whiskey glass, which the cunning barman-scriptwriter sets a little distance away from him on the bar. The backs of his fingers touch it first, and then his hand opens and takes hold of it under the eyes of the man in the black suit, mesmerized by the blind act. The hand brings the rim of the glass to the nose, and the nostrils breathe in the fumes of the triple distilled whiskey.

Sorry, the man in the black suit apologizes, I didn't notice you were blind.

Not completely, he says with an ingratiating smile, I see patches of light and shade. I can see your silhouette. But I can hardly distinguish between your face and your suit.

And he brings his face close to the jacket of the man's elegant suit and puts out a hesitant hand:

May I? Touching complements what remains of my vision.

Go ahead, the owner of the black suit presents the fabric of his jacket to the fingers of the visually impaired soldier, who notes an unmistakable fact: the man is looking at him with intent curiosity, as if he too is trying to clarify to himself who this blind man reminds him of, or where he knows him from.

The beginning scriptwriter-barman looks at them through the gleaming glass he is holding as he polishes it to a high shine, and sees a picture that ignites his imagination: two strangers permitting themselves the kind of intimacy that exists only between co-conspirators about to carry out a prearranged plan together. More and more the pair look to him like a dangerous hit team seconds before an act of violence. To be on the safe side he moves a little to the right, so as to be within reach of the black C-Z pistol lying under the counter with a bullet in its barrel.

Fine cashmere, pronounces the blind soldier, rolling the 'r' in a heavy Sicilian accent.

You understand something about fabrics, says the owner of the black suit admiringly.

Syracusians are well known for their sharp senses, he embarks on a fishing expedition, but since the guy doesn't take the bait he tries another direction:

I've been looking for a suit like that for years, he announces.

Is that so? The owner of the black suit says in surprise, Did you ever see a suit like this before?

A few years ago I was in some place in Scotland. They had cashmere suits there but there was a problem with the trousers. One of my legs is a little shorter than the other.

Were you born like that?

I was hurt in an accident. They removed a piece of the bone.

Now the barman-scriptwriter is sure the two men are exchanging loaded messages, and he pricks up his ears so as not to miss a word.

That place in Scotland, the man in the black suit presses a point in the code, do you remember where it was exactly?

Yes, it was a big commercial center on the high road, between villages, says the blind man.

Did they make whiskey there too?

Whiskey with a brown color, almost like Macallan, but very soft and friendly.

Auchentoshen? suggests the man in the black suit.

No, says the blind man, even though the place, as far as I remember, isn't far from Dunbartonshire. It's on the A-9, about eight or nine miles North of Pitlochry, or St Andrews....

Bruar?

That's it! The blind man leaps on the fateful code word: Bruar! Is the suit from there?

Yes and no, says the owner of the suit: there's a store here that imports these suits from over there.

Here in Manhattan? The blind man exclaims, barely able to conceal his excitement.

When you go out of the pub, the cashmere man directs him, turn right, walk to the corner, turn right again, and go into the third store from the corner. Go to the men's department and ask for Winnie. She'll take care of you.

Thank you, says the blind man, thank you very much. He finishes off the rest of the Bushmills, puts the glass down carefully on the counter, and holds out his hand to the owner of the cashmere suit. When the latter shakes his hand, he notes that he has a rapid pulse rate, an unhealthy heart and a defective blood supply. The man is quick-tempered and impatient, but on the whole a short-distance runner, he sums up to himself and starts to limp out of the pub, but at the last moment he changes his mind. He stops and asks the barman for directions to the toilet. The barman offers to lead him there, but he declines the offer politely and firmly:

No, thanks, I have to get along alone in the world. Just give me exact directions.

The barman gives him instructions including directions, distances, and the number of steps to be descended, and the bleeding soldier sets out with measured steps and disappears down the stairs.

What a guy, says the barman admiringly, trying to get a lead into the labyrinth of this close and mysterious relationship. He wonders what war the man was wounded in.

But the man in the cashmere suit refuses to volunteer any information. On the other hand, as soon as they hear the toilet door slam shut, he makes haste to get hold of the person called 'Winnie' on his cell phone and inform her of the imminent arrival of a purblind Italian customer with a limp, worth investing in. Give him a good time, like you know how, and get what you can out of him.

Then he leaves a crumpled ten dollar bill on the bar and hurries out without waiting for change or saying goodbye.

At the same time, in the toilet, the blind-Italian impersonator takes out his cell phone and punches a number. He's on hold, merde, he curses in French. He hangs up and decides to wait half a minute and try again. But suddenly the cell phone vibrates in his hand. He looks at the display. Yadanuga is getting back to him. He touches the green button and takes the call.

Hello, Shakespeare, says Yadanuga's warm baritone from the other side of the world, you called me?

Tell me, Yadanuga, he whispers, can you imagine Adonas's mug without a beard?

Whose mug? Yadanuga can't make out what his friend is saying.

Tino the Syrian, nu, the one we called Tino Rossi because of his egg-yolk tenor, says Shakespeare.

Are you talking about Adonas the maniac who murdered Jonas? asks Yadanuga.

Yes, says Shakespeare, I think I've tracked him down here in Manhattan.

For God's sake! Shakespeare! protests Yadanuga. What are you getting into?!

I'm sure it's him, says Shakespeare. The trouble is he's shaved off his beard. But judging by the walk and the voice it's him. Shut your eyes, turn on your visual imagination, and describe his face to me without the beard. How do you see his cheekbones and chin?

Close that case, Shakespeare! You finished Adonas off with your own legs four hundred years ago!

I didn't finish him off, Shakespeare insists. I lost sight of him in the dark. I'm telling you this character has a lyrical tenor that's unmistakable.

Intelligence reports said explicitly that his body was found in the Libyan desert, exactly where you lost sight of him, Yadanuga tries to remind him.

Forget our intelligence, Shakespeare snaps in an angry voice. We've already seen what they know.

In this case the information is accurate, protests Yadanuga. The Belgian pathologist confirmed that the guy died of dehydration and a torn liver.

I saw the Belgian pathologist's report too, says Shakespeare, but how do you know that the body he examined was Adonas's?

Get it into your head, Yadanuga pleads, Adonas is dead!

Not for me, says Shakespeare in a voice that reaches the pricked-up ears of the barman, who is amazed to hear Hebrew coming from behind the toilet door.

You killed him before the flood, says Yadanuga. Leave that ghost alone, Shakespeare!

Thanks, Yadanuga, says Shakespeare, you've never been so unhelpful as in this case. I'll leave him alone when I've turned him into a ghost.

The barman takes a little notebook labeled 'Ideas for scripts' out of his pocket, and while the blind man lingers in the toilet he writes: 'The cashmere man, the blind man, Winnie' and adds in brackets: 'The cashmere man called Adonas—a neo-Nazi anti-Semite. The blind man—an Israeli impersonating an Italian. Apparently a Mossad agent. Winnie—apparently works as a sales assistant in a men's fashion store round the corner. Investigate.'

When Shakespeare comes out of the toilet he is not surprised to find that the man in the black suit is gone. His hasty disappearance from the scene reinforces his suspicion that this is the man he has been searching for for eighteen years.

The man who was here, is he a regular customer? He asks the barman in Italian English.

I don't know, replies the barman in Hebrew. I've only been here a week. This is the first time I've seen him.

How did he know where you're from? Shakespeare asks in Hebrew.

From the accent I suppose, says the barman.

Now it is clear to Shakespeare that he has to meet Winnie, but he decides to make it hard for her to identify him.

If you see that man, he says to the barman, who interrupts him:

I have the feeling that the anti-Semitic dog won't show his face here again.

What makes you think so?

He got out of here like a crook running from the scene of the crime, pronounces the barman.

If you run into him anywhere by chance, here's the number of my cell phone. If you get voice mail, leave a message that Adonis is alive, and he was seen at such and such a place.

Adonis or Adonas? inquires the scriptwriter.

To you—Adonis, says Shakespeare.

No problem, says the excited scriptwriter and holds out his hand and introduces himself: Turel Shlush.

From the famous Shlush family?

A branch of the family, says Turel modestly. I'll help you get your hands on this Adonis.

That's music to my ears, Shakespeare shakes Turel Shlush's cold hand. If you leave a message, say it's from Tyrell.

And what should I call you? asks Tyrell of the icy hands.

Invent a name, Shakespeare challenges him.

Not Fellini, says Tyrell, not Zeffirelli, not Antonioni—you know what? I can't find a name to fit you.

Why not?

Because you give off something terribly confusing, confesses Tyrell with a kind of naive embarrassment that touches Shakespeare's heart.

I'll tell you my real name, says Shakespeare, but don't pass it on.

It won't cross my lips, Tyrell swears without saying 'I swear'. I was in an undercover unit in the army. I know what a double identity is.

Call me Hanina, says Shakespeare.

Hanina! repeats the astonished Tyrell. The last name in the world I would have given you.

Why? Hanina pretends innocence.

Because you're not a Hanina! You're a Maoz, a Giora, a Tavor, says Tyrell, never a Hanina! I can't call you Hanina!

Then call me 'S.N.F.'

Which stands for what?

Secret nameless friend, says Shakespeare and leaves the pub.

The barman is happy to be left alone in the deserted pub, in this damp, solitary hour of a winter afternoon. He hurries to take out his notebook. He turns to a new page, writes the heading 'Secret Nameless Friend', and begins to write feverishly.

3

Nobody loved Hanina. Hanina was once in love with a woman, but even when he loved he wasn't beloved. There was nothing about him that people love to love. Hanina himself, a sturdily built man, didn't love any of the two hundred and forty eight body parts he had received from nature, and he refused to accept his body until he had laboriously reshaped every single part of it. Be it his jaws or his chin, his fingers or his toes. Already as a youngster his legs seemed to him too short and thick. Exhausting exercise, cruel self-discipline, endurance developed to the limits of the ability of the nervous system to bear pain—and even beyond, to the point where the pain is so intense that it numbs pain—finally resulted in the ability of his short legs to carry him distances that Olympic long-distance runners could only dream of, and his terrifying kicks sent more than a few believers, who had joyfully joined the holy war in the knowledge that the pleasures of this world are very small compared to those of the next as promised in the Repentance Sura of the Koran, to Paradise.

The shortness of his legs had stopped bothering him long ago, and their remarkable power, of which we will hear more later, had turned into a source of private amusement and practical jokes, such as the limp he just adopted, and which he now abandoned as he entered the elegant store. He made for the men's department and proceeded to the suits section with a springy, almost dancing, step, his darting eyes boldly appraising the shapely sales assistants and challenging them: let's see you recognizing me now, Winnie. If you've got any sense, we'll have a secret that Mister Adonis, who sent me to you, doesn't know. Who are you, Winnie? Are you the slender black sales assistant with the ample breasts and the shaved head? Or are you the other one, the one with the childish face and the boyish haircut, wasp-waisted and stringy limbed, like the long-legged Segestria Perfida spider?

While his eyes are darting from one to the other the black sales assistant approaches him and asks how she can help him.

I'm looking for a black cashmere suit, he says in a French accent.

She asks for his size and as he answers her the long-legged spidery wasp intervenes and points out to her colleague that this dangerous man belongs to the impudent race of the short-legged. She conveys this strange diagnosis in a whisper, but she makes sure that it will reach his ears. The provocation is like a surprising opening move in a game of chess.

Wait until you see how thick they are, he winks at the treacherous spider with his non-aiming left eye, while his aiming eye, which has seen the whites of the eyes of quite a few men in the last second of their lives, penetrates her with the sharpness of a laser beam.

I can't wait to see! The long-legged spider laughs suggestively and adds a question:

Hey, who are you spending the holiday with?

With a secret nameless friend, says Shakespeare.

Wow, the spider exclaims enthusiastically, a secret nameless friend! I'm dying to meet him!

He's standing in front of you on two short legs, which are just long enough to reach from his ass to the floor.

I'm spending the holiday alone with a secret nameless friend too, says the Segestria spider.

The question is whether we'll be alone together or apart, says Shakespeare.

Being alone on Christmas is like being a parrot in a cage in a deserted pub, whistling 'Strangers in the Night' to itself, says the spider with the stringy limbs.

They exchange cell phone numbers, and after abandoning the idea of the suit, he sets out for his meeting with the director of public relations in the pharmaceutical firm.

4

The meeting in Sol Lewis's office goes on for hours. Sol doesn't talk. He has a DVD presentation that does the work for him. He clears his throat like an opera singer about to break into an aria, and then he produces a special voice, monotonous and metallic, by whose means he commands the system to bring up the ultimate-love-pill project, all in one zero two. The DVD goes into action, and the Barko projects onto the shining screen the lecture delivered by Sol Lewis himself, and intended for the ears of the directors of the advertising agencies selected to enter the final stage of the competition for the rights to design the advertising campaign to promote the all-in-one new pill produced by Biomedic Org-Chemic Industries. The figure of Sol Lewis now fills the screen. He is sitting behind a desk, upon which three thick volumes are lying, his head as bald as a potato, his flushed face ruthlessly shaved, his thick neck strangled by a blue tie, and speaking directly to the camera. His lecture is very methodical, very clear and organized, and he repeats three or four times every message he wants to convey to the directors of the advertising agencies who have reached the short list before the finishing line. Hanina waits for Sol to stop the screening and give him the CD, so that he can pass it on to Mackie, otherwise known as Yadanuga, 'the art director of my office', he explains to Sol Lewis, but Sol has no intention of foregoing the pleasure of watching his skilled and eloquent performance in the company of another viewer. Hanina stares with empty eyes at the figure several times larger than life talking and talking and talking on the screen in front of him, and tries to pretend that he is riveted by the sea of verbiage. There is no doubt that this nudnik derives sexual gratification from the use he makes of his mouth in order to spew out more and more words, more and more well-organized sentences, whose sole purpose is to clarify to the directors of the advertising agencies, and their creative and technical teams, what Biomedic Org-Chemic Industries expects them to convey, by means of a striking image and a thirty second clip, to the potential purchasers of the pill which is about to grant them total satisfaction and blissful happiness in their emotional, sex and love lives.

Three times, each time slightly differently, Sol Lewis explains to them, that in contrast to its predecessors, the new pill is intended for both men and women; that it increases not only the capacity, but also the desire of both sexes—and in addition to its amazing ability to lengthen the male member by three inches if taken for three months, it also has the ability to lengthen the duration of the sexual act and to shorten the recovery time between the orgasm and the new erection. But the main thing, Sol explains—and in this too the pill is essentially different from all its predecessors—is that this astonishing all-in-one product by Biomedic Org-Chemic Industries not only arouses the sexual mechanism, it also has an wonderfully beneficial effect on the emotions it enables participants in their orgy of pleasure to derive from their sexual interaction. In other words, Sol Lewis repeats for the benefit of those who have not yet understood the message, this pill awakens and arouses love between the two participants in the above sexual interaction.

And for anyone who has not yet grasped the significance of the revolution this wonder pill is going to bring about in our lives, Sol Lewis repeats for the third time, couples who take the pill in the afternoon will find themselves falling madly in love during the course of dinner, especially since red wine in the amount of up to three quarters of a pint per person increases the effect of the pill twofold, both on the emotional and the functional plane, and thus, after drinking two glasses of wine, or after emptying a bottle together, our happy couple will reach a pre-climactic state in the flaring of their passion for each other, while the climax of their mutual love will of course be reserved for those who continue the journey of desire with the help of the pill to the full realization of the act of love, in the laundered and squeaky-clean formulation of Sol Lewis, whose thick tongue occasionally licks his fat pink lips, and whose eyes pop out of their sockets behind his gleaming glasses.

Somehow the screening comes to an end, not before Sol Lewis reminds his listeners in the advertising agencies that they are expected to convey this entire complex package of messages by means of a single image, which will be developed in the course of a thirty second clip, and whose content will be conveyed to the viewer by means of a visual message alone. 'Let the picture talk', Sol exhorts his anonymous listeners, 'let it talk to the Chinese, to the Portuguese, to Germans and Russians in the very same language. Let it persuade the educated viewer in a language that will also be clear to a goat herd in the Caucasus', he repeats the message for the third time, and concludes his speech with the magic formula: 'Remember that everyone wants to be happy. And when you say 'happy' you say love, passion, intimacy, potency, excitement, enjoyment, pleasure, satisfaction.'

Impressive, says Hanina. Very impressive.

The result of many hours of hard work, says Sol.

I'll show it to my team, promises Hanina, I'm sure it will be a powerful source of inspiration for them.

Give it your best shot, Sol urges him, I know that the Japanese team have already invested a huge effort in the project.

My people will do their best, promises Hanina.

That's not enough, Sol warns him. If you want to win, you'll have to outdo yourselves. In the past you've proved that you can do it, if you see what I mean.

Don't worry, Hanina reassures him. I was in command of a team that took care of international terrorists.

No, really! exclaims Sol in excitement. What do you say! His face turns red, his eyes are damp, his potato nose quivers, he looks as if he has taken one of his own magic pills. What do you say! He says again, and his voice betrays a longing for closeness to the tough, virile man standing in front of him, and for a moment it seems that he will be unable to resist the impulse to fall on the object of his desire and clasp him to his bosom in a tight embrace.

But the agitated Sol is still at the stage of foreplay:

You killed terrorists with your own hands? He whispers in an aroused voice.

With my own hands, admits Hanina and displays hands equipped with short, thick fingers of equal length. Sol stares spellbound at the hands of his interlocutor, and suddenly he takes one of Hanina's hard hands in his hand, which is as soft as a warm roll, and declares with profound emotion:

I'm rooting for you. My grandmother's mother's name was Leah. Lewis comes from Leahles. When they arrived in America they changed Leyeles to Lewis.

Wos zogs du! the words escape Hanina.

Where's the Yiddish from?! asks Sol.

From my parents, says Hanina. They spoke to each other in Yiddish.

I only know a few words, apologizes Sol, and lists his Yiddish vocabulary: *meshuga, a zoch un wei, a yachne, shul, davenen, a kurvele.*

Apropos the *kurvele*, says Hanina, have you tried this pill yourself?

God forbid, says Sol. If I had to try all our products I would have been making *fartzen in zamd* a long time ago.

You know that expression? marvels Hanina.

My parents used it, Sol recalls and is flooded with longings for his parents, who for many years have been breaking wind in the Jewish cemetery in Brooklyn.

Can you let me have a few of the pills? asks Hanina.

Just for you, says Sol. They're not packaged for marketing yet. I have to warn you that they're still in the experimental stage. And it goes without saying, don't pass them on to anyone else and don't talk about them to anyone.

You're talking to a graveyard of secrets, says Hanina.

I know, Sol whispers admiringly. I know.

5

Hanina emerges into the city, where a wintry wind is raging, howling in the narrow passages quarried through it by the skyscrapers like tunnels in the bowels of a mountain. He strides down the street illuminated by thousands of sparkling Christmas lights, and as he calls the young sales assistant on his cell phone the fingers of his left hand play with the packet of Sol Leyeles's pills in his pocket.

Hi honey, he says, this is the dangerous man with the short leg here.

Hi, she says, do you want to come round?

If you want me to.

Very much, she says, but I have to warn you that it will cost you something.

Sure, he says, in this life the only thing you get for nothing is death.

It's five hundred dollars till midnight, or a thousand for the whole night.

Including breakfast? he asks.

You're a real piece of work! She laughs with a sound of tinkling bells from the other side of the satellite wandering through space. For you—including breakfast.

Dinner is on me, he says after she gives him the address. And he adds: Including red wine.

6

After clicking three locks and drawing back two bolts, she opens the door and sways and shies away from him like a praying mantis in brief black running pants and a black tank top, all arms and legs of a still-growing adolescent girl. Her long skinny legs shoot up like two bamboo canes from black Doc Martens, high and heavy, as if she has just returned from a hike in the country. The contrast between the clumsy masculine boots and the stork legs underlines her boyish appearance, and he wonders if he isn't getting involved with a minor here. The wide bracelets on her wrists draw his attention to the vein-slashing scars underneath them. He looks up and meets her narrowed eyes, weepy eyes that examine him with feline curiosity. She sees that he has registered the scars and sends him a smile that may be naive or embarrassed, or maybe it comes from bottomless sadness and terrible bitterness, because her full lips stay sealed when she smiles, and he asks himself if they express sensuality or disgust, and the narrowed weepy eyes, are they alive or dead? A dark grasshopper silhouette against a background of Manhattan's sea of lights, whose waves break against the glass of the huge picture window, which takes up an entire wall of the one room apartment, whose area he estimates with a comprehensive glance at thirty-five square meters. He notes to himself that there is only one entrance, that the kitchenette adjoins the living space, with no dividing wall, takes a quick look inside the open bathroom door to make sure there's nobody there—and thus, in the habit acquired during the years of pursuit and liquidation, he concludes the screening procedure and answers the questionnaire he internalized during those stormy years, the strict compliance with which saved his life and the lives of the members of his team, until the Alsatian caught it in India, and Jonas ended his life in the team's last liquidation operation, in the terrible pursuit in the desert of Tino the Syrian, who he is now trying to reach through this young woman, facing him here in all the enigma of her youth. He hands her the bottle of Cote-de-Ventoux he bought in the wine shop on the corner of 14th Street, and says:

Half's yours, the rest's mine.

And when she laughs, and starts tearing off the paper, and he is sure that this apartment is not a trap—only then he closes the front door behind him and takes care to bolt at least one of the locks.

You don't have to worry about the window, says the perfidious spider, who picks up on his warning and control system with the senses of an alley cat, you're on the twenty-first floor, and that window doesn't open.

Fortunately, he says without going into details. But her sad smile confirms that she has taken in everything unsaid hiding behind that single word, and they both know that both of their suicidal pasts are now filling the empty space between them.

In the meantime she strips the bottle of its wrapping, and the tissue paper rustles in the silence.

Coat de Ventooks! she cries in a New York accent.

You know it?

I'm not sure, she hesitates, although the name rings a bell.

Have you ever been to Combs d'Arnevel? he asks.

Comb Darnavel? No, where is it?

In France, he says, in the North-East of the province of Chateauneuf du Pape, this wine comes from there, and I almost died there.

What from?

An agricultural problem, he says. Somebody wanted to fertilize a vineyard with my corpse. I preferred to fertilize it with his.

And we're going to drink his blood tonight? she says provocatively.

Are you a vegetarian?

Do I look like a vegetarian? She says with a wry smile.

No, he admits. Although it would be alright even if you were.

From what point of view?

This wine goes well with lamb, fish and vegetarian dishes as well.

You took all eventualities into account, she expresses her appreciation.

It's become my second nature, he reassures her.

Since that night in the vineyards of Arnevel? she guesses.

Long before that, he says.

But since then you celebrate with this wine?

When I take a risk.

Do you feel threatened?

Yes, he admits. Very threatened.

By me? she asks.

No, he says. By my id.

Do you still believe in Freud? she asks.

Who do you believe in? he asks her in return.

Who do you expect me to believe in after my Lacanian therapist tried to persuade me that it was okay to try to commit suicide, if that was the first step I had to take in the process of my individuation in order to be who I am? She laughs with weepy eyes.

A Lacanian therapist in New York?!

He's Hispanic, she explains. He was a student in Paris in the sixties, a student of Guattari and as crazy as him. Antipsychiatrist, anti-philosopher, anti-human.

What's his name?

What does it matter, she says dismissively, Ramon Gasparo, a name to forget. He would tell you that you're simply afraid to fall in love, because the thing you call your id, is the sexual attraction and the sex that begin in the place where the ego ends.

This spider is a trap, he says to himself. She's a lot more sophisticated than she looks, or else she's just trying to make an impression with a bit of bullshit she learnt by heart to turn on clients looking for an intellectual whore.

So, she says, was that just an overture, or is your id really threatening your ego?

The whole system, he says, trying to access the depth and breadth of this consciousness confronting him. Dangerous volcanic activity has been taking place lately, deep down in the bowels of the mountain, far below the tunnels and shafts of the abandoned mine.

Take a hot bath with lavender oil, she suggests, and relax.

I'll leave the door open, he says.

It doesn't bother me, she reassures him.

She starts filling the bath. The phone rings. She glances at the display and freezes like a rabbit thrown into a cage with a python. The phone goes on ringing until the answering machine comes on. An unmistakable velvety tenor rises from the machine and commands her softly: 'Pick up the phone. You're there. I know you're there. Bryant's waiting for you at his place. Take a taxi and go there now. If you don't pick up the phone I'm coming round, and it'll be bad. I'm not kidding. I'm waiting on the line.'

Should I answer? asks the secret nameless friend.

No, she says. I'll answer.

She picks up the receiver and answers in the voice of a frightened child:

Hi, Tony, is that you? I was in the bathroom. I'm working. I've got somebody here. I can't come to Bryant's now. No, I can't go out at midnight either. He took me for the whole night. No, it's not the blind Italian. He's Japanese. Not a businessman. A wrestler. Judo I think.

Ikido, barks the secret nameless friend in a Japanese accent, Ikido-ka.

Yes, she says into the phone, it's him you hear. You don't want to talk to him. He doesn't speak English well.

The secret friend signals her to hand him the receiver. She gives it to him and he informs Tony in Japanese English that he has hired the lady for a week, and he doesn't like to be disturbed.

For a moment there's silence on the other end, and then Tony's velvety voice returns:

A week?! The fucking bitch took you for a week? Give her to me!

You not talking to girl, says the Japanese wrestler in broken English. I take her till January two.

Give her to me right now! Tony raises the volume of his tenor by two decibels.

Talk quiet, says the Japanese, or you talk through my ass.

Sir, the tenor called Tony softens, you can't have her for a week. She's not free. It's impossible. You can only have her for one night.

I stay with girl how much time she likes, states the Japanese in a tone that brooks no argument, and adds: And how much time I like.

She can't do what she likes, Tony tries to explain.

You mistake, the Japanese corrects him in a quiet voice. She can. She free person.

What the fuck are you talking about? Tony erupts. Free person my ass. She does what I tell her. She's full up all week. You can have her for two hours max. In two hours time you're getting the hell out of there.

Forget it, says Hanina quietly.

Don't fuck with me! Tony's voice is menacing.

Why not? asks Hanina like a child in third grade.

Why not?! Tony yells as if he can't believe his ears. And suddenly he changes his tone. Hey! You're no fucking Jap.

Oh, no? says the fucking Jap in surprise.

That's not how fucking Japs talk, pronounces Tony.

How do fucking Japs talk? inquires the fucking Jap.

Fucking Japs don't answer a question with a question, states Tony, and adds: If you see what I mean?

So how do fucking Japs answer? The Jap answers a question with a question.

I'll tell you what you are, Tony spits out in a voice full of loathing.

Suddenly there's a long silence on the other end of the line.

Hello? The non-Japanese challenges his silent interlocutor. You promised to tell me what I am.

You know what you are, says Tony, you're a sonofabitch son of Satan.

You're wrong, I'm Satan himself in person. Body and soul.

You think everybody's afraid of you? Tony's voice seethes with hatred. I'm not afraid of you!

Who's 'you'? asks Satan in a Satanic tone. Who are you talking about?

I'm talking about you, the man called Tony refuses to elaborate, you!

But who is this 'you'? Satan persists. Are you talking about devils?

You people are worse than devils, Tony says heatedly, you're a curse, you're the fucking disease of the human race!

You still haven't told me who you're talking about, says Satan in an amused tone.

You're everywhere, you're like the sand on the seashore. A person can't go anywhere in this town without bumping into you. In the streets, the offices, businesses, stores, hospitals, restaurants, courts, the opera, the newspapers, television, the media, the banks, you push in everywhere like cockroaches crawling out of the sewers!

Are you talking about some kind of animal? Satan wonders.

Animals? What animals? What are wolves or snakes compared to you. You're wild animals in human form! A person only has to read your history to understand who you are.

Really? Satan pours more oil on the fire burning in the heart of his interlocutor. What for instance did you find in our history that helped you to understand something?

You tortured your prophets, accuses Tony. You threw them in jail.

What do you say? Satan goes on provoking him. That's really terrible!

The prophets told the truth about you, pronounces Tony.

You speak like a scholar, says Shakespeare, how did you end up dealing in women? Via drug dealing? Is it connected to something you did in your past?

It's connected to your fucking mother, Tony embarks on a monologue composed entirely of obscenities and curses.

The longer the outpouring of curses continues the more certain Shakespeare becomes that the voice over the phone is indeed that of Tino the Syrian, in other words 'Tino Rossi', who he himself had given the name of 'Adonis' when he came up with the first plan to liquidate him with the help of a Lebanese hunter who received a handsome sum in the course of a nocturnal boar hunt in the valley of Lebanon. Certain as he is, all he has to go on is the sound of the voice implanted in his memory, which he learned to know in the course of listening to Adonis's phone calls. But the more he tries to concentrate on this voice, the more the memory dims, until he begins to doubt whether it is indeed the velvety voice that caressed his ear two decades ago. He needs to make him go on talking.

What exactly did the prophets say? he throws him a bone.

They said that you're all a terrible plague, that there's nothing healthy in you, that you're a rotten stinking sore that can't be cured, from head to foot....

'From the sole of the foot even unto the head there is no soundness in it', he hears the voice of Meir Blechman, the Bible teacher, who liked to stand before the class and declaim the terrible lines from Isaiah with pathos: 'Wounds and bruises and putrifying sores: they have not been closed neither bound up, neither mollified with ointment.' And Tony continues:

Your lips tell only lies, and your tongues speak only evil, and your hands are filthy with blood!

'Your hands are full of blood', he hears Blechman's voice again, getting in the way of his attempts to identify the familiar stranger.

You should all be loaded on old freighters, and drowned in the middle of the sea, like rats in a trap!

Do you know who you're talking to? Hanina tries a different tack.

I know, says Tony, I'm talking to a rat.

What do you know about this rat that you're talking to? asks Hanina.

I know everything I need to know.

Did you ever meet him, this particular rat who's talking to you now?

It's enough to know one rat in order to know all there is to know about all rats, pronounces Tony.

I'm afraid you don't yet know everything about rats, says the rat.

You're all sons of dogs, sons of apes, sons of asses! The zoologist gets carried away.

Make up your mind, says the rat, sons of dogs, apes or asses?

You think you're so smart? You're always smarter than everyone else. You think you can screw the whole world. You treat other people like animals. Like insects. You think you're permitted everything, because of what was done to you. Let me to tell you: what was done to you is nothing compared to what's waiting for you. This time nobody will come to your defense. This time we'll finish you off.

Why don't you start with one rat? Hanina suggests. No reply. Hello? calls Hanina, hello? Mister exterminator? Hello?

Hanina decides to use his final weapon:

Sir, I'm sorry to inform you that you'll never see Miss Winnie again. Not on the second of January and not ever. You can cross her off the list of the girls who work for you.

And that's just the beginning. I'll take them all away from you, one by one.

The silence on the other end of the line goes on for two or three seconds, and then the stranger's voice comes on again, and it seems to have undergone a change:

Why are you provoking death?

It's a habit, replies Hanina.

Wait till we meet! Tony says in a menacing voice.

Why wait? Give me your address, and I'll be happy to pay you a visit right away, says Death and winks at Winnie, who looks at him with wide open eyes.

I know where you are, blusters Tony, and you won't get away from me.

I'm always at your side, says Death.

What do you mean? Tony loses his confidence.

Your hands sweat, your pulse is rapid and irregular. Your heart's not healthy. You're not at your best. I won't let go of you until you're mine. And let me tell you, my word is worth more than a contract with a lawyer from Chicago, promises Death.

A strangled cough and the sound of throat clearing rises from the receiver.

What's the matter, inquires Death, is your throat dry? Never fear: you won't die before we meet, and that will be sooner than you think.

Go to hell! screams Tony. I'll find you!

Let me make it easier for you, Death offers generously, here's my cell phone number, and I'll always be happy to tell you where I am. Have you got something to write with?

You can stick your fucking number up your ass!

Death is unfazed by the obscenity. He dictates the number, and hears the victim clicking the digits into the memory of his electronic diary, or his cell phone, and after he finishes he asks:

What's your fucking name?

For you—Shylock, replies Death, you want me to spell it?

Go and get fucked!

At the moment we're not in the mood, Shakespeare laughs, but if we feel like it, I promise you we will. Do you have any more requests or suggestions?

You'll be sorry you ever met me, Tony promises.

One of us will be sorry, says Death, but we will meet.

Silence. Then the phone slams.

Who told you my name was Winnie? she asks.

Your fucking pimp, who sent you the blind Italian.

The minute you walked into the store, she confesses, I knew it was you.

Even though I didn't have a limp, and I wasn't particularly blind either?

Yes. For a second she withdraws into herself. At that moment I took it all in.

What did you take in?

You, she says. And a few other things.

What exactly?

That I'd been waiting for you for a long time.

Don't try to give me that shit, he clips her wings.

I'm not, she vows. I need you. You can save me. If you want to. But I don't have the right to ask it of you.

Everyone has the right to ask for help, he says.

But I know the danger I'm placing you in.

You want to free yourself of that scum?

Yes, she says, very much, but....

Consider it done, he says.

It won't be so simple, she brings him back to reality.

It's up to him, he says. If he lets go—

He won't let go, she states.

Then we'll arrive at the moment of truth.

Aren't you afraid at all? She examines him through narrowed eyes.

How long have you known him? he asks her. Maybe the answer will come from her, or at least a clue that will enable him to ascertain that this man is indeed the same Adonas who evaded death twice, in spite of the claims of intelligence.

I've known him for two years, she says. Why do you ask?

What do you know about him?

I know he has a collection of firearms and knives, and that he's a computer and cell phone freak.

What's his surname?

I don't know, she says. Both the girls who work for him and the clients call him Tony, or 'The Singer'.

Why 'The Singer?' he asks.

Because of his voice, she says, and she adds: He sings beautifully.

Have you seen him naked? he asks.

What do you want to know? she asks.

Distinguishing marks, he says.

Where?

On his stomach.

I've never seen his stomach, she says.

What have you seen?

Nothing, she says.

He doesn't go to bed with you? Hanina is surprised.

No, she says. He does it standing up. From behind. With his clothes on.

Do you know where he lives?

I know one address, she says, but I think he has more than one.

Does he travel a lot?

Yes, she says. He's always on the move. He keeps changing his cars and he owns a yacht, I think, and sometimes he disappears for a few days.

Does he play a musical instrument? he asks.

Play a musical instrument? She sounds puzzled. Not that I know.

No, he says to himself, she's not helping me to identify him.

What are you going to do? she asks apprehensively.

He said things he deserves to die for.

I'm on probation, she says, and I don't want to get into any more trouble than I'm in already.

It's got nothing to do with you, he reassures her. It's between him and me. And don't worry. He deserves to die, but I won't be his executioner. On the other hand, I won't save him when he's hovering between life and death either. Can I go and bathe?

Yes, she says, your bath is ready.

Excellent, he says, talking to him is like a roll in the gutter.

Can I ask something else? Don't call me Winnie? For you I want to be Melissa.

Melissa, he tries out the name, why not?

He goes to the bathroom, and when he starts to get undressed the phone rings again. Melissa looks at the display and says as if asking permission:

It isn't Tony. It's a private client of mine. A pervert who comes over the phone, but he pays good money.

You're a free agent, he says. Do what you like.

But my time is yours, she says carefully, trying to establish the nature of their agreement and the relations between them: You hired me for a week?......

I didn't hire you, he says. I rented a room, not the landlady. If that's okay with you.

It's fine with me, she says, still having difficulty understanding him.

She picks up the phone and listens. Every now and then she says 'Yes'. She covers the mouthpiece with her hand and turns once more to the nameless man whom she understands less and less:

Are you sure you don't mind me being on the phone while you're in the bath?

If anything bothers me, he says, I'll tell you.

He takes a glass, pours himself a double shot from the bottle of Jameson standing on the unpolished oak of the work counter in the kitchen, and goes into the bathroom.

Are you naked? she asks in a nasal simper over the phone. Today I want you to take everything off and give me all your magnificent body. My pussy's so wet, I want you in the raw.

He strips off his clothes and gets thoughtfully into the bath. She opens a book lying on the little table next to the telephone, puts on a pair of reading glasses with narrow cats-eye frames, and as he sinks into the warm caressing foam he sees her through the open door, sitting opposite the galaxy of Manhattan shining in the window and whispering into the receiver, in a husky voice full of phony lust, a passage of hard-core porn which she reads from the book in her hand. He listens to the banal text professionally performed by this half-woman half-child, and he doesn't feel a thing.

Suddenly it seems to him that he's playing a part in some scene from a script written by somebody else. Maybe that kid in the pub, Tyrell from the undercover unit. The director yells 'action', and he sees the assistant director signaling him to take a sip of the sweetish Irish whiskey and not to look at the camera. He reaches for the glass standing on the black marble slab at the side of the bathtub, which is apparently intended for uses such as this, raises it to his lips, and sips. He rolls the whiskey round in his mouth and now it is clear to him that he is indeed acting in a movie.

This is a true story, he hears the voice in the trailer say, the story of the secret life of the undercover agent H.R., otherwise known as Billy the Bard, or Shakespeare for short. A story of desperate manhunts, daring assassinations, friendship between men, love sanctified in blood that won't let our hearts forget. In his ears he hears the words of the song that for some reason, when sung by twenty-year-old girls in khaki uniforms, still thrills him to this day.

No, none of this is real, he says to himself, this isn't happening to you, you're not in New York, this girl isn't a whore, her name isn't Melissa or Victoria, just as your name isn't Bill or Shakespeare. All this is happening in some crazy Hollywood studio, but what can he do when the loathsome voice of that son of Satan goes on echoing in his head, and he feels his fingers moving of their own accord at the ends of his arms dangling over the sides of the tub, scenting action, itching to grip the handle of a pistol or a dagger and do what they do best.

And when he raises the whiskey glass to his mouth again, he is suddenly sure that the mind making up the script has already set a date for the unavoidable meeting between him and Tony—whether the guy is really Tino Rossi or not, he knows that the meeting will take place. If he knows anything it's that the scene of this meeting, from which only one of them will come out alive, is already written and only waiting to be executed. It hasn't yet been decided where it will take place, on the deck of a yacht in the middle of the sea, or in the desert, or in a cellar, or in an abandoned loft piled with junk, but he is already being led to this fateful meeting like a blind man, and he hears Shakespeare's familiar voice speaking to him in the second person: You'll pretend to be blind. You'll wear a faded, shabby khaki-beige raincoat, stained with oil and wine and mud, you'll cover your eyes with dark glasses and your head with a bald latex wig, topped with an old hat, not a fedora, a bowler hat!

Yes, that's clear, an ancient bowler hat from a hundred year ago. You'll appear to him like a nightmare, like a character in an old Irish play, groping your way with a white blind man's cane...and you'll have a dog too, of course! A seeing-eye dog. The dog will go in first. And before the maniac understands what's happening, you'll follow on the heels of the dog, who got away from you—that will be the excuse, that will set his mind at rest, explain what you're doing there, but no, he's already seen you as a blind man, you can't use the same trick twice. Lure him to the desert. Yes. It began in the desert, and it has to end in the desert. If he really is our man—

7

Is that what you call a smoking break? A powerful voice interrupts him.

Hanina turns round and sees the bronzed face and the cropped platinum hair gleaming like frost on Mona's skull. He examines her clean cut jaws and chin. The cleavage between the firm pomegranates of her breasts under the tight red sweater descending to the walnut colored leather pants hugging her sturdy thighs and muscular calves—

Hey! Hello! Nino! Are you with us? demands Mona. Hanina nods, and she continues with her rebuke: We've been sitting and waiting for you for half an hour.

Half an hour? Hanina mumbles absent-mindedly, the words meaning nothing to him.

Aren't you feeling well? Mona comes up to him and lays her soft palm on his forehead.

I'm all right, Mother.

Mother? repeats the astonished Mona incredulously: Did you call me Mother?

What?! Hanina stares at the powerful woman who manipulates sail ropes in the wind as if they were strands of wool. He looks through her and for a moment he sees the wild laughing girl with the almond eyes, who would challenge him to swim out to sea in the middle of the night.

The met at sea, they fell in love at sea, and now the sea divides them, he hears the voice of the scriptwriter Turel Shlush, making up a story about him and Mona in the third person plural.

We didn't meet at sea, he corrects him, we met in the unit. Mona was an intelligence officer—

I'm trying to make your story a little more romantic, insists Tyrell. The formal meeting took place in the unit, but the intimate meeting was in the sea, when you swam naked in the moonlight.

When did we swim naked in the moonlight? He interrogates the scriptwriter.

You've forgotten, Tyrell rebukes him, you've forgotten a lot of things.

More and more Shlush's voice surprises him as he writes scenes from his secret life. He sees him sitting opposite the computer screen, speaking the shooting instructions and typing. Conducting a dialogue in the name of the characters involved in the scene and typing the lines. And sometimes he addresses him directly in the second person, as he writes:

What do you know, man? What can you do? What can you expect?

He has no doubts as to the origins of Tyrell the scriptwriter. He's a branch of his own tree, cut off years ago, when he decided to become a man of action, but lately he has begun to show signs of life, to exercise his voice in speaking in the second person to the man called 'Hanina', or in talking about him in the third person. He hears this undercover scriptwriter saying 'I think', 'I want', 'I feel', while wondering to himself if this is really what he thinks, wants and feels. To himself Tyrell never says 'I', only 'you' and 'he'.

Strange, why don't you ever say 'I' to yourself? Think about it, he instructs Tyrell, try to think about it once.

Okay, promises Tyrell. The man will think about it.

What's happening to you? he asks the nameless computer man sitting deep inside him, beyond Hanina and Shakespeare and Tyrell. Are you going crazy? And he hears the voice mimicking his own voice addressing Mona and speaking to her in his name:

Carry on with the meeting. I'll be down in a minute.

Nino, she says to him, we have to make a decision. We won't go on without you.

I'm coming, the voice says to her, and at the same time whispers to Hanina: 'You're not going back there. Even if you go back there, you won't be there. So why don't you tell her?'

Are you holding talks from here? she says suspiciously as she turns to the door of the elevator and prepares to return to the conference room.

Who can I hold talks with from here?

With God, she retorts with her dry humor and points to the sky.

Ah, says the nameless man, thanks a lot!

What for? she wonders.

For giving him a name.

Who? She knits her brow in perplexity.

God.

Ah, she says, and sniffs.

I just need a bit of air, he hears Tyrell speaking in his name from his throat, and he's glad that for a moment, by chance, a name has been found for the anonymous narrator talking to him and about him in the third person, and sometimes also speaking in his name in the first person, and releasing him from the onerous duty of talking to others.

Thanks a lot, God, he says to him, and God answers politely:

You're welcome.

We're waiting for you, she addresses him again from inside the elevator, a second before the stainless steel jaws, shining in the light of the full moon, close on her, and she is swallowed up in the belly of the monster and disappears from view.

8

The cell phone vibrates in his trouser pocket. A text message. He looks at the display.

'Where are you, you shit? You're a miserable coward like all the rest of your rotten race. Big mouth and small balls. You're even afraid to tell me your name.'

Hanina keys in his reply:

'We'll meet'. And he signs: 'Shylock.'

Why did you give him your cell number? asks Melissa.

To get to know him, he explains.

I can tell you everything you want to know about him, she says.

Not everything, he corrects her. You never saw him naked. Anyway, you know Winnie's Tony, but you don't know anything about Shylock's Tony.

Can you explain yourself? she asks.

A person is matter that can take on any attribute. Every new meeting creates a new person, who didn't exist until that moment. I hope that, from the minute you met me, a woman that Winnie didn't know existed before is being revealed to you.

That's definitely true, she says.

Do you know her name yet? he asks.

The minute I saw you I thought her name was Melissa, she says, but now I'm beginning to know her a bit better, it seems to me that she's called Timberlake, or Timber for short.

And are Timber's mother and father also Melissa or Winnie's parents?

No, Timberlake states firmly, Winnie and Melissa aren't Timberlake's sisters. They aren't related at all. Winnie's mother was an alcoholic, and her father was a good man, but weak.

And Timberlake's father? he asks.

Timberlake's father was a hangman, she says with absolute certainty.

A hangman, he reflects aloud, that's interesting. I'd like to have met him.

Let's talk about you, she changes the subject. I hope you too are no longer the same person who met Melissa.

No, he admits, I'm somebody else.

And what's the name of the different person talking to Timberlake now? she inquires.

The name of the different person talking to Timber now is Samael, he says.

Samael, she repeats the name to herself, Samael...a magic name.

What else can you tell me about Tony? he asks.

You were interested in his stomach, she recalls.

Right, he tenses.

I know it's his vulnerable area.

What? he says in excitement. What do you mean by 'vulnerable area'?

Everybody has a sensitive area in his body, where illness attacks when he's under stress, and with him it's his stomach.

How did you come to that conclusion?

His left hand is always massaging his stomach in the area of the diaphragm and the liver, like you massage a painful or wounded place. And he suffers from chronic flatulence and heartburn too, and I have the impression the upper sphincter of his stomach doesn't really work, it may be completely ruined.

Where do you get that from?

Sometimes the smell of a corpse comes out of his mouth, she says.

This immediately puts him in mind of Marcus, who they called 'Stinker' in the unit—who divided the human race into two: the sissy majority, who were prepared to compromise on any old whiskey, but couldn't come near a bottle of Laphroaig, and the tough, uncompromising minority, who were crazy about this whiskey, so redolent of iodine, seaweed and carbolic acid, that in the time of prohibition in America the bootleggers were able to trick the authorities and sell it officially as a medicine. And when the news that Adonis had been killed in a 'hunting accident' in Lebanon arrived, Marcus assembled all the members of the unit, and in honor of the occasion opened a bottle of Laphroaig 57.3 percent, the original strength reached in the barrel after distillation, and compelled all the fighters to drink a toast in pure, undiluted whiskey—and afterwards invited them all to a second round, in which he added two parts of water to the whiskey—to enable them all to enjoy the aroma of the peat, smoke and sea, as well as the bitter sweetness released in the mouths of those brave enough to overcome the initial fierceness and roughness of the drink. But as they were celebrating with the taste and aroma, or as some would say the reek of this whiskey, which seared itself into the memory like the murder of a prince or a president, a correction of the original report arrived: Tino the Syrian had not been liquidated. The Belorussian bastard, who had German and English blood flowing in his veins, had only been mortally wounded by shrapnel from the boar-hunting bullet, and although they said there was a chance he would not survive the wound, later on it transpired that he had not only recovered, but been transformed by the failed attempt on his life into a wounded animal on the rampage, until they succeeded in locating him again, and the second assassination attempt ended in the death of Jonas and the terrible pursuit in the desert, where he succeeded in giving them the slip at the last minute and vanishing into the darkness, in spite of the intelligence version, which relied on the report of the Belgian pathologist, who was an undercover agent, according to which their man had given up the ghost in the desert, after he had become dehydrated and his liver stopped functioning, but there was no knowing if this was the truth, or only a rumor he himself had spread in order to get them off his back for good—

Where shall we escape to? she interrupts his thoughts.

I have a place in Santo Domingo, he hears Shakespeare picking up the story he had started telling Bridget.

Santo Domingo! she exclaims enthusiastically.

Have you been there? he asks.

No, never, she admits. What's it like?

Full of villas. He starts giving her a detailed description of an island landscape—white villas, each of which is crazier and more grotesque than the next, for they all embody the dreams of heaven on earth conceived in the minds of people with no imagination, and the island as a whole looks like a parody of a bourgeois paradise, with little gardens and trim lawns in front of the houses, little pools and barbecues in the back yards, and the villas are surrounded by hedges with thorns as long as fingers, and in the tourist season, which is in winter, they fill up with noisy foreign tourists, most of them from Germany, and then the pubs and bars too are full of bored men, avid for little holiday adventures—he goes on painting a picture of whose relation to reality he has no idea—but on the day that the tourist season comes to an end all of them get into their hired cars and make for the airport, and for a few hours the roads are jammed, and the charter planes take off one after the other into the depths of the green tropical sky, and the next day the villas stand silent and empty, and only the stray cats prowl the gardens which seem to have been abandoned in a hurry, as if the panic-stricken inhabitants left suddenly, fleeing for their lives, and here and there security guards patrol the streets, their cars driving slowly down the deserted streets, and a few bored maintenance men in white overalls water the abandoned gardens, and anyone who stays on after the exodus of the seasonal visitors feels profound loneliness and boredom from which there is no escape, for the deserted pubs only deepen the sense of isolation, especially in the afternoon hours, especially on the days when tropical storms rage and the rain comes down from the sky like curtains of gray water, and you can sit there in an empty pub, downing glass after glass of Bahama-mama or Winnie-wacky-woo—

Winnie-wacky-woo, she cries gaily, I like the sound of that!

Then full steam ahead for the Caribbean islands! he commands the crew, leans with both hands on the deck railing, and waits for the ship to sail into the night sea. The white solar heaters, and the glass panes of the reflectors attached to them, glitter like thousands of fishing boats at night by the water in Tel Aviv. He looks down into the back yard of the building. A dilapidated oven lies on its side next to a smashed glass door, with an old exercise bicycle rusting beside it. Full steam ahead for the Caribbean islands! he commands again from the heights of the bridge, but the many-storied monster stays still, immobile as the Cutty Sark standing in dry dock in Greenwich, refusing to spread its sails and put out to sea.

Sorry, Captain Antoniu, no more voyages tonight.

9

Captain Antoniu, he hears them calling his name, Captain Antoniu dos Shaninas do los Rugashivas.

He disliked not only his legs, but also his arms and all the other parts of his body, and he couldn't stand his name either. He gave expression to these feelings in a poem. No, not a poem, an epoch making poetic novel in verse, composed of a cycle of seventy-eight, no, a hundred and seventy-eight, poems, like 'Eugene Onegin', whose opening poem began with the words:

Hanina did not choose his name.

This poem-novel, which heralded a new era in poetry, a return to classical meter and rhyme, was immediately translated into seventeen, no, twenty-seven languages, and rose to the top of the best-seller lists in eight, no, eighteen, countries.

In the opening poem, stunning in its simplicity, the mysterious poet, dos Shaninas, succinctly sums up his attitude towards himself in the following words:

Shaninas did not choose his ma,
Shaninas did not choose his pa,
And on the night it came to pass,
Nobody thought of Shaninas.

There is no need to quote the poem in its entirety here. As soon as it was published, shortly after the death of the poet, its lines became a byword for the new poetry, and the public is already well acquainted with them.

Indeed, it was only after his departure that the full extent of his astonishing creation would be revealed. A box full of papers closely covered with his cramped writing would be found under his bed, in the modest room in which he lived his secret life, in the heart of the teeming city which paid no mind to the intellectual giant passing like a shadow through its streets, always wearing the same hat. No, not a hat, a beret. No, not a beret, a peaked cap. A dark brown leather cap. Almost black with use.

On the fiftieth anniversary of his death, when the bronze statue of the poet, in which he was seen sitting at a table in the little cafe where he was a habitue, was unveiled, the television would interview women with necks generously wrinkled by the pleasures of life, and they would declaim his poems to the camera in voices full of emotion, and confess with damp eyes and no inhibitions: 'His lines turned us on, his words wet our panties', and one grandmother in a wheel-chair would gush in the ears of her blushing granddaughter: 'His poems simply stripped you bare. When I read his poem 'Take your baby my love/ Take my prick in your hands' for the first time I couldn't breathe, I panted so hard my mother came running in a panic to see what had happened.

Yes, Monsieur Rejvani, you should have been a poet. How did you allow them to tempt you into imprisoning the joy of your youth in liquidation operations, and bury-ing the rest of your life in advertising? First you murdered for them, and now you're selling them vegetables, chickens, fruit, banks, computers and quack medicines. Take all those lost years and throw them into the trash. In your soul you remained a poet, of that there is no doubt. You introduced direct speech into poetry. The simple description of what people see when they close their eyes and live moments of happiness. When a loving hand touches them in the exact places they want to be touched. Write the poems that nobody will write in your place.

The fact that one day Hanin stopped writing poetry led to much speculation in those distant days and gave birth to rumors that Haninai had not really written those wonderful poems, published in the collection 'Shock poems', himself, but that he had come into possession of a notebook belonging to an anonymous comrade in arms, a solitary youth who had fallen in battle. Straight off the boat, or the plane, the anonymous poet Yohanan had landed in the slaughter fields of the most terrible war of all the wars in the war-sick East. He had time to meet a nurse with a braid. He had time to fall in love with her, to spend the night talking to her, but when he set off in the morning he remembered that he had forgotten to ask her name. On his way to his last battle he told his story to Honen Avihai, and made him swear that if he fell in battle, Heynan would give the notebook he carried on his body to the girl with the braid who had never left his side.

But the shady Hananya had published the poems he found in Yohanan the anonymous warrior's notebook under his own name, shamelessly, and after he published the last of the poems in the notebook the wellspring of his poetry had dried up forever. But this rumor gave birth to a further rumor, according to which H. N. Hanialik himself had invented the rumor about the solitary fallen soldier's notebook, and also taken care to spread it.

One literary researcher, in his attempts to arrive at the truth among the rumors, discovered to his astonishment that Honen, with his reputation as a social butterfly, with all the girls hanging round his neck, didn't actually have one close friend, and everything those considered close to him knew about him came from rumors, and none of them could point to the source of those rumors. Yes, he didn't have a single friend.

10

....Apart from Yadanuga—a corruption of 'Yad-anuga' or 'Tender Hand'—who now emerges from the jaws of the elevator which previously swallowed Mona. First his solid head appears, crowned with a mane of silver curls, beneath which his eyes, full of childish wonder, twinkle mischievously, then his broad shoulders push their way out, and finally this overgrown infant emerges in all his ungainly height. Yadanuga pierces him with a sharp look—one of those precise looks which always ended in a body lying at the side of the road, or sitting at the wheel of a car with a hole between the eyes—and asks in an amused tone of voice:

What's the matter with you, Shakespeare? Everyone's waiting for you.

For Yadanuga he's Shakespeare, just as for him Yad-anuga is Yadanuga, and not Yudaleh Nugilevski, who to his widowed mother is still her good little boy Yudinka, who leaves a soccer game in the middle if she calls him, and comes running to ask her what she wants him to do. And in high school he was the tough daring athlete Roofy, who even then excelled at walking on the parapets of high roofs and acrobatic riding on the Matchless Motorcycle his uncle Yehiel Nugilevsky-Nagil brought back from the army. And in the assassination squad, where they served together, he was discovered to possess a delicate hand, capable of skewering a lizard on the branch of a jacaranda tree with a commando knife at a distance of eight meters, and therefore he was Yadanuga in the team of the 'Cunning Cooks', of which only the two of them had survived, and Hanina uses this ineffable name only when no strange ear is in the vicinity, and Yehuda Nugilevski too calls him Shakespeare only under the same conditions. In the presence of the other employees of the advertising agency Yadanuga becomes Mackie, and Shakespeare becomes Hanina.

Yadanuga, says Shakespeare, and then he says again: Yadanuga...

And since at least three seconds, if not four, of silence pass between 'Yadanuga' and 'Yadanuga', the latter responds with a short 'What', leaving all options open, and Shakespeare repeats once more:

Yadanuga....I didn't sleep all night. And he immediately corrects himself: Maybe I slept for two hours.

What's up? asks Yadanuga, who reads his friend like an old book full of pencil lines. Don't tell me you're still stuck with Adonis's ghost.

It's much more complicated than you think, says Shakespeare.

I thought you came back because you'd recovered from that illusion at last.

It's not an illusion, says Shakespeare.

Listen, says Yadanuga, after you called from New York and told me you were on his tracks, I spoke to Tzibeleh. He got into the archives and went over the report by the Belgian pathologist, who by the way died a couple of years ago—

I know the de Odecker document off by heart, says Shakespeare, and it's no longer relevant.

The de Odecker document isn't relevant?!

Look, says Shakespeare, even if this guy isn't Adonis, although I think he is, I've gotten somebody else involved, someone who has nothing to do with the affair, and this person's life will be in danger as long as Tony is free.

Tony? says Yadanuga in surprise. But he wasn't called Tony. He was called Tino.

Yes, confirms Shakespeare, his official name was Tino the Syrian.

He wasn't actually a Syrian, Yadanuga tries to clarify something forgotten to himself. He was some kind of English-Spaniard or German-Italian wasn't he?

He was a Belorussian of English-German descent, Shakespeare corrects him.

Right, right! Yadanuga's memory grows clearer, like a distant dream whose details suddenly, at the magic touch of a word, or a sound, or a picture, begin to emerge from the mists. His name wasn't Tino at all!

No, that was his alias in their network, Shakespeare fills in another detail.

Right, his name was Anatol! Yadanuga eagerly adds another details to the mosaic emerging from under the sands of oblivion.

Anatol? Shakespeare introduces a doubt into Yadanuga's heart, without offering an alternative.

Just a minute, just a minute, not Anatol, Yadanuga corrects himself, Anthony....Anton!

Do you remember his face? asks Shakespeare. Could you draw his face for me without the beard?

How can I draw his face for you without the beard? protests Yadanuga. All they gave us then was a blurred photograph... you could hardly see anything. That's why we came too close to him. Because we weren't sure if it was him.... And Jonas paid for it with his life.

What exactly do you remember?

In the photo he had a black beard that covered half his face. That's all I remember.

In the period when we were looking for him, you made all kinds of sketches of his face, says Shakespeare.

Yes I did, says Yadanuga, but years have passed since then.

Can you find those sketches?

How can I? I don't even remember what I drew them on.

You had a little Kohinoor notebook, with an orange cover.

You know how many of those notebooks I've been through since then?

Perhaps you could try to reconstruct his face from memory, take off the beard and add twenty years?

Shakespeare, Yadanuga laughs despairingly, I can make you twenty sketches, what good will it do?

I don't know, admits Shakespeare. On every trip it seems to me at least five times that I've seen him. In the end it's just some guy. But this time I have a feeling—

You don't want a repeat performance of the story with that poor waiter from Islay, warns Yadanuga.

That's the problem, says Shakespeare. That's why I'm asking you what you remember. Your visual memory is the only thing I have to rely on.

What do I remember....Yadanuga tries to fish up details. I remember something with brown and white.

What brown and white?

Is there such a thing as a brown-white wine?

A brown-white wine?! It sounds like that bastard wine whose taste changes from bottle to bottle.

Right! It was called 'Vino bastardo' I think, the wine he liked, a sweet Spanish wine, don't you remember they gave it to us to taste, so we would be able to identify it?

Wait a minute, wait a minute, Shakespeare remembers, bastardo...that rings a bell.

And he liked white carnations with red stripes.

That's it, says Shakespeare. He was wearing a white shirt with red stripes, or maybe the opposite: a red shirt with white stripes.

A lot of people wear shirts like that, Yadanuga tries to dampen down Shakespeare's excitement, without success.

No, no! Shakespeare protests, the shirt had a white collar, and he was wearing a brown tie.

All that means is that he's got terrible taste, Yadanuga demurs, but it doesn't prove that he's our man.

He's our man, pronounces Shakespeare.

Where did you meet him? Asks Yadanuga.

In Manhattan, in an Irish pub. He was sitting there drinking muscatel, into which he poured creme-de-cassis from a flask he took out of the inside pocket of his jacket.

How did we come up with the name 'Tino the Syrian'? Yadanuga wonders.

Don't you remember? When they gave us his profile, they said that he had a lyric tenor, and he liked chansons from the thirties; and because he was called Anton, and he was one quarter Russian, we called him 'Tino Rossi', and later on, when we found out that he trained in Syria, and for a while he acted as a bodyguard to that old Nazi who lives in Damascus—we turned 'Tino Rossi' into 'Tino the Syrian'.

Even if it is him, he's no longer the same person. He must be forty-five today...Yadanuga reflects on all the years that have passed together with the secret *gloria mundi* of their stormy youth in the quartet of the 'Cunning Cooks'.

Listen, Yadanuga, confesses Shakespeare. Weird things are happening to me. I need a break.

And Yadanuga, aware of every nuance in his friend's voice, lays a beefy hand on Shakespeare's shoulder and says:

Shakespeare, we'll make a decision, and after that take a break, go where you want.

Where I must, corrects Shakespeare, if I take responsibility for my actions.

You take responsibility, if I know you, says Yadanuga, but now we have to come to a decision, and you, as the boss and the CEO of the firm—

I can't sit there, Yadanuga. I can't!

Those two yuppie pipsqueaks raise my revulsion level too, confesses Yadanuga, but we haven't got a choice. Mona's tending in their direction. You have to throw all your weight into the ring. Come on, let's go down.

That's not the point, Yadanuga. The revulsion level doesn't bother me.

What is it then, Shakespeare? Talk, because you're beginning to worry me.

Something's happening to me, Yadanuga, and I don't know how to tell you. I don't even know where to begin.

Yadanuga doesn't say a word. He takes a flat bottle of Knob Creek out of the pocket of his leather jacket, takes a sip of the whiskey, and hands the bottle to Shakespeare.

What's this, says Shakespeare in surprise, you've changed to Kentucky straight bourbon?

Lately, says Yadanuga, I prefer whiskey without memories.

Shakespeare takes a sip of Yadanuga's whiskey without memories, and in his head the expanses of Mid-west cornfields open up, with the country roads, and the isolated farms scattered between them, and on one of them, in the shade of the giant elm trees, in the place where he had parted from her for the last time, Bridget sits on an old wicker chair breast-feeding the small, pink Hugh. Before he drives out to the road, he waves to her from the car window and calls: Wait for me here, under the elm, and a the same moment the sentence rings in his head in French, in the voice of the Alsatian, the voice in which he would say softly to every corpse they parted from: *Attendez moi sous l'orme*, and he knew that he would never see her again, or the little son, who would grow up without a father. That's the biggest favor you can do him, Shakespeare eased what remained of his conscience, and stepped on the gas, and drove away.

11

Yadanuga looks at him, draws on his whiskey bottle, and says to himself that he knows him like he knows himself. In other words, hardly at all. He is shrouded in absolute darkness, and out of the darkness pictures emerge like cars from the road tunnels in the North of Italy. One minute they're racing along the road twisting between mountains stunning in their savage beauty, and the next they're swallowed up again in the maw of the next tunnel. Sometimes he tries to attach names to these pictures. The names are very strange, and more than shedding light on the content of the pictures, they actually increase their obscurity.

One of these pictures now pops out of the dense darkness in Yadanuga's head, labeled 'Binbad the Bailor', and he laughs.

Shakespeare looks surprised, and Yadanuga apologizes, explaining that all of a sudden, because of the way 'Tino Rossi' had turned into Tino the Syrian', the words 'Tinbad the Tailor' had suddenly popped into his head. Shakespeare, Shakespeare, you and your crazy codes! To this day the French police are still puzzling over 'Zinbad the Zailor'. How did you come up with it?

Shakespeare doesn't answer. Shakespeare isn't here any more. Shakespeare is already there. In the dark night, on the road climbing to the isolated villa near Nice, which said backwards is 'Sin', which gave birth to 'Sinbad the Sailor', and Stephen Dedalus, or perhaps Mr Bloom, gave birth to 'Binbad'. And the pictures flicker and chase each other in the darkness. Four men in overalls get out of the French Electrical Corporation minivan and enter a dark isolated villa on a hilltop. Between the pines the lights of Nice, capital of the Azure Coast, twinkle in the distance, and Yadanuga sings softly 'Tomorrow my friends we shall

sing as we go into battle'. The Alsatian silences him: If
you have to sing, sing 'Frere Jacques'. The armed goon
stationed at the entrance to the villa shines a strong flashlight on their faces and overalls. What's the trouble, the
Alsatian inquires, and the goon explains that the electricity
suddenly shorted, but all the fuses are okay. Where's the
fuse box here, asks the Alsatian, and the goon says, come
with me. He turns into the entrance. Jonas raises his hand
as if to scratch his head, and a terrible blow aimed at the
back of the goon's neck leaves the latter sprawled lifeless
on the stairs. In the dim drawing room eight men are seated
at a round table in candlelight. They raise their heads and
look at the four technicians. Good evening, the Alsatian
greets them, you'll have your light back on in a minute.
And indeed, light bursts in brief flashes from the toolboxes
in the hands of the electricians accompanied by a dry hic-
cuping sound. Chairs turn over. The technicians hurry to
the fallen men and take care of each of them personally.
A flash and a hiccup for every head. The eyes of Shakespeare's personal patient suddenly snap open. Shakespeare
looks straight into the whites of his eyes and whispers:
This is for Munich. And adds another flash and another
hiccup, right into the aiming eye, which sprays onto the
overalls emblazoned with the initials of the French electric
corporation: EDF, 'Électricité de France'.

Hey, Shakespeare, he hears Yadanuga's voice and feels
the weight of his hand on his shoulder, where are you?

In the villa in Nice, says Shakespeare.

It was brilliant, says Yadanuga. Connecting up to their
phone, and then cutting their electricity, letting them dial
the electric company and complain of a short, and the Al-
sation reassures them: Oui, monsieur, we're sending you a
team of technicians....right away, tout de suite, monsieur!
How did you think of it, Shakespeare?

I had the mind of a writer, Shakespeare mourns for Hanina, and I sold it. And now I'm paying the price.

Have you been diagnosed with something?

Diabetes, Tyrell the scriptwriter gives him the second answer that occurs to him. Never the first, banal one.

That's nothing, Yadanuga tries to console him. If it's only diabetes—

Neglected and deteriorating, Tyrell continues improving his new invention, examining its possible implications for what comes next. I walked around with it for years. Somehow I knew. This dissolving flesh showed the signs. Pins and needles in my feet. Attacks of numbness in my fingers. Attacks of blurred vision.

You didn't go to a doctor? Yadanuga pretends to be surprised at his friend. In truth he is simply astonished at Shakespeare's ability to set in motion improvisations in which he himself enjoys participating, without knowing where they will lead and where they will end.

Why go to a doctor? Shakespeare laughs. So that he'll tell me that I should have died three hundred years ago? That the fact that I'm still alive is a medical scandal? That my cardiac arteries are a mess? That I have to stop ruining women's reputations and drinking myself to death?

The question is if you prefer to go blind, Yadanuga goes on playing the game. Or to lose your organs one by one.

I hoped to croak before my body landed up in the hands of the butchers, Shakespeare plays another card, but my heart refuses to die.

I'm sorry I gave you the whiskey, says Yadanuga, and asks himself how and when the moment of truth, which ends every game, will arrive.

Don't be sorry, Shakespeare laughs at himself, those drops won't change anything now. And the best joke is, it's caught up with me exactly when I'm suddenly dying to live, and even if I've only got one more year, I'm not prepared to give up a single day.

We've finally come to the point, reflects Yadanuga. Now the guy's beginning to talk about something that really happened to him. But he immediately warns himself: don't forget you're talking to someone for whom imagination is reality and reality is imagination. Now, go figure what happened in reality, what happened in imagination, and what happened in the no-man's-land between the two, where this man lives his life.

What's her name? Yadanuga mounts a frontal assault, which causes Tyrell to leap for his script and start scribbling a new scene:

Francesca, he throws out the first name that comes into his head, the devil knows where from.

A nun? wonders Yadanuga.

How did you know? Shakespeare begins with growing curiosity to reveal the biography of a woman whose identity is still unknown.

I don't know, admits Yadanuga, a kind of hunch. How did you meet her?

Through a friend of hers. I was in Florence, I went to the Accademia to see Michelangelo's David, there were two girls standing there, one of them in a nun's habit and the other in the uniform of a novice.

Since when do you know the difference between a novice and a nun? Yadanuga tries to frustrate Shakespeare's unexpected move with a clumsy mate.

I heard them talking, Shakespeare laughs at his contestant's amateurish move. I heard the nun saying to the novice: Do it for me, Isabella. Find out what his business is. You can do it, I can't. You haven't taken your vows yet.

I didn't know that nuns weren't allowed to talk to men, Yadanuga marvels at his friend's powers of improvisation.

They're only allowed to in the presence of the Mother Superior, explains Shakespeare, and adds: And even then—they're not allowed to show their face to a man, or if they do show it, they're not allowed to talk.

What do you say, marvels Yadanuga.

To cut a long story short, the novice comes up to me and says: My friend, Francesca, took a bet with me that you're a gynecologist. So I answer loudly, to let her friend hear too: What's the problem, did your brother get you pregnant? And before the words are out of my mouth Francesca bursts into lewd laughter, and I felt as if midsummer was breaking out in the dead of winter in my heart.

Are you serious? marvels Yadanuga.

The laugh didn't come from her belly, it came straight from her Diana-bud, which opened up and made the Cupid-flower blossom in my dormant garden. Suddenly I understood why Orthodox Jews are so afraid of a woman's voice.

And what happened afterwards? inquires Yadanuga.

We began the evening with black cuttlefish soup and celebrated the night in her hotel room.

With the nun?

What nun? He laughs. If I tell you, you won't believe it.

Spit it out, Shakespeare!

In good time, Yadanuga.

Whatever. And the next day you said goodbye—

The next day we got on a plane.

A plane?!

She took me to meet her parents in Vermont. They live in a big wooden house, in a forest of maple trees. They make maple syrup for a living. Maple wine. Maple liqueur. Their house is steeped in the aromas of maple and cinnamon.

Never mind the maple and the cinnamon, what's the girl like?

The girl is maple and cinnamon too.

What does that mean?

Her hair is maple syrup. You never saw a color like it in your life. Not only on her head. On her mound of Venus too. And her lips—cinnamon. Reddish-brown.

Are you talking about her mouth or her pussy?

Both. But what drove me crazy were her eyes.

Cinnamon or maple syrup?

No no, Shakespeare gravely dismisses Yadanuga's attempts at humor: Her eyes are something you've never seen. Their expression is the cleanest thing I ever saw. Clean as clean can be. The innocence of a child, and the sexuality of a woman of thirty-three. When she came to say goodbye to me, her hair was wet with rain. She was wearing a white shirt, and over it a man's brown leather bomber jacket.

White and brown, Yadanuga reflects aloud. Hanina takes it in, but Shakespeare goes on telling his story without a break:

Her cheeks were flushed with running in the rain. She came into the room, sat down in an armchair, breathing hard with flared nostrils, and looked straight into my eyes. For fifteen minutes we sat like that, looking into each other's eyes. I had such a hard-on I was afraid to move. In the end she stood up and said: I'll miss you. I have to go to work.

What does she do, your nun?

She works for the police.

A cop?! Yadanuga is stunned by this completely unexpected turn in the development of the character. Where in the hell is he taking me, he wonders, is there a story of getting into trouble with the law behind this tale being spun by his compulsively fiction-fabricating friend? And aloud he asks: Are you trying to tell me that you've fallen in love with an American policewoman?

Not a policewoman. She's a criminologist. She investigates particularly serious crimes.

What are 'particularly serious crimes'? Yadanuga has a hard time hiding the suspicion awakening in his heart.

Exposed neck crimes, Shakespeare replies with a confidence that amazes Hanina, who suspects that this time even Shakespeare has reached a dead end. He hopes that Yadanuga will let it go, but Yadanuga is as stubborn as a Canaanite mule:

'Exposed neck crimes'? What exactly is that?

You don't know?

No, says Yadanuga. It's the first time I've ever heard of it.

Hanina almost admits that it's the first time he's ever heard the term too, but Shakespeare preempts him:

Haven't you noticed that lately all kinds of people in the media, artists and academics, are wearing jackets with Chinese collars, over black tee-shirts that expose their necks?

So.....?

Have you ever thought about what kind of crimes are typical of this population group?

What kind of crimes?

Think about what's characteristic of this sector, suggests Shakespeare. These people travel a lot. They fly to congresses, lectures, exhibition openings. They come for one night to some little town in the Bavarian alps, the next day they're giving a lecture in Elsinore or Helsingborg, and two days later they're spending the night in Edinburgh or Paris, and before they return to Yale or Cambridge, they manage to fit in a trip to Bali to take in the Barong Festival.

So? demands Yadanuga, whose head is beginning to spin.

These people are developing a multiple identity syndrome. On the one hand—one identity is not responsible for what the other identities do, and on the other hand—it's very difficult to keep track of their activities, because they're here today and somewhere else tomorrow. Do you understand? The investigation of exposed neck crimes requires sharp senses, special insight and tremendous skill, explains Shakespeare and thinks of the unavoidable murder, the liquidation of the maniac who might be Tino the Syrian and who is definitely threatening the life of Winnie a.k.a. Melissa Timberlake, and he concludes with the fateful words: And that's what Francis does.

Nice story, says Yadanuga. Now let's hear the simple truth.

That is the truth, Shakespeare tries to sound as convincing as he can, but Yadanuga isn't buying it:

Bill, he says, I really enjoyed your flight of fancy, but enough is enough! Come back to reality. Tell me the sordid truth, without any embellishments. You got yourself involved in a dangerous, criminal affair, and you involved someone else as well. Am I right or wrong?

The truth is she is called Melissa. A New Yorker whose parents got divorced when she was four, and ever since she had lived with her alcoholic mother, who would come home drunk in the early hours of the morning, every time dragging a different man behind her to finish the night with. At the age of twelve she ran away from home for the first time, and became a streetwalker.

You got mixed up with a New York whore?

She's a sales assistant in a fancy shop on Sixty-something or Eighty-something Street off Madison Avenue in the daytime, and at night she's an unhappy prostitute.

Go on, says Yadanuga.

A highly educated girl. Doing a doctorate on a family of British hangmen, says Shakespeare, and Hanina's voice breaks. He puts the bottle to his lips, takes a healthy swallow of the bittersweet Knob Creek, and finishes with an Arabic curse.

A whore doing a doctorate on a family of hangmen?! Shakespeare! There's a limit! protests Yadanuga.

She's from a family of hangmen herself, explains Shakespeare. Her grandfather was a hangman. He executed the Nazi war criminals at Nuremberg.

Yeah, sure! laughs Yadanuga. I suppose you met him too, and he gave you a piece of the rope that hanged Hans Frank or Baldur von Schirach.

No, says Shakespeare. Her grandfather was killed in a work accident. He sat down on an electric chair in order to demonstrate the routine to a group of apprentice executioners, and someone, apparently a cleaning woman, raised, or forgot to raise, the switch by mistake.

Good going, Bill! says Yadanuga. Shakespeare himself would never have come up with an invention like that.

I didn't invent it, Shakespeare defends himself. It's what she told me. By the way, a lot of hangmen ended their lives on the gallows. There was a well known case of a hangman who had a stroke at the moment he was hanging the convicted man, and there were also a number of gangster-executioners, who were sentenced to death and executed, which proves that the death penalty is evidently not a deterrent.

And is the prostitute a real prostitute? Yadanuga asks again, to make sure he understood correctly.

The mother of prostitutes, says Hanina. She receives customers at home, and at the same time she does phone sex as a sideline.

Where exactly does she work as a sales assistant? asks Yadanuga.

What do you know, says Hanina, I've forgotten the name of the store!

Aha! Yadanuga hurries to widen the crack that has suddenly opened up in the story. What kind of store?

Fashion, says Hanina. What's the name again? Something that sounds like a killer. Not Rudolf....

Stephane Kellian? suggest Yadanuga.

Not Kellian....

What were you looking for there? Yadanuga attacks.

A cashmere suit.

For a woman?

No, for me.

A men's fashion store, says Yadanuga.

Both. Men and women. I think it's something like Lars.

Larson?

Is there a fashion designer called that?

I think so, I'm not sure.

No, it wasn't Larson. Maybe Karlson...

Karl Lagerfeld?

Lagerfeld rings a bell....

A cashmere suit you said? Is it supposed to be a Scotch fashion house?

Today they breed goats you can comb cashmere from in Mongolia too, in China, even in Texas, in Florida, and other places too, says Shakespeare.

When did you suddenly start taking an interest in cashmere? Yadanuga fails to conceal his surprise.

He was wearing a cashmere suit, says Shakespeare.

Who?

Adonis, says Shakespeare. Her pimp.

Ah-ha!...Yadanuga begins to put the strands he's succeeded in untangling together, but Shakespeare doesn't give him time to breathe:

Apropos cashmere—I'm not talking about the raw material. I'm talking about the mills and the wool industry, where the Scots are apparently still in the lead. Although it seems to me that the Italians are beginning to catch up with them, and they may even have gotten ahead of them by now.

Maybe, says Yadanuga, with the strands he's managed to untangle getting tied up in a new knot.

Why don't you throw out the name of some fashion house, maybe it will ring a bell, requests Shakespeare.

McLarn? Yadanuga takes a shot in the dark.

McLarn? ponders Shakespeare. McLarn....we're getting there, but no.

Leave off, says Yadanuga. It won't come to you if you worry about it.

Suddenly I'm not sure it was on Madison either, says Shakespeare.

What difference does it make if it's Madison or Lexington, Yadanuga tries vainly to get to the point.

Something strange is happening to me. To my memory, I mean, complains Shakespeare and looks at his friend in a plea for help.

There are hundreds of clothing stores in Manhattan, Yadanuga says reassuringly. You probably saw something you liked in a display window and went inside without looking at the name of the store, and when you saw her you forgot about the suit, because she grabbed all your attention.

That's true, confirms Shakespeare, but it's a little scary when whole sections of reality vanish into the mist like ships, until suddenly you aren't even sure anymore if there was a ship there in the first place. Tell me, doesn't it happen to you sometimes, that for a minute it seems to you that something that happened didn't happen at all?

Or vice versa, says Yadanuga, sometimes it seems to me that something that never happened actually did happen.

Yes, Shakespeare agrees, sometimes the border is completely blurred, and sometimes it simply doesn't exist.

Let's get back to the girl, Yadanuga suggests. You said she was doing her doctorate?

Yes, Shakespeare replies absentmindedly. She gave me her phone number. I call, ask if I can come by. She says to me: You can even stay the night. A thousand dollars a night, including breakfast.

Fuck-and-breakfast, says Yadanuga. And you went there?

I couldn't refuse, Shakespeare reflects aloud. It was a cry for help.

She talked to you about the price, and you heard a cry for help?

Lately, confesses Shakespeare, everything sounds to me like a cry for help.

We're in trouble, states Yadanuga.

Yes, Shakespeare agrees. Imagine all the human despair in the world in the laughing face of a child as fragile as Segestria Perfida.

As what? demands the baffled Yadanuga.

It's a kind of spider with long thin legs the breadth of a hair.

You want to know something funny? says Yadanuga. A few days ago I came across a spider exactly fitting that description, when I stepped into the bathtub.

And what did you do?

I flushed it out with the shower hose, confesses Yadanuga. It went down the plug hole.

Murderer, says Shakespeare.

What was I supposed to do?

You should have put a sheet of paper into the tub, and breathed gently on the spider, so it would crawl onto the paper of its own accord, and then taken it to an open window, and blown gently onto it again, so it would fly outside to freedom.

Why all the blowing? inquires Yadanuga.

Because its legs are so thin and delicate, explains Shakespeare, that any touch could break them, and the trouble is that they don't grow again.

It seems to me that she touched a sensitive spot in you, says Yadanuga.

I stayed for seven days and seven nights, laments Hanina, and we didn't fuck once.

What happened? asks Yadanuga in concern, were you afraid of breaking her legs?

She wasn't interested.

And you? asks Yadanuga.

You'll be surprised, he admits, but I wasn't either.

I'm not surprised, says Yadanuga. Spiders with long skinny legs never gave rise to any irresistible lust in me.

Nor in me, admits Shakespeare.

So what did you do there for seven days and seven nights? demands Yadanuga.

Nothing, he says. Most of the time we did nothing.

Did you talk?

A bit, he says. Nothing to write home about. We talked a bit about vampires.

Vampires?! What's there to say about vampires?

Nonsense, Shakespeare says dismissively. She chatted about vampires, and I answered her with any rubbish that came into my head. Nothing serious.

Seven thousand, Yadanuga calculates. You could have taken a suite overlooking the park, and still had enough left over for analysis.

When we parted, she didn't want to take the money.

You're kidding me.

She didn't want it! In the end she agreed to take something as a Christmas present.

And you didn't touch her all week?

I touched her, and she touched me. But nothing else, says Shakespeare. Nothing. We just rested.

Yadanuga holds out his hand and Hanina passes him the bottle. Yadanuga swallows, corks the bottle and lays a tender hand on his friend's shoulder:

What are you still doing here, Bill, he says. You're not really here at all. Get on a plane and go to her.

Yes, Hanina agrees sadly, I guess that's what I'll have to do.

And now let's go down to the meeting, Yadanuga concludes, and put all your weight in the right place.

They turn round and step into the elevator, leaving the night and the cold, hard, pure moon behind them.

12

Smoke. Bluish-gray smoke stings his eyes. And the sweetish smell of grass. He passes his hand to and fro like a fan in front of his eyes, to get rid of the cloud suspended between the Himalayas, and out of the mist three burning dots smolder in front of his watering eyes, perhaps the cigarettes giving rise to all this smoke, or perhaps the eyes of Shiva, the Indian god with the third eye, which can see within, but when it looks out has the power to burn and destroy everything in its path. This third eye pierces the smoke like some kind of ancient laser beam. Smoldering like a red diamond in the head of an upright lingam, or in simple English, an erect penis. Hanina strains his eyes and manages to see through the smoke that this lingam is actually their energetic young graphic artist, Golan, whose two wives, Sati and Shakti, are supporting him on his left and right, each with a cigarette flickering in her mouth. Hanina rubs his eyes and waves away the smoke, and it turns out that Sati is Moran, the ideas woman, who brought Golan to your advertising agency, and Shakti is your wife Mona, Hanina, Tyrell Shlush the scriptwriter reminds him, beginning at this moment to develop a subplot, because from the way they are sitting on the right and the left of Shiva-Golan, the upright lingam—it is quite clear that they will be impregnated by him, and perhaps they have been already, and the only question is which of them will give birth to Skanda, the six-headed monster, and which of them will give birth to the elephant-headed Ganesha, but a second look leaves no doubt that Mona-Shakti will give birth to Skanda, and the young Moran-Sati will give birth to the elephant man, or the man-elephant, and what does it matter anyway who gives birth to what, it is perfectly clear that from this three-sided fuck only monsters will be born.

Why are you stuck in the door? He hears the voice of Shakti-Mona.

This place smells like Shiva's temple in Bangalore, says Shakespeare, to himself or to Yadanuga, who responds, 'I thought it reminded me of something bad...'

13

And suddenly they're there, racing along the thickly overgrown red dirt path, their straining lungs breathing the sickeningly sour-sweet smells of rotting tamarind and passion-fruits, as they drag the Alsatian with them, grunting and foaming bloodily at the mouth. And like a pesky fly buzzing round their heads, they are accompanied by the fateful moment when the guy with the beard realized that the four men following him are not innocent Shiva devotees, coming to beseech the god of the many faces, but members of a death squad who have been hot on his heels all the way from Frankfurt to Bangalore, and who are now closing in on him—and in the fraction of a second, before they can grab him, the knife glitters in his hand and is buried in the Alsatian's stomach. In the twinkling of an eye Jonas's iron hand comes down on the back of the murderer's neck, and the sound of a dry cracking of bones is heard, and the bearded man with the round face and the swollen lips falls broken-necked on the white marble steps, limp as an empty sack.

But what has been done cannot be undone. The Alsatian spits though his teeth: The dog stabbed me in the liver, and immediately loses consciousness, and someone has to take command in his place. The few tourists on the steps at this early morning hour take in the scene and run for their lives, but one skinny Japanese man turns his Handycam towards them and films them, and Yadanuga pats his cheek, snatches the video camera from his hands, removes the mini video-tape with a skilled, tender hand, returns the empty camera to him, and suggests in basic English that he go and piss somewhere else. The terrified tourist doesn't need to be told twice and he runs down the steps as fast as his legs can carry him. In a matter of minutes they will be surrounded by police. The way to the car is blocked, says Jonas, and at that moment Shakespeare takes command and orders: 'To the river'. They reach the jetty. Hundreds of boats lie on their sides in the sand along the bank. They turn one of them over and push it into the water, lay the Alsatian in the bottom, and the boat slides into the water amid the tangled vegetation. The slow tide takes them out. They ply the oars, now they are far from the shore. And Jonas, who all this time is trying to give the Alsatian mouth-to-mouth, says fuck it, we've lost him. The Alsatian's face turns a poisonous green, the color of tattoo ink. His lips are turning purple. His eyes open and for a split second his pupils reflect the green tropical sky, and then they suddenly go dull and they no longer reflect anything. They look at each other.

They each wait for somebody else to say it, but all of them, with their throats choked up, maintain the right to silence.

And that's the moment, says Shakespeare, that you stand up in the middle of the boat and produce a bitch of a monologue, God only knows where from:

What a genius you were. What a noble mind was destroyed here. Always, when we stood at a loss confronting the impossible, you would analyze the situation with your Cartesian French mind, going straight to the heart of the matter with the elegance of a knight, cutting to the chase with a stroke of a Samurai's sword and the sharp intelligence of a Yeshiva scholar from Alsace. And now you lie here, at the bottom of a fishing boat, on a foreign river in a foreign land, a marvelous miracle of a man, and it's all over for you, over and done, and we have nowhere to take you, friend. Forgive us, Danny, we're giving you up to the river.

As one man they lift Daniel Altwasser, who for the first time Shakespeare has dared to call by his name, and lay him very gently in the water, over the side of the boat. The tide takes the body, rocks and spins it for a moment, until it slowly sinks into the brown water. But the Alsatian never disappeared. At this very moment he's here with us, muses Yadanuga, and he senses the reluctance of Shakespeare, who is standing in front of him rooted to the spot, to enter the conference room, which is full of smoke and steeped in the fragrance of marijuana, like the Temple of Shiva in Bangalore. But here the sweetish scent is coming from the joints which Moran is rolling with her long fingers. And he says to himself exactly the same words he said then, as they stood in the boat and looked at the body as the muddy water spread over its monk's habit and stained it brown, like coffee seeping into a white sugar cube: We talk wildly. We come up with all kinds of random sentences. Belonging to a world that doesn't yet know why things happen. Surrounded by senseless killing and meaningless death. And what do we understand? Nothing.

14

Shakespeare Shakespeare, thinks Yadanuga, where did you find those words at that moment on that muddy river, words which described what our lives were with such precision. And in his head, from darkness to darkness, a selection of action scenes rush past, as if they had been cut out of many movies and stuck together into one sequence. A mustachioed man, wearing a well-tailored ultramarine suit, gets into a maroon Renault 16 next to a public park, slams the door, starts the engine, and breaks into body parts flying between fragments of metal inside a ball of fire that scorches the foliage of a chestnut tree, bright with the fresh new green of the end of spring, and then a coded knock in Morse, dash-dash-dot-dot at the hotel door, and a fat naked man, his paunch spilling over the top of his green boxer shorts, opens the door in the middle of the night and gets a bullet between the eyes from a silencer that coughs into his face at point blank range, and he falls backward on the carpet, and the crown of his limp penis peeps in one-eyed astonishment from the opening of his shorts, and a man's voice on the telephone says 'Pronto' in Italian with a heavy gutteral accent, and a finger presses eight-one-zero, and from the other end of the line an explosion is heard and after it the long shrill whistle of a disconnected line, and four men in the overalls of the French electric corporation skip like goats and spray eight men sitting round a table with miniaturized machine guns, and chairs turn over, and a fisherman's cabin goes up in flames, and a boat blows up at sea, and people with arms and legs outspread fly like black cardboard cutouts against a background of glaring gold, and the voice of the Alsatian sings a line from a song by Yves Montand with cheerful irony '*Et tout cela pour rien*'—and all this for nothing.

God, how much we killed and were killed. So many lives were lost in order not to reach the place we've reached, and here we are at exactly the place where we didn't want to be. And the lives that were lost are lost. We have to talk about it one day, Shakespeare. We have to sit over a bottle of Lagavulin one night and talk about it. Not Lagavulin. Its presence is too powerful, and it will take us straight to Islay, to that poor waiter, Bousidi, whose only crime was that he looked like the identical twin of the real Bousidi, and this resemblance cost him his life. So not Laphroaig and not Lagavulin and not Talisker. We'll sit over a more neutral brand of whiskey. Calm. Without memories. Not from the Western Isles, whose soil is soaked in peat, but from the Highlands, from the heights of North Scotland. Balvenie, or Oban, or Glengoyne. Or perhaps from the lowlands, velvety triple distilled Auchentoshan. We'll sit, you and I, and try to understand what it was, this Marathon, in which the streets are suddenly filled with crowds of runners, seventy thousand runners stampeding like herds, flooding and packing the squares and avenues to suffocation, spilling into the streets and alleys, a human tsunami flooding a city, the earth trembles from the thudding of the soles on the roads and the pavements, a hundred and forty thousand feet pounding the asphalt, and the shop windows and the facades of the buildings echo, and the air trembles with the sobbing of the desperate breathing of the lungs inhaling and exhaling two hundred and eighty thousand liters of air a second, and suddenly the last runners go past, and the race is over, the streets are empty, and a profound silence descends on the still city, and you stand there wondering: What was it, all that? Where did they come from? Where were they running to? What did they want? Where did they suddenly disappear to? What the hell was it, this crazy story that was our lives—

Where are we?

15

Shakespeare's voice interrupts the torrent of images flooding the cellars of Yadanuga's consciousness, and Mona repeats the sentence, and directs it to a precise address:

Moran, so where exactly are we?

Well, says Moran, and turns to Hanina, before you went up to the roof—

He knows what happened before he went up to the roof, Mona interrupts her and says in the commanding tone of a skipper: Tell him what happened when he wasn't here.

Moran takes a breath. Her nostrils flare and quiver. A beautiful mare about to break into a gallop, he says to himself, trying to banish Melissa, who wears reading glasses on her slits of eyes, which look as if they have just been bathed in tears, and who is reading to someone over the phone passages from a book with a yellow cover, which shows the photograph of a man with a bald head and a lifeless face in a tuxedo, embracing a naked young Thai girl.

He asks himself why she needs this book for the pervert on the other end of the line, since there is nothing new about the description she is reading him. He has no doubt of her ability to successfully improvise a text of the same kind, full of names for the male and female sexual organs and tediously banal descriptions of what happens to them in the act of sexual intercourse. Apparently she prefers to read these things from a text written by someone else, a translation of some French novel, since this frees her from the need to search for words or to involve herself in the dreary transaction taking the place of real intimacy. He looks at her through the open bathroom door and sees her contemptuously deceiving her customer, who is fully aware of the deceit, but at this moment, in some kennel of loneliness, in one of the tens of thousands of cells of human habitation in this city glittering in a festival of light in the window, he is sitting on the lavatory, or leaning over the sink, and masturbating, with his face contorted in an expression of bestial stupidity. Apparently she gathers from the sounds on the other end of the line that the guy is about to come, for instead of continuing with her reading, she starts to puff and pant, with an expression of utter boredom and indifference on her face, and if she feels anything at all, it's presumably an itch under her right elbow, for while her right hand holds the telephone, the fingers of her left hand move to scratch a spot just under the elbow on her right arm, and after they've finished scratching there they climb up her forearm and scratch there too, and when she's done scratching she inserts her skinny pinkie into her left ear and probes inside it, and he watches her from his bubble bath, and steamy vapors cover the big window and turn Manhattan from 12th Street North into a shimmering Milky Way in the darkness, and her pants and moans over the phone grow faster and more frequent the deeper her matchstick pinkie digs into her ear, and now her mouth gapes open in a jaw-splitting yawn, of which she takes advantage to let out a deep groan, as if she has discovered within her a vast reservoir of hidden air, and she cries, now, baby, stick it into me, all of it, oh yes, she roars, go on, shout, she whispers, and afterwards she puts the phone down and opens her mouth in a yawn even bigger than the one before, and she gets up, and stretches in front of the steamy window, and swings her long arms round behind her, making her shoulder joints crack loudly, and then she senses his presence close to her, and she turns round and sees him standing opposite her, wrapping a white towel round his waist, and she asks him in a businesslike tone if he wants to fuck now, or a little later.

Not now, he says, infected by her yawn.

I hope that conversation didn't bother you, she yawns a third time.

A job's a job, he says. We all have to earn a living.

And suddenly the phone rings. She looks at the display and says:

It's him.

Hanina takes in the number, engraves it in his memory, picks up the phone and says:

I'm waiting for you, maniac.

There is silence on the other end of the line, and Hanina returns the receiver to its cradle.

What did he say? she asks.

Nothing, he says.

He wanted to check if you were still here, she says.

So now he knows.

I'm living on borrowed time, she says. One day that lunatic will kill me.

He won't touch you, he says.

I can't take him hitting me anymore. He keeps accusing me of being lazy. However hard I work, it's not enough for him.

I can testify that you work even when you're resting, he laughs, and adds: Or maybe the opposite...

In the end I'll kill myself, she says, and that scares me.

When a person really wants to kill himself, he tells her, he should kill whoever put him in that situation.

This time they won't let me off so easily, she says, I'm not a minor any more. Besides, Tony's not Patrice. He's a professional killer. He'll kill me ten times before I can give him a scratch.

If you permit me, I'll help you, he hears Shakespeare sharpening a quill.

You help me just by being here, she says. These days between Christmas and New Year's Eve are the worst for me. Because anyone who's lonely all year is doubly lonely then, and the demand for whores goes through the roof.

Shakespeare is a little taken aback by her casual use of the vulgar word 'whore', which comes to English from the German 'Hure', which is close to the Arabic word 'huriyeh', which reminds him of the Hebrew word 'hor', or hole, and the noble one 'horin', freedom, which reminds him of the Indo-European root 'karo', from which are derived the Italian 'caro', the French 'cher', the Hebrew 'yakar', and the English 'cherish', 'caress' and 'charity', but also the ancient German 'Horaz', which is close to the Israeli 'harman', or lecher, which is reminiscent of the Sanskrit 'kama' which means love or desire, giving rise to the famous 'Kama Sutra', that Hindu codex of love and marriage, and who knows how far the bard of Stratford's musings would have taken him if the huriyeh of Manhattan hadn't interrupted him in mid-flight:

Tony has one client, a deaf-mute, a kind of kinsman of his, who's into orgies. This maniac's ordered three whores for New Year's Eve. And who's supposed to provide them for him? You guessed right: me. Believe me, it isn't easy to find a girl who's free on New Year's Eve. So where am I going to get the other two? And if I don't do what Tony tells me—he beats me up. That's his language with women. The last time I failed to come up with three whores for the deaf-mute's harem, to make him feel at home, Tony gave me a black eye. I holed up in a motel, I didn't want to see anybody. My problem is that when he hits me I hit the bottle. So I was sitting at the bar when this guy came up and bought me a drink. He was nice to me so I went up to his room with him. At first he was nice, but suddenly I realized even though I was pretty drunk by then, that he was trying to pimp me to three Hispanic butchers who worked at a slaughterhouse near the motel, and I saw that if I said no it would be bad. So I said I was going to my room for a minute to take a pill, and I went out to the road and got away from there as fast as I could. I haven't got the strength for that kind of stuff anymore. I've had about as much as I can stand. I'm teetering on the edge here. Do you understand? She's pleading for her life, and the slits of her eyes are suddenly flooded with tears.

Yes, he understands why she gave him her telephone number, and he wants to tell her: Goodbye, it's been nice to know you, but the Secret Nameless Friend says to him, you can't do that to her, not now, not like this, not after you got her into trouble with that filthy pimp, who even if he isn't Adonis deserves to have his nose stuffed and his mouth sprayed with insecticide. And suddenly he feels his fingers moving like snakes' heads in the air.

Tell me, he asks, does he like to sing?

When he's driving, she says.

What songs does he like?

All kinds, she says. Cole Porter, Donizetti arias, all kinds.

Where does he live, he asks, and the information flows from her mouth precise as the designation of a target.

16

And that's where we are now, he hears Moran's voice, and sees her eyes looking at him, and realizes that all this time he has apparently been staring into her gray-green eyes without taking in a word she said, and he hears himself say 'Yes', and Mona says: So what do you say?

What do I say, he says. What do I say....

He looks from Mona to Golan and from Golan to Yadanuga. They are all waiting for him to speak. He's their boss, and they're waiting for him to open his mouth and speak, to say something at last. To settle this idiotic question, which Yadanuga has suddenly decided for some reason to turn into a matter of principle. As if it's the be-all and end-all. Whether it's legitimate to involve children and old people in the promotion of the pill for enhancing sex and feeling.

You want to know what I say, he repeats. Stand a big prick under the balcony in Verona, opposite a cunt overflowing with love, and write: 'Romeo, oh Romeo' or words to that effect.

There is a moment of silence, as if a siren has gone off and everyone is standing to attention in memory of the fallen in all the wars, or as if someone has pressed the 'pause' button on the remote, and just as the siren ends, and the silence is suddenly broken, and life bursts out again full of noise and fury at having been cut off, Mona bursts out first and demands indignantly:

What's happened to you, tell me, have you gone completely crazy?

What's the problem? he asks.

What's the problem? She demands. You ask what the problem is! We've wasted two days on arguing, examining every detail, analyzing every tenth of a second in Golan and Moran's script, and we need a decision, because we can't drag it out any longer if we don't want our competitors to finish us off with a knockout in the first round, and I don't think it has to end like that at all, I think we have an excellent chance of winning the contract, because we've got a real ace, yes, I have no hesitation in stating my opinion, and I think it's time to say openly: Golan and Moran's script is a sure winner, and Mackie's proposal is a non-starter.

That's your opinion, he tries to put down a bridge-head of a couple of words, but she immediately opens the floodgates and a mighty torrent of verbiage floods his little bridgehead and sweeps it away, and the whole torrent begins with one little word:

No, she says, it's not my opinion, these are the facts, this is the reality. We've had a week for brainstorming. And you kept quiet. Ever since you returned from New York, you've kept your mouth shut most of the time. If you thought that everything people said was idiotic, that we were going in the wrong direction, you should have said so. I don't recall hearing you say anything that contributed to the discussion. Not an idea, not a direction, not a concept, you were completely passive. Paralyzed. And now, after everything we've been through, after all the arguments and the confrontations and the shouting, you come and dismiss it all as if nobody's invested hours and days of work here, and you still have the nerve to come up with that imbecilic joke—a prick standing opposite a cunt on the balcony in Verona—

It isn't a joke, he says.

A bad joke, she snaps.

It isn't a joke, he insists. It's exactly what Sol Lewis wants: one image, to convey that his fucking pill simultaneously enlarges the penis, arouses it, and empowers it, and all in thirty seconds, so it seems to me that my suggestion—

Hanina, she cuts him short, pronouncing his name as a kind of reproach concealing a threat, you know that the future of our entire firm depends on winning this contract. And we're competing with giant advertising agencies in the US, in England, in Japan, in Italy and in Germany. If we're on the short list of six finalists we've got Moran's brain and Golan's work to thank for it. This time you didn't

contribute a thing, and if we'd gone with Mackie's first proposal we would have been out of the running a long time
ago. Now we haven't got any more time to lose. We have to
decide between Mackie's second proposal and the development of Golan and Moran's idea. Allow me to remind you
that this is why we called this meeting, at your initiative.
We've been arguing all night long, and when the time came
to decide, you asked for time out to go up to the roof and
think. I was sure you would come down with a decision,
and what happened in the end?

I told you what I suggest. I think that....

We heard, she interrupts him. What's your opinion of
what Moran said?

When? he asks.

A minute ago.

What did she say?

I told you about the ideas that came up here while you
were gone, about how to develop our original idea, says
Moran.

I think the ideas are excellent, Mona supports her. You
don't agree?

Try to remember something she said, he urges himself
and concentrates on Moran's face and her eyes staring at
him in bewilderment, but her face, and her pouting lips,
which part now to say something, undergo a rapid trans-
formation before his eyes and turn into the buttocks of the
fucking Frenchwoman whose text Melissa read over the telephone, and again the Frenchwoman's hand slips between
her parted thighs, and in a minute he's going to get a hard-
on, and in order to nip this embarrassing and uncontrollable
development in the bud he utters the only words that he's
capable of producing at the moment:

A prick with a hard-on under the balcony in Verona,
and a cunt overflowing with love, and Romeo—

I don't believe it, says Mona in despair. I don't believe it! We're going to lose the contract because of you! This firm is going down the tubes. And it's your fault.

Is this what you meant?

The erect lingam, Golan—who all this time had been sitting in silence and playing with the mouse, absorbed in the screen in front of him, as if he wasn't there at all—has been there all the time. Now he taps the keyboard, presses Enter, and on the giant presentation screen there appears a giant pill in the form of a balcony, under which a mighty black phallus stands upright in all its glory, swollen veins twining round it like wisteria branches on a casuarina trunk, a pair of lovesick eyes gazing from its head, while it smiles lasciviously at a pink vagina crowned with curly chestnut hair, whose dripping lips are parted like the petals of the Venus Slipper orchid. And from the parted lips a balloon emerges with the words: Romeo, oh Romeo.

When did you do it? demands Hanina in astonishment.

While you were arguing, replies Golan indifferently.

But how did you have time? asks Hanina admiringly.

No big deal, says Golan dismissively. I downloaded the penis from the Mapplethorpe site, and the vagina is a water lily I processed with Photoshop.

Amazing, says Hanina.

But Mackie demurs: He was talking about Romeo and Juliet, not Othello.

What's the difference? asks Golan.

Romeo wasn't black, explains Mackie.

No problem, Golan dismisses him. He concentrates on the mouse and the keyboard, clicks a few times, brings up a color table, selects a shade and drags it to the black penis, whose perimeter he outlines with a dotted line, after which he selects the shade of the black phallus and does the same thing with the vagina-lily, click-click, and the races switch before their eyes on the presentation screen: a Caucasian penis pink as a boiled ham rises lustfully opposite an African vagina-lily, dark and desirous as a black iris.

Any other comments? asks Golan.

No, says Hanina, it's perfect.

Ye-es, Moran agrees thoughtfully, perhaps it is perfect, but it will outrage the feminists, the fundamentalists, and the anti-defamation leagues. And besides, the judges will reject it outright because it's an outmoded concept which has no chance of being accepted.

Why not? demands Hanina.

What, in one word, characterizes the whole 'New Age' scene? asks Moran.

Fundamentalism, he quotes another book he read on the transatlantic flight home from America.

No, says Moran, write it down: mystical shit.

That's two words.

She ignores his comment, sell people a carrot as a carrot and they won't buy it. But if you hint to them that the carrot contains a substance that in combination with the oil of pitango seeds brings about a mystical connection to the embryonic experience together with continuous triple orgasms, they'll buy the carrot, and also search the internet for pitango seed oil. Do you get it? Advertising today has to speak to our generation, and it isn't simple. Because our generation is very difficult to characterize, it has many faces. We were born with a mouse in our hands. In other words, we roam at our ease, open everything curiously, but we are quickly disappointed, and easily abandon things that disappoint us. We believe only in ourselves, and we like buying things that we ostensibly discover for ourselves, because we're a very creative generation, we create as easily as we breathe. We are actually multi-cultural, we pick up Spanish from *telenovelas*, English from the internet, and we feel completely at home with chaos and high-tech and virtual reality. For us complexity is pretension, and our motto is being connected, connect to yourself, connect to your friends, connect to what's cool, what's groovy, what's hot, connect to the latest trend, the post-trend, the post-post, because basically we're dying to belong, to be part of what's happening, to land a good job, to earn a fortune, to make your first million before thirty, and we're optimistic, but also a little hard, tough, maybe even a little crude, we don't buy a horse without examining its teeth under a microscope, which is a metaphor of course, because we don't buy horses. We can be very diligent and very precise, you can't sell us slogans or grand metaphors. We try new brands willingly, even eagerly, but we don't stick to any brand. We're interactive, we like to influence, but we're also selective, and we buy only what we need, and that too with a critical eye. Our motto is simple: 'It's cool to be smart'. But we hate smart alecks, we like things that are direct, pure and intimate...

And all this is in your and Golan's proposal?

More or less, says Moran. If you look carefully, you'll see that something almost imperceptible changes in the faces of the children after they take the pill. Suddenly the look in their eyes seems to grow older, it becomes wet and eager, and then lustful and passionate, and in the end satisfied and calm, because Golan went to a porno site and selected the look in the eyes of a woman before, during and after orgasm, and put it in the little girl's eyes after she swallowed the pill, and he did the same with the old grandfather, who takes the pill while he's looking at the little girl, you can see that suddenly he looks like a twenty-year old in love, and the little girl suddenly looks like a woman of thirty, who knows what it is and who's just experienced it, and it works instantly on the subconscious of the viewer, because this change in the expression of the eyes during orgasm is something you recognize in a tenth of a second. We did a lot of experiments on our friends to make sure. It arouses the desire in the viewer to imitate them and to take the pill himself. It works like a peepshow. It appeals to you on your most animal level, and the whole thing is conveyed through the eyes alone, without anyone being able to say what did it to him. We tested it with our friends, and none of them could say what did it to him.

What did what to him? Yadanuga attacks from his corner.

I don't want to tell you, because your attitude is negative in advance, there's no point.

Tell me, suggests Hanina, my attitude isn't negative in advance.

When you saw it for the first time, didn't it turn you on? she asks, and offers him her eyes, and he sees in them the eyes of Melissa offering him her lips, wet, eager and yearning, and he feels his penis swelling, and he admits that yes, it turns him on.

That's what you want to achieve with your commercial? Mackie attacks her.

Yes, she says simply, a commercial should titillate. Like the beginning of an affair, like a good book that you can't put down. It should be sexy like an 'in' quarter of the city, arouse unsatisfied cravings in you together with a promise of satisfaction—

'I desire you more acquaintance, but retain it—' Hanina hears Shakespeare speaking from his throat.

What's that? asks the startled Moran, and Hanina explains:

'A Midsummer Night's Dream'. And Shakespeare translates silently: 'I want to fuck you, but I'm controlling myself.'

So what are we going to decide? Mona presses them.

17

What are we going to do, asks Hanina, and Melissa stands in front of him dressed in old jeans and a sloppy white T-shirt, holding a wooden spoon and stirring the wine simmering on the electric plate which glows with an infrared light. With her other hand she sprinkles nutmeg into the steaming punch, which gives off intoxicating scents of cloves and cinnamon, and her eyes look straight into his, and she says to him for the first time, with utter simplicity:

You know, my secret nameless friend, I'm gonna miss you.

Speak to her, the scriptwriter urges him, I've written you a dialogue with her. Tell her who you are at last. Give her a name to hang onto. Tell her you're Maoz Tzur, or Giora Bar-Giora. Something heroic. Tell her you don't know who you are. Maybe you knew once. But that's not certain either. Maybe you never knew. This silence is becoming intolerable, the novice scriptwriter says nervously, we're not in a Bergman or Godard movie here. You're acting in an action movie. Man, make a sound.

Cock-a-doodle-do, says Maoz Tzur.

Make a sound like a bulbul or a crow, pleads Tyrell. Tell her tra-la-la or cra-cra-cra. Tell her you don't know if you're a man or an animal. And if it's an animal, then what kind of animal. A mole or a monkey-bird. Tell her it's the bird migration season. The time when all winged creatures are commanded to arise and depart the land of their birth and the graves of their forefathers, to forget their friends both dead and alive, and to fly in the direction indicated by the bird compass implanted in their brains or their DNA.

You know, he hears himself declaim the strange text which the scriptwriter puts in his mouth, once people thought that when autumn came in cold climates, birds took off for warmer climes, but today we know that this isn't true.

So what is the truth? she asks, without wondering why he has suddenly started talking about bird migrations.

The migratory instinct of birds is apparently connected only to direction, he goes on reciting the novice scriptwriter's tedious text, without understanding why he's saying what he says.

But how do they know when the cold days are coming? she asks.

Something changes in the sound of their voice, he declaims the next line.

The birds know that autumn's coming by the sound of their voices?

They're very sensitive to sound, he says. You know they can hear ultrasonic frequencies?

And vampires? she asks.

It's well known that vampires transmit sounds on ultrasonic frequencies, and they pick up echoes returned by various objects on their inner sonar. That's the only thing that enables them to fly between trees in the dark without bumping into the branches.

And before he can shut him up, the novice scriptwriter involves him in a weird discussion of vampires, which the spidery girl embraces with enthusiasm, and into which she draws him too:

Why do humans suffer so much when they fall in love with vampires? she asks.

Simple, replies the last scion of a vampire dynasty who has just this minute been born. Human beings want to possess the objects of their love. They don't understand that it's impossible to possess a vampire.

Because thanks to its sonar system, the vampire will exploit every crack and loophole in order to escape into the dark, she guesses.

Obviously, replies the vampire Sisera, sipping the hot spicy wine offered him by Yael, the wife of a nameless jealous friend, and now imagine what happens when two vampires fall in love with each other, he hears himself repeating the idiotic text, without the faintest idea of what he's talking about.

Usually it's a sad story, she muses aloud.

Because if both of them are searching for cracks in the dark, it will all be over very quickly, without any warning signs, he completes her musings.

So why do they start with each other in the first place, she wonders.

Because they get tired of the possessive instincts and emotional blackmail of human beings, he reads the next line of dialogue from the prompter, and thinks that it contains a measure of truth.

And when the female vampire suddenly leaves the male, doesn't he pursue her? she wants to know.

Never, he states firmly.

'Never say never', says her id, quoting the universal id, and now it's a conversation between id and id, whispers the delighted scriptwriter, and it can go on forever without putting any effort into it at all.

A true vampire never pursues anyone who leaves it, the words slide smoothly out of his mouth. It will never harass anyone who abandons it, or nag it with stupid questions like, what have I done to deserve this.

And he won't try to look for her in order to find out why she suddenly broke off contact? She isn't convinced.

Never, he follows the inexperienced scriptwriter. That's the difference between vampires and human beings: human beings are sure that they deserve to be loved. When love ends, they look for the logic, because they believe in reasons, circumstances, meaning. In any straw they can grasp at. Vampires, on the other hand, know that they don't deserve anything. They don't believe in anything. When somebody loves them, they regard it as a miracle. And miracles, as vampires know, suddenly vanish, for no reason, just as life ends.

That's true, she agrees, but it doesn't make them happy.

No, he agrees, vampires aren't happy creatures, but they have the strength to withstand it.

What's the source of their sadness? wonders her id, which uses her young voice with whorish charm.

The source of their sadness is not known, says Shakespeare.

In sooth I know not why I am so sad, Melissa unthinkingly quotes Antonia's opening lines from the first scene of 'The Merchant-woman of Venice'. It wearies me, she goes on quoting, you say it wearies you.

It won't weary me, Shakespeare reassures her, I have to write the fifth and last act, even though my inspiration dried up after the fourth act, which is why the last act is going to be lousy, but Melissantonia isn't reassured:

But how I caught it, found it, or came by it, what stuff 'tis made of, whereof it is born, I am to learn....

Me too, such a want-wit sadness makes of me, that I have much ado to know myself, admits Shakespeare, without remembering which of his characters he is quoting now, although he is clearly quoting someone, because he himself feels neither sadness nor witlessness at the moment, only emptiness, an abyss of emptiness gaping between them, and all the contradictory statements that he makes, and all the conflicting acts that he performs, circle round the edge of this abyss, and apparently this is the strange force attracting them to each other: a black hole, which is signified by

black-hole bypassing sentences, such as the next sentence
that comes out of her mouth:

When a vampire encounters an ordinary human being,
who falls in love with it, it doesn't help it to understand
anything about itself.

And Shakespeare supports her:

But when a vampire meets a vampire—

What happens when a vampire meets a vampire? She
asks, and her direct gaze bores a long dark tunnel inside
him, leading to a vast underground space, hollowed out of
the bowels of a mountain in which no one imagines there
to be winding passages, opening into dark secret cathedrals,
where an eternal silence has reigned since the day the voices
of the anonymous miners who quarried these underground
galleries were stilled.

When a vampire meets a vampire, Shakespeare embarks on a voyage to an unknown land over the simmering
cauldron of wine she has brewed for them, for the night of
the vampires—

18

We'll continue the meeting tomorrow, Mona cuts sharply
into the train of his thoughts, and before he can recover she
commands:

And you're coming with me.

He leaves the conference room behind her and follows
her down the corridor. She stops in front of the elevator,
and he stands next to her. She presses the button. They wait
in silence. The numbers change over the elevator door. The
elevator rises from the ground floor, reaches their floor and
comes to a halt with a click. The stainless steel jaw gapes.
Mona steps inside, and he steps in after her. He looks to see

where she is taking him, to the roof or the ground. She takes him below ground, to the parking level. The elevator stops.

They get out. Only a few cars are scattered here and there in the underground lot, deserted at this late hour. They walk silently to the blue Land Rover. Mona walks with a brisk, resolute step, and he trails behind her, contemplating the tight walnut colored leather pants, the red sweater whose neckline reveals the curves of her breasts, and notes her athletic build, the pomellas of her firm buttocks, her muscular calves and thighs, and the strong tendons of her ankles, twining like roots into her running shoes. As she walks she whistles to herself a kind of improvised cover version of Roberta Flack's 'Killing me softly', which she turns into a kind of jazzy march. Accompanied by the clattering of her keys, which are attached to a steel ring ten centimeters in diameter and look like the keys of a mediaeval prison warder. She's in a belligerent mood, he says to himself, and as if she has read his thoughts, she turns her head and surveys him with an amused expression. For a moment it seems to him that she is about to open her mouth, but no. She throws her key ring into the air, catches it with one hand, right on the remote of her Land Rover, and presses the button with an imperceptible sleight of hand. The Land Rover whinnies and snorts with the joy of a wild horse that knows its owner, and its eyes flash her two mischievous winks, and already she jumps in and sits behind the wheel, starts the engine and engages the automatic gear with a movement full of dynamism and power, as if she's operating the lever of the manual gear box of an old Titanic truck, or at least a Mac Diesel from the middle of the previous century. He hardly has time to take his place beside her before the wild beast leaps forward with a powerful thrust that sticks him to the back of his seat. With a savage screech of its tires the monster veers and tilts sideways, scraping the curb of the sidewalk as it makes a right turn, like a plane changing direction after takeoff. He wants to tell her to be careful, but before he can open his mouth Mona presses the button that transfers the gearbox into sports drive and steps ferociously on the accelerator, humming to herself a tune she picked up from a French commercial many years ago, in the days when she was an Intelligence officer in their liquidation squad and drove a Mini Cooper, whose gear stick was equipped with an overdrive button: '*La conduite sportive à la portée de tous*'. The engine growls threateningly and the Land Rover cuts across an intersection at a red light, weaving in a slalom like a drunken cruise missile dancing a samba between cars screeching to a stop or getting out of the way in a panic. Mona leaves behind her a cacophony of hysterical hoots and curses, which only egg her on to give the hundred and fifty fire horses imprisoned under the hood their heads. And in this way they burn through another two red lights with traffic swerving right and left in front and behind them the last tenth of a second before or after they enter the intersection, borne on the wings of a terrifying demon chariot. Hanina puts his hand on the handbrake, ready to pull on it with all his might the moment they enter the collision course opposite another vehicle or post or tree at the side of the road. The speedometer needle goes into the red and hovers next to a hundred and eighty. Mona's eyes are focused on the dense darkness in front of them, through which the headlamps carve a tunnel of light. From time to time the rear lights of other cars flicker in the gloom, rushing towards them with dizzying speed. Mona passes them and leaves them far behind like a vampire, yes! Like a vampire gliding through the darkness and flitting between the branches of the trees without so much as touching a leaf. His hand remains resting on the handbrake.

19

He's on the back seat of the Harley Davidson which Yadanuga races at the speed of a plane taking off—swerving
acrobatically between giant trucks and private cars, leaving
behind Fiats, Alfas, Lancias, and even one Lamborghini, red
with shame or anger, which they fly past like a rocket, when
suddenly a patrol car leaps out of the lay-by at the side of
the Autostrada del Sol, five hundred meters ahead of them,
and it is clear that it intends to stop them, or even to open
fire on them, and Yadanuga yells into the fierce wind, 'Hang
on with all your strength—we're taking off!' and he tightens
his grip on Yadanuga's waist, and the motorcycle veers to
the left and leaps over the wide strip of lawn dividing the
lanes, and they fly over the traffic hurtling in the opposite direction, and Yadanuga makes a masterly landing on the bicycle lane on the other side of the busy motorway, and they
race against the direction of the traffic, and he bursts out
laughing at the imagined sight of the flabbergasted faces of
the policemen, and 'What are you laughing at?' asks Mona,
who is now racing the Land Rover towards the parking lot
next to the marina, and he says: I remembered a certain
liquidation, and he wonders why they had given that terrorist the strange code name of 'Santa Rosa', they had always
called their targets Abu-something, and only 'Tino Rossi'
was the exception to the rule, and suddenly they were told
that the next one on the list was 'Santa Rosa'. But in fact
they never told them who the man they were required to
remove from the world was. They restricted themselves to
general information: So-and-so is responsible for the deaths
of such-and-such a number of people. Here's his picture.
Here's his surveillance file. The addresses where he stays.
His daily schedule. Habits. People he meets on a regular
basis. The address of his mistress. When he goes to her.

When he leaves. Choose your own MO. Access routes. Escape routes. If you're caught, you haven't got a father or
mother in the world. You're on your own with God and the
devil. That's it. Any questions? No questions. Get to work.

20

Come, she says.

They go down to her boat. A white sloop emblazoned
with the strange name 'Cadenabia'. Mona had bought it
from a Greek Cypriot skipper who had made her promise
not to change its name. He too had acquired it under the
same name, from an Italian grain dealer, who told him that
the name had brought him a lot of luck. Mona unfurls the
beautiful sail, which swells with the wind that at this quiet
early-morning hour is blowing from the land to the sea.
She seizes the mainsheet with her right hand, and tilts the
sail to an angle of thirty degrees to the boat, which slides
soundlessly out of the jetty. Now Mona leans over the side
of the sloop and increases the windward angle of the sail,
and the craft picks up speed and skips lightly over the little
breakers which Mona calls 'ducks'. Or so he understands,
because just then she announces that they have a choppy sea
ahead of them, and when he asks her how she knows, she
replies: 'Look at those ducks.' Hanina doesn't know if this
is her own private metaphor, or an accepted term for little
waves of this kind, which for some reason break far from
the shore.

Ducks are a sign of an approaching storm? he asks
anxiously.

A choppy sea isn't a storm, she replies with a certain
contempt and throws him a yellow life belt: Put it on, she

instructs him, and hold the helm in a straight line with the prow, if you can.

Hanina wonders to himself what the difference is between a choppy and a stormy sea. He has never been attracted to the sea, and in spite of Mona's increasing expertise on matters concerning the sea and seamanship, Hanina is not well up on nautical terms, and he doesn't even know the names of the parts of the sailing boat, never mind the type of the sail, not to mention its various components. As far as he is concerned there's a boat, a prow and a stern, a helm, a mast and a sail. All the rest are poles and ropes without names or meanings. Mona shows no inclination to include him in the intimacy she has developed over the years with this mysterious entity. The sea is her territory, and she guards her exclusive sovereignty over her vast and rebellious realm jealously. When two or three times in the past he had brought up ideas for improving the protection of the exposed metal parts, or suggested up-to-the-minute survival kits, which he had come across in the guerilla warfare magazines he continued to receive in the mail, she dismissed his suggestions with utter contempt, and he had stopped showing an interest. He contemplates her skill and efficiency with balancing the boat with the help of her taut body, stretched like a powerful spring over the side. She holds strongly onto the pole to which the bottom of the sail is attached, responding to the slightest movements of the boat which slides with a faint swishing sound over the fathoms of water, and gaining the greatest amount of speed possible from the wind, sailing over the ducks heralding the approaching turbulence.

He looks at her pear shaped head, with its short, boyish crown of platinum bristles, and wonders what goes on in the depths of her mind. What submarine plants grow there? What drunken old ships are wrecked there? What deep water fish glide majestically between silent engine rooms, whose metal parts are covered with plumes of sea weeds and algae? From one of the empty spaces rises the head of a little girl with short, boyish, wet hair, a head which is all water and whose eyes are a fount of tears.

Timberlake. Timber-lake. Timber.

With a tumbler of whiskey in her hand—

21

She lounges on the thick carpet, indifferently exposing her unfeminine body with its long skinny limbs. Holding a tumbler of whiskey in her left hand, and lightly brushing the calf of his left leg with the cobweb fingers of her infinitely long right arm. Her touch is not sensual, her fluttering fingers do not give rise to any desire, which is precisely what is so good and suits him so well in this strange strait of his life, rocking like a drunken boat whose engines died in the middle of the sea, borne along aimlessly by the waves.

You really don't want to fuck me? she asks.

No, he says, I hope you're not insulted.

Not in the least, she says. It's the last thing I need now.

They lie supine side by side, and he listens to her quiet breathing.

You're not just being considerate, she wants to make sure.

I'm lying next to you naked, he says. If I felt like fucking, would I be able to hide it?

You don't suffer from impotence? she asks directly.

No, he says, and I don't have any need to prove it.

Because if you have any problems performing, I can give you Viagra, she says.

I've got something much better in my coat pocket, he reassures her, and I don't need it.

Something better than Viagra? She asks with interest. What is it?

A Midsummer Night's Dream pill, says Shakespeare. Good for both sexes. Gives rise to emotional and sexual excitement, produces a terrific erection, shortens the recovery time and lengthens and thickens the male sexual organ. You want to try it?

Do you want to? she asks.

I don't need it, he says.

That's good, she says, I'm sick and tired of disturbed men.

So am I, he says.

Maybe you're sick and tired of disturbed women, she suggests a correction.

That too, he says. But I've had more to do with disturbed men.

Are you gay? she asks.

I don't know, he says. I never tried.

Then you're not gay, she pronounces. A queer knows he's a queer, just like a Jew knows he's a Jew.

Are you a rabbi? he asks.

Why? Do rabbis turn you on? she laughs and covers his penis with her palm and stringy fingers. A deep sigh breaks from his chest.

Why are you sighing? she asks in surprise.

A Jewish reaction, he says.

I hope I'm not making you suffer, she says.

No, he sighs again, we sigh when we're happy too.

I had a Jew once, she says.

A boyfriend? he asks.

A client, she says. A Hasid from Queens. I even remember his name: Bornstat. He looked like a plucked chicken, but when he took out his thing, I got a shock. It was something between a piano leg and a fireman's hose. I didn't want to insult him, so I said: Sorry, I'm done working for the day. But he insisted: The rabbi sent him to a prostitute, because his wife refused to go to bed with him. I told him: Go to your rabbi, ask him to give you his wife.

The Hasid was insulted, made a scene, Tony came and beat me up: Because of you we'll lose the whole Yeshiva.

I hope it didn't turn you into an anti-Semite, he says.

I don't hate people more than they deserve, she reassures him.

He laughs, and she plays with his pubic hair and asks: How do you learn to sigh?

It's simple, he says. You need to be chased out of a few countries, be the victim of pogroms, have your house burned down, your grandmother and grandfather and all your aunts and uncles murdered, and after a few hundred years of treatments along those lines, it comes of its own accord, without any effort.

I understand, she laughs. I guess I won't learn to sigh in this incarnation.

They lie there relaxed, without wanting to do anything. The noise of the city beyond the window, a cacophony of screaming tires, screeching brakes, the groans of the tortured iron of the subway, sounds like a chorus of howling wild animals in a distant jungle.

It feels so good to be able to hold your cock without it starting to stiffen, it's really nice to hold a soft dick, she confesses, and after a minute she adds: But maybe it's not so nice for you.

If it didn't feel nice I would remove your hand, he says. You can leave it there if it feels good to you. It feels good to me.

What kind of business did you have with disturbed men? she asks.

I killed a few of them, he says. There are still too many left.

Did you do it for fun?

No, he says, I performed a mission.

Who for? she inquires.

For the human race, he says.

After a further silence, during which the only sound is that of their breathing, his deep and slow and hers quick and light, she asks:

Can I come closer to you?

As close as you like, he says.

She turns onto her left side, and the skinny string of her body clings to his. The unripe peaches of her breasts brush against the sides of his ribs, the taut skin of the drum of her belly touches his waist, her pubic hair tickles the edge of his buttocks, and when she lifts her thigh and lays the stalk of her long leg on his leg, and tucks her sharp knee between his knees, he feels the lips of her open pussy licking the skin of his thigh like a blind puppy groping with its wet nose for its mother's teats and greedily fastening onto the nipple—and all this time his penis stays still in the web of her fingers weaving it a nest. For a while they lie like this, profoundly at rest, far from all the labors of the flesh, and then her voice begins to trickle softly between her warm lips into his ear.

22

I'm so tired, she whispers, I'm so glad you don't want to fuck me and I can just lie next to you and rest, rest for one night like a normal human being. You don't have to pay me for tonight.

I spend the night in expensive hotels, he says, and enjoy myself less. I'll pay you what it would have cost me to go to a hotel.

There's no need, she says. I have the money to cover tonight.

You mean to pay that slimebag Tino?

Tony, she corrects him, and adds: Every profession has its own code of ethics.

You have a strange way of speaking, he says.

What's wrong with the way I speak?

Nothing, he hastens to reassure her, it's only that sometimes you use high-flown language, sometimes you even quote Shakespeare.

I'm writing a doctoral dissertation, she says.

What's the subject?

The Samson family.

Who were they? he asks.

Hangmen, she says, a family of hangmen. The profession passed form father to son.

That's interesting, he says. How did you get onto it?

My grandfather was a hangman's assistant, she says. He helped to hang eleven war criminals at Nuremberg.

Good for him, he says. He did a good job, your grandfather.

Not really, she demurs. They hanged them on an improvised gallows, and he sawed the holes in the floor for the trapdoors.

So what wasn't good about it?

The holes were a bit too small, and when the hanged men fell through them, they bumped against the sides. The fall was arrested, and instead of breaking their necks and dying instantly, they hung on the noose for ten to fifteen minutes until they choked to death.

Even better, he says.

You're a cruel man, she remarks.

No I'm not, he protests, but there are bastards who deserve to die slowly and in great agony. I'd be glad to shake your grandfather's hand.

That would be difficult, she laughs. He died in a work accident, on the electric chair. He sat on it to give a demonstration to apprentice executioners. It's not clear how it happened, but the electric current was connected, and by the time they switched it off, he was already fried like a fish.

So that's your specialization, the family history of executioners?

You know that these people had a sense of mission and great professional pride?

I'm not surprised, he says, and I'm sure that they were happy people too.

I understand that you're in favor of the death penalty, because you yourself carried out—

Yes, he interrupts her, there are people who don't deserve to live. There are people I'd be happy to kill.

People who harmed your parents? she asks.

How do you know? he exclaims.

I have a third eye, she says, like Shiva and like you.

You know something about Indian mythology too?

I had a lot of spare time, she says, and noting to do except read.

Were you in jail?

Eight years, she says. Two years in a juvenile facility, the rest in a lifers' wing.

It wasn't for soliciting or vagrancy, I imagine.

No, she confirms, I was barely sixteen when I was sentenced to life in prison.

Who did you kill? he asks.

Patrice Terramagi.

She pronounces the name Patrice Terramagi as if it was John Kennedy or the Prince of Wales at least.

Patrice Terramagi? He pages through his memory and fails to connect the name with any well known personality. Was he some prince or African president?

Neither a prince nor a president, she replies. Just a piece of dogshit my mother scraped off the street.

So what are you doing free, he asks, did you escape from jail?

No, she says, after eight years inside my lawyer got me a retrial, and the sentence set a precedent. Thanks to my case continuous abuse is now recognized as cumulative aggression, and a woman who kills someone who abused her for years can claim that she acted in legitimate self-defense, even if there was no immediate threat to her life, but only one more act of abuse, even a small one, in a long series of cumulative abuse.

How long did he abuse you? He asks. For months? Years?

For ever, she says. For ever. My parents separated when I was five. They were both alcoholics. My father moved to another continent and disappeared from my life. I stayed with my mother, who would come home late at night. Always drunk. Ever time with a different man. They would screw her for two or three days, and bugger off. If anyone stayed with her a little longer, it was a sign that he was completely down and out, that he had nowhere to put his stinking bum at night. But even the most fucked-up homeless only stuck it out for a week at most before they ran for their lives from her attacks of rage and fits of weeping and craziness and threats of suicide. Now try to imagine what kind of a lowlife this Patrice was, if he stayed with her for three years, until the night I stuck a barbecue skewer into his heart.

He stayed with her because of you, he states.

Good guess, she confirms. The first night she brought him, after he fucked her, he got into my bed and raped me.

You were only thirteen, he calculates.

Twelve and a bit, but far from innocent, she laughs her bitter laugh.

I already had a history of running away, vagrancy, drugs, prostitution, arrests, committal to a psychiatric ward for observation, removal from home by order of a judge in juvenile court to an institution for minors, which I couldn't stand, because it was like a prison, and being a vampire, I found a crack in the dark and ran back home, to my alcoholic mother. And when two policemen come to look for me, to take me back to the institution, I shut myself in the bathroom and slash my veins, so they'll return me to the hospital, to the psychiatric ward, and maybe this time I'll be able to persuade them to recommend to the court to let me stay with my mother. But the social worker testifies that my mother is drunk twenty-four hours a day, and she does me nothing but harm. And I tell the judge that my mother drinks because she wants me at home, and the judge asks me, why does she want you at home, and I say, because she's my mother, but this judge wasn't born yesterday, she's seen all kinds already, and she says to me, tell me the truth, Pipa, your mother wants you at home so much that she drinks twenty-four hours a day because she misses you so much? And I say, yes, your honor, I swear on my life that I'm telling you the truth! And she says to me: Why does she miss you so much, Pipa? Tell me why she needs you so much? And for a minute I want to tell her the truth: Because my mother knows that Patrice only stays with her because of me, because he's dying to fuck me, and my mother knows it, and she doesn't care that this is the price I have to pay so that this maniac will stay with her and fuck her too even though she disgusts him with the crazy scenes she makes whenever she gets drunk, in other words, at least twice a day, but I know that I can't tell the judge the truth, because then she'll remove me from home forever, so I keep quiet, and the judge understands my silence, and she says, Pipa, for your own good I'm sending you back to Mulberry Woods,

in other words, the institution, and as soon as they take me
back there I stick my fist through the window, and cut my
hand to pieces, and I'm back in the hospital again, and I
plead with the social worker, that if they don't want to send
me back to my mother, then let them look for my father in
Australia, and send me to him, but the social worker says
to me, face up to reality, and I pick up a vase that's standing next to my bed and throw it right in her face, and two
orderlies come running and strap me to the bed, and while
I'm lying there strapped to the bed like a person sentenced
to death waiting for a lethal injection, I ask myself what's
wrong with me, what, am I so different from everybody
else? Am I mad? Am I going to spend the rest of my life in
closed wards in mental hospitals? Or in jail as a murderer?
Or maybe one day I too will find someone who cares about
me, and who'll want to live with me and set up a family
with me, and we'll have children who I'll bring up the way
you're supposed to bring up children, and not the way I was
brought up by my mother, who never related to me like a
mother to a daughter, and even when they let me go home
for a visit, on Christmas, Patrice fucked me and slapped me
around, because he came quickly and he hated me for it,
as if it was my fault, until I stabbed myself in the stomach
because I was so sick of him, and they took me back to
the hospital, and afterwards I told my mother that a gynecologist there said I'd done myself so much damage that
I probably wouldn't be able to get pregnant—so what did
she say, my mother? You're better off this way, otherwise
you would have had at least ten abortions before you turn
seventeen, ooh, you hug me so good, she suddenly says in
the middle of all this outpouring, hug me tight and don't let
go now, and she twines herself around him, and her whole
thin body quivers in the too strong hands of the man whose
penis is sleeping like a soft warm baby in her hand, and

her matchstick legs wind round his hairy grizzly-bear leg, and he says to her, don't talk if it makes you feel bad, but it makes me feel good, she says, it makes me feel so good, but if it's hard for you to hear, it isn't hard for me, he says, on the contrary, it does me good, how does it do you good, the terrible story of my lost youth, how can it do you good? I don't know, he says to her, but it does me good, maybe because I went through a few things that weren't so nice in my own life too, not nice things, she laughs her bitter laugh, yes, he says, not nice things, that were put into deep freeze and left for years covered in a thick layer of ice, which is apparently beginning to crack. And after that time for some reason they sent me home, the words start to gush out of the gaping wound in her childish face again, and for a few days Patrice was careful and didn't dare to touch me, he was apparently frightened by what I had done to myself with the scissors, and perhaps he felt that what I had done to myself I was capable of doing to him too one day, if he went on torturing me, and he loved his own skin too much, that piece of shit, but after a few days his need overcame his fear, something about me turned him on, I don't know what, what does it matter anyway, I began working the streets on a regular basis, I did quite well, there are perverts out there that need little girls to turn them on, and that gave him a good reason to slap me around, all of a sudden he turned into my moral guardian, whenever I came back from work he would grab hold of me and hit me again and again, until I cried, and that gave him a hard-on, my crying, and when I caught on I began to fake it, I would begin to howl at the first slap, to cut it short, but it didn't solve the problem, because the minute he came, always too quickly, he would begin to blame me and say that it happened to him because of me, and that I did it on purpose, moving and making him come, and it wasn't true, because I didn't even move a muscle, because I don't feel a thing when the creeps are fucking me, not pleasure or pain, nothing, because I'm not there at all when they press up against my body and shove it into me—but it didn't help me, straightaway yelling: Why did you move? You whore! And straightaway blows. One night I came home finished. Three stinking homeless guys threatened me with a box-cutter and raped me and robbed me of all the money I'd made, and when I got home, Patrice was waiting for me with two friends of his, and I begged him, Patrice, leave me alone tonight, but he said, tonight I'm gonna to stick it to you, and then I'm gonna give you to my friends, and I said to him, not tonight, and he began slapping me around, and I began to cry, and as usual it gave him a hard-on, and he pushed me up against the kitchen sink and bent me over the sink and pulled down my panties and shoved it into me from behind, and as usual he came right away, and he started to curse me and hit me, and bending like that over the sink which was full of dirty dishes, I grabbed hold of a steel barbecue skewer, and I turned round to face him and I stuck it between his neck and his collarbone, and it sunk in as if it was slipping into butter, and suddenly he looked at me in great surprise, and there was such a sorrowful look in his eyes that I almost took pity on him, but it was already too late, he collapsed and crumpled onto the floor like a rag, and suddenly he jerked and kicked and hit the garbage pail that was standing there, and the pail overturned and the garbage spilled onto the floor, and that's it.

You did an absolutely professional job, he says, and explains: A matador strike.

What's that? she asks.

The connection between the neck and the collarbone. Soft tissue all the way, from the lung and the aorta straight to the heart.

I didn't know what I was doing, she says. And suddenly she has second thoughts:

Hey, if one of us is professional, it's apparently you. But you don't say much. I have to guess everything.

What do you want to know? he asks.

You won't tell me the truth anyway, she says.

What do you like hearing before you go to sleep, the truth, or a bedtime story?

Tell me a story, she says, and snuggles further into his big body.

23

Imagine a hilly landscape, he says.

Is it winter or summer? she asks.

Which do you prefer? he replies with a question.

Winter, she presses against him and nestles into him, everything covered with snow.

Yes, he says, deep fluffy snow, and the sky resting like a blanket of gray cotton-wool on the mountain tops and the white forests, and a snowy road winds between abandoned log cabins around which big rusty cogwheels are scattered, only their upper halves peeping out of the snow, and coils of steel cable whose wooden spools are sunk in the snow, and the road disappears into a gaping hole in the mountainside.

An abandoned mine shaft, she says, I like it already. Go on.

Through the opening you can see narrow rails, leading into a tunnel hewn out of the rock, lower than the height of a man and no wider than his outspread arms, and the pale light filtering in through the tunnel entrance soon fades, and the darkness is absolute, and from here on you can only continue by lamplight.

Don't stop, she requests, and he goes on leading her down the tunnel, and stops for a minute to tell her that the tunnel was quarried by copper miners in the Middle Ages, between five and ten centimeters a day, the traces of their chisels are still etched in the rock—and after ten long minutes of stooped walking in the tunnel you reach a little square, which we'll call Andreus Square, a square roofed with iron beams supporting its ceiling, and from Andreus Square three new tunnels branch out, the one on the left half full of water, the lake tunnel.

A lake in the bowels of the mountain? she asks.

Yes, he confirms. A lake the color of Bordeaux soup.

What kind of soup is that? she wonders. I've never eaten Bordeaux soup.

Of course not. If you'd eaten Bordeaux soup, you wouldn't be here now.

Is it a kind of poison?

It's a kind of fungicide used against leaf blight, once it was also used to spray potato and tomato fields.

Where do you get all this information from?

I grew up in a country village, he replies.

What's its color? She goes on questioning him.

The houses are white, with red-tiled roofs.

No, she says, I mean the Bordeaux soup.

A kind of venomous blue, he says, a kind of turquoise.

Go on, she requests.

Where were we? he asks.

In Andreus Square, she reminds him. You said there were three tunnels branching off from it, and the left one was half-full of water—

Yes, he confirms.

And the central tunnel? she asks and in her mind's eye she sees the three tunnels branching off from the underground square.

The central one is the track tunnel, because of the rail tracks.

And the one on the right?

The machine-hall tunnel, he recalls.

Go into the tunnel of the turquoise lake, she requests, and her fingers stroke his feet, feeling for something hidden there, and her electrifying touch sends currents through him that make the roots of his hair tingle and stiffen his nipples.

He takes her into the lake tunnel. Walking is difficult and progress is very slow.

Why, she asks, and he explains that at the entrance to the tunnel the water reaches only to the ankles, but the floor is very slippery, and the ceiling is so low that you have to walk at a crouch. But the deeper you penetrate into this tunnel, the more the water gradually rises. At first you don't feel it, because the slope is very mild, almost imperceptible, but after advancing slowly for five minutes, you find that the water is already above your ankles, and after another five minutes you're splashing in the water that reaches halfway up your calves. And you have to move in absolute silence.

Why in silence? she wonders and her fingers focus on a very specific area on the arch of his foot, next to the ball of the big toe, and the currents advance to the bottom of his stomach, close to the surface of the skin.

You have to keep quiet in order not to disclose your location.

To who? she asks.

To the character guarding the person you went into the belly of the mountain for.

But he can see the light of your lamp, she says.

Only if he has glasses that can distinguish infrared light, he says.

And does he? she asks in suspense.

I don't know, he says, I'm taking a risk.

Go on, she says and her fingers hover over the sole of his foot, and he doesn't know any more if they're touching or not touching, but the heat and the maddening tickle reach the root of his nose.

He goes on advancing at a slow, silent crouch. In the infrared light of the miner's lamp set in the middle of his forehead the walls of the tunnel look greenish.

Like Shiva's third eye, she comments.

Exactly, he agrees. Now the water already reaches his knees. But precisely here the ceiling of the tunnel begins to rise, and it seems that the walls too are moving a little further apart. There is no longer any doubt that the tunnel is widening like the neck of a bottle of Beaujolais. Now he is hugging the left wall of tunnel.

Why the left? Her fingers travel down the slope of the arch of his foot, and he abandons himself to the sweetness seeping into his blood like chartreuse and remembers the beginning of the chase, in the mountains next to Grenoble, and since his tongue is heavy now, and his silence continues, she repeats her question, Why are you hugging the left wall of the tunnel?

Because the space suddenly opening out is the 'Hall of love and creation', he says, and if you go on doing what you're doing to me now, we'll end up fucking.

I see, she says and looks at his penis, do you want to?

Whatever you want, he says.

How about going for a run? she suggests.

Suddenly the axes hidden under their coats come out and land on the German officer's head, and at exactly the same moment a column of women returning from work outside the camp arrives, and they see the officer with his head split open, his face bathed in blood, and they start screaming and running in all directions—

Don't you feel like going out for a run? she asks again, interrupting the uprising in Sobibor at the precise moment when several women faint at the sight of the officer twitching on the ground, and there's no chance of organizing and imposing order, and his father stands there with the bloody axe and shouts: 'Forward, comrades! For the motherland, for Stalin, forward!'

Let's go, he says, let's go out for a run. I haven't had a run for two days now.

24

She rises from the carpet, light as air, opens the closet door, throws him a gray track suit made of a soft, silky synthetic material, and while she herself slips into a snow-white track suit she apologizes for not being able to provide him with running shoes big enough to fit him.

My Eccos will do the job, he reassures her and slips the huge feet he inherited from his father into the means of transportation that undefeated man taught him to value above all, in other words, shoes.

'Shoes aren't an article of clothing, sonny. Shoes are vehicles. Never put on shoes that you can't set out in at any moment on a thousand kilometer march', his father passed on to him the wisdom that had saved his life, and at this moment, as he ties the laces of his Ecco shoes—with the shock-absorbers under the ball of the foot and the heel, the soles whose angle of contact with the ground is precisely calculated, to facilitate the movement of the foot from the heel to the toe and soften as much as possible the shocks to the spinal cord with the landing of the foot on the ground, and thus to reduce to a minimum the fatigue of the body systems when running—at that moment six hundred exhausted and humiliated people break out to life and liberty with a cry of 'Hurrah', but the dash for the armory is cut

short by a burst of machine-gun fire from the watch tow-
ers. People fall. The body of runners splits into two. One
group makes for the main gate, where they kill the sentries
with the guns they seized from the soldiers whose heads they
smashed with their axes, and run towards the forest. Others turn left, to the fence. They cut the barbed wire and run
through the minefield. And what did you do, Daddy? I attacked the officers' barracks with a group of prisoners. One
of the officers, who opened the door and came out to meet
me on the steps, got it from me with an axe on the head. I
grabbed his revolver, and we attacked the fence behind the
barracks with axes and wire cutters. The fence is behind
us, the minefield is behind us. We run forward. The fence
is already a hundred meters behind us. Another hundred.
Another hundred. Faster, faster! To cross the open ground.
To get outside the range of the machine-gun fire. To reach
the forest. Here are the first trees, but the firing goes on,
Daddy, don't stop, run, run deep into the forest. What's
that? Gunfire? No, it's the branches breaking under the soles
of our shoes, blessed art thou, Luka the shoemaker, who
made these shoes, blessed art thou and blessed be thy name,
because the minute you discover that your shoes aren't up to
it, will be a minute too late.

It's all right, he reassures his father who stops for a moment between the trees, to take a breath, and turns his head
to look for Luka, for Mishka. It's all right, Daddy, I've got
my shoes on—

Are you ready? she asks and finishes lacing her Nikes.

I'm ready, he says and ties the laces of his Eccos with a
double knot.

25

They step out of the elevator into the ground floor lobby, and the dark-skinned doorman, gazing sleepily at the midnight mass being broadcast from the Church of the Nativity in Bethlehem, stares at them in astonishment:

Now you're going jogging? You know how cold it is outside?

We'll heat up the night, Melissa reassures him.

Fare you well, says the doorman, and adds in concern: Your suit is cold.

You're from Morocco, states Shakespeare.

Right! exclaims the doorman. How did you know?

By the text, says the author of 'The Merchant of Venice' and leaves the doorman open-mouthed behind him. He opens the thick glass door for Melissa and invites her to go out into the cold with a theatrical flourish, continuing to quote the Prince of Morocco:

Farewell heat and welcome frost!

And they run out into the freezing deserted street.

Now we have to run. As fast as we can. Spilt up into small units and take different directions. The Polish Jews run in the direction of Chelm. To the area and the language they know. Us Soviets run East. The machinegun fire is behind us, getting further away all the time, giving us the exact location of the camp we're escaping from. Fire away, bastards. All you're doing is helping us find the right direction. The sounds of the firing grow fainter and fainter. Until silence falls.

At first the cold stings their faces and penetrates their track suits, but after fifteen minutes of running up the deserted Fifth Avenue, as they cross 40th Street, she suddenly says:

You run fast.

Should I slow down? he asks.

Are you in a hurry to get somewhere?

No, he says to her, we're already out of the range of fire.

Then slow down a bit, she requests, without asking what fire he's talking about.

You set the pace, he suggests, I'll coordinate myself with you, Luka.

Luka? She's bewildered. Who's Luka?

Someone thanks to whom I'm here.

Thanks to him you came to New York?

Thanks to him I came into the world.

Is it your mother?

It's someone who made my father shoes that saved his life.

Luka, she says, I love him.

So do I, he says.

You don't know what you did to me, she says. All the time I'm in the belly of the mountain. Inside the tunnels of the mine. I can't find my way out.

Maybe it's the roundness of the space surrounding you like half a globe, he says.

No, she says, it's the lake.

Ah, you're still with the lake...

I can see it, she says. The color of Bordeaux soup. In the air there isn't even the faintest movement to disrupt the absolute stillness freezing the surface of the water.

Exactly, he confirms.

Take me further, she says.

You advance slowly, along a narrow path, which slopes slightly upwards and curves at the corner of the left wall of the space, goes round the lake and leads to a tunnel that leads into the hall of the fingers, if you're following me—

I can see every detail, she whispers, panting from the run: You have an awfully long breath. You talk as if you're not running.

Are we running? he asks. I never noticed.

Don't be mean, she says. Take me further.

Where are we? he asks.

In the hall of the fingers, she reminds him.

Its name on the map is Ignatius Cavern, he says, but I call it the hall of the fingers. The name of the hall of love and creation too is actually Karol Cavern. But everything in the world can have many different names, depending on your point of view, one man calls a certain woman 'my wife', another calls her 'my mother' and a third 'my lover'.

Let's get back to Ignatius Cavern, she says. Why did you call it the hall of the fingers?

Because it's a fan of five narrow paths stretching over a deep chasm, which start out from a crescent and end in a single track that disappears into a dark winding tunnel.

A threatening place, she remarks.

Threatening and dangerous, he agrees. It's almost like walking a tightrope. Especially when you have to cross one of those narrow paths with the help of the infrared lamp on your forehead and infra-glasses.

How deep is the chasm underneath you? she wants to know.

Between eighty and a hundred meters.

How do you know?

Ten times four square divided by two equals eighty.

What's that?

Something I dimly remember from high school, he tells her. But maybe I'm wrong.

You're talking to me in Chinese, she laughs.

Halfway across I dislodged a stone with my foot and the thud reached me after four or five seconds.

Scary, she says.

Very scary, he hops over a pothole in the pavement.

What gives you the strength to go on?

Luka, he says.

What do you mean? she asks.

We understand the beginning only when we reach the end, he says.

Don't try to be clever.

I'm not being clever. You're told that as soon as you arrive at the right place you'll know it's the right place, and then you'll also know what to do next.

You're arrived at the right place, she whispers.

The only thing that counts here is patience. A lot of patience. Sometimes you have to wait for hours before you take a step. Or make a movement. You have to be able to lie behind a bush for hours without moving a finger. If you don't have patience—

I do, she reassures him. I could lie with you for hours.

And so could I with you, he says, but we're running.

It's good for me, she pants. Running with you is so good for me.

And for me with you too, he says.

You take my pace into consideration, she says.

I'm half a step behind you, he says.

I feel it. You don't put pressure on me. You're not in competition with me.

Who needs competition, he says.

Men, she says.

I'm not a man, he says.

Yes, I saw, she laughs.

Seriously, he says. I'm an error of nature. I should have been born a woman.

You're making fun of me, she says.

Not at all, he says and hears the neighbor women, sitting and drinking tea with his mother at a soft twilight hour. A red sun dips into the narrow strip of sea visible between the mountains, and he tries unsuccessfully to transmit to

the paper with his paintbrush the sense of beauty that over-
whelms him, or perhaps it's the promise of happiness, and
then he hears behind his back Ceska saying to his mother,
that boy should have been born a girl. He's so gentle, she
adds, and his mother sighs: Yes, sometimes I fear that he's
too gentle for life.

But you're laughing, she protests.

I remembered something, he says. Once I was in Paris.
Before I returned to my country, I went to buy a dress for
my mother, and I tried it on to see how it would look on
my mother.

Is she as big as you? she asks in surprise.

I'm not big, he says.

You're big, she says. You don't know how big you are.

My mother wasn't big, he says. She was a small woman.

So why did you try on the dress? she asks.

For fun, he says. For a laugh. I came out of the changing booth wearing the dress, and all the sales girls gathered
round and started shrieking like a flock of parrots escaped
from the zoo.

Go back to that moment, she says.

I'm there, he says. Completely.

Why did you put on the dress you bought for your
mother?

Her question casts him back suddenly to that night in
Nice, when they impersonated workers in the French Electric Corporation. To the moment when it seemed to him
that he saw a shadow slipping out of the room. Someone
escaped through the window, he says to the Alsatian. Impossible, says the Alsatian. They told us there were eight people
here. But I saw someone, he insists. You're mistaken, states
the Alsatian. In any case, we're getting into the van and getting out of here as quick as we can. Jonas and Yadanuga
back up the Alsatian, and a few years later it costs Jonas his

life, and you too, Shakespeare, almost pay with your life, in the running duel in the desert. The craziest marathon of your life.

A penny for your thoughts, she says.

What? he wakes up.

I asked you why you put on the dress you wanted to buy for your mother.

Because the night before we eliminated a few terrorists, he says.

I'm not surprised, she says.

At what? he wonders.

Suddenly you looked as hard and sharp as a German decapitation axe, she says.

A German decapitation axe? He puzzles over the strange image.

Yes, she says. German executioners in the middle ages had an instrument like that.

The middle ages are now, he says. The old gods are taking their revenge. Barbarity is coming back in a big way.

A combination of barbarity and religion, she says. I experience it every day.

The streets of this city remind me exactly of the tunnels of that abandoned mine in the Austrian alps.

So don't leave me alone, she requests.

Sorry, he says, I didn't realize I was putting on speed.

You sure were, she pants. I thought you were about to take off and fly.

Why didn't you say anything?

I was curious to see how fast you could run, she confesses. You run as if all the devils in hell are after you.

It won't happen again, he promises.

Do you know where we are? she asks.

Yes, he says. We're on the way to Executioner's Square.

Executioner's Square? she wonders.

Do you want to go there? he asks.

Yes, she says.

OK, he says, you're my navigator. What's this?

They enter an area illuminated by thousands of neon lights.

I'm damned if I know where we are.

Look up, he says.

She raises her eyes to the winter night sky studded with billions of stars.

Now look ahead. What do you see?

A big empty parking lot stretches out in front of them, illuminated in a cold neon light.

What am I supposed to see? she asks.

Do you see elongated shapes lined up in a row on the ground?

What are they? she asks.

Fighter planes, he says.

OK, she says in a half question, willing to go along with the story he's telling.

A full squadron of state of the art Super Phantoms, equipped with extra-large drop tanks to lengthen the flight range, and armed with miniaturized nuclear bombs weighing a quarter ton each. Can you see them?

I see exactly what you see, she encourages him to continue his story.

Each plane carries ten such bombs under each wing.

Exactly, she confirms, ten bombs under each wing.

Can you hear the music? he asks.

Yes, she says. What is it?

He wants to tell her that it's Beethoven's Ninth, playing from some window open to the night, but he hears the novice-scriptwriter Tyrell's voice explaining that it's the Air Force band conducted by Ziko Graciani playing a selection of marches.

Just a minute, she stops him, who's Psycho Greatshiani when he's at home? And he tells her about the great conductor whose band accompanies the best of our aviators on their way to their planes before particularly dramatic missions, like the one in which they are about to take part. He asks her if she doesn't want to change her mind, and she assures him that she's with him through fire and water, and they pass together before the reviewing stand, leading behind them the men of the legendary Squadron 505, and opposite the stand he commands his men 'Mark time', and they jog a little on the spot, because when your body is so hot you shouldn't come to a full stop, and the Commander of the Air Force and the Prime Minister and the Defense Minister approach them at a quick march, with the old Prime Minister hurrying ahead, his white mane waving in the wind like two flames on either side of his large head, and the Commander of the Air Force and the Chief-of-Staff can hardly keep up with the brisk strides of the short, resolute man, who when he reaches them asks them hurriedly in his clipped, metallic voice how they feel as they set out on their mission, and Melissa declares:

This is the mission I've been dreaming of since I was a child!

Is the mission clear to you? the Prime Minister asks her in the voice of a man of iron.

Yes! answers Melissa. To destroy the forces of evil in the world!

Excellent! The Prime Minister gives her a mighty comradely slap on the shoulder. Go in strength and bring us salvation!

Ziko Graciani gives his band a sign and to the blare of the trumpets playing the 'Ode to Joy', the pilots and navigators climb into their cockpits, close the canopies, Hanina presses the ignition button, and the air of the vast subterranean hall vibrates with the thunder of the engines of the thirty-two Phantoms, which pair off and move slowly along the underground runway carved out of the belly of the mountain. Hanina pulls a lever, and the heavily laden Phantom leaps forward with a terrible roar, accelerates and shoots out of the bowels of the mountain through its gaping maw, which spits into the air one after the other sixteen pairs of mighty steel birds, which climb into the sky and rip it to shreds in a storm of thunder.

And then there's silence. An ocean of silence. And into this cosmic silence, in the middle of the blue sky thirty-two tiny dots advance in four arrowheads. Below them lies the Mediterranean, a basin of solid glass between the yellow of the African deserts and the green of the forests of Europe. Above the boot of Italy they veer right, and start flying over land. The green of the forests turns to the grayish olive green of the olive groves of Umbria and Tuscany, and it grows darker and darker, turning into a poisonous green with shades of black. Blacker and blacker.

Now they're above Germany. And here's Munich. And in the heart of the city a vast square, black with hundreds of thousands of black uniforms and black boots. An open black Mercedes approaches a stage crowned with flagpoles as tall as skyscrapers, flying red flags emblazoned with huge black swastikas. A man dressed in a black uniform with a little black moustache under his nose stands in the black Mercedes and raises his arm in a salute to the crowd that cheers him like one man from a single hoarse throat, and the cheer rises above the city buildings and reaches the ears of the pilot, who smiles a small smile under his helmet and asks his navigator over the radio:

How long has he got to live?

Two minutes and sixteen seconds, he hears the navigator's voice in his earphones. The timing is perfect. Down there they are punctual to the minute and up here to the fraction of a second. Punctuality is about to meet punctuality. The black Mercedes stops in front of the stage, and the owner of the little black moustache jumps out and bounds onto the stage. The crowd roars Zieg Heil. The man raises his hand and the roar of the crowd is immediately silenced. Now he roars into the microphone suspended in the center of a metal ring like a spider waiting for its prey. The man's screams are magnified a thousandfold, they echo from batteries of hundreds of powerful loudspeakers surrounding the square.

We're on target, Hanina hears the navigator's voice over the radio. He looks right and left, and against the background of the clear sky he sees the other pilots sitting tensely in their cockpits, their hands on the joysticks into which the firing buttons are set, waiting for a signal from him. He raises his thumb and then turns it down. He sees the other pilots nod in confirmation, and he winks at them before yanking the joystick, veering left, and commencing a dizzying dive towards the stage. The owner of the black moustache has sixty seconds left in which to enflame the souls of his audience with the venomous hatred about to drown nations and countries in blood and fire and columns of smoke, but suddenly words fail him, the crowds standing at the foot of the stage raise their eyes to the sky—a vast field of faces with gaping mouths and staring eyes, of circles with three holes punched in them, one hole for the mouth and two for the eyes, and all those millions of holes turn to the sky, and from the sky a quartet of thundering iron monsters swoops down on them, and the owner of the moustache sees what all that multitude sees: blue stars painted on white circles under the steel wings and on the bodies of the powerful planes, and he turns to the fat man with the swollen face standing at his right, and asks him in confusion: What is that, Hermann?

And Hermann replies, pale with horror: Those are shields of David.

Why shields of David? the terrified man with the moustache asks the no less terrified fat man.

It looks like a Jewish air force!

A Jewish air force? The owner of the moustache demands in horror: Did you say a Jewish air force?

But before the fat man has a chance to reply, Hanina presses the red button on his joystick, and all the people standing on the stage rise into the air in a great ball of fire, break up into arms, legs, heads, guts, livers, gallbladders, kidneys, testicles and backsides, which fall from the sky like a bountiful rain, and in the meantime Giora squeezes the white button on his joystick, and as he pulls on the joystick and raises the nose of his plane and climbs high into the air he catches a glimpse of the bright flash that turns the square beneath him into a field of statues strewn with columns of basalt rock or black clay. And when all thirty-two Phantom jets of the illustrious Squadron 505 reassemble from the corners of the Kingdom of Evil into a single cluster, which rises to the borders of the atmosphere above the European sky, on their way home to the base in the belly of the Mountain of Justice, the pilots see through the canopies of their cockpits the smoke rising from the burning airfields, and the mangled remains of the armored divisions that were about to flood the continent, and then the boy Hanina radios Air Force HQ, to announce that the mission has been accomplished, but to his astonishment there is no answer, and he calls again: Nest, this is Eagle, Nest, this is Eagle, do you read me, over! And nobody answers. Does anyone hear Eagle, he calls, does anyone hear Eagle? But the communications network is silent. And suddenly the realization penetrates his mind. Since he destroyed the Third Reich, the Second World War never broke out, there was no Holocaust, and accordingly there is no State of Israel either, no IDF, no air force, no illustrious Squadron 505. And on the other hand, since there was no Holocaust, there are no Holocaust survivors either. His father never landed up in Sobibor and his mother never found refuge with the partisans in the forests. They never sailed on an illegal immigrant ship to Palestine, they weren't sent to a detention camp in Cyprus, they never met, and thus there is no Hanina. And if there's no Hanina, there's no Phantom attack on the Third Reich either, and the Holocaust does happen, and Hanina does exist......

Who's Hanina? asked Melissa, running next to him and breathing heavily, even though she's as light as a silk scarf.

Hanina, he tells her, was a dreamy child, who destroyed all the evil people in the world. And before he wiped out the Third Reich with Phantom jets, he defeated the Roman army besieging Jerusalem with a medium machine gun, and now he's hovering in the air in his Phantom, with nowhere to land....

He does have somewhere, says Melissa, he has a place with me.

She changes to a fast walk, and he walks next to her, and he's not Hanina, or Shakespeare, or Tyrell the novice scriptwriter: he's just a man without a name or an identity, stamping his feet in the cold New York night and breathing clouds of vapors from his mouth and nostrils.

I feel so good, she says, waving her thin arms round in circles as she walks, I haven't felt so good since I was a little girl!

And suddenly she stops and asks:

Do you know where we are?

No, he admits, I haven't got a clue.

We're in front of the house, she says.

What house? he asks.

This is where my private Adolph Hitler, Tony Fritshke lives, she says to his astonishment, with a bitter smile.

There's a light on in his window. I can see him lying there on his stomach, on his thick carpet, his feet waving in the air over his ass, his presents scattered around him on the carpet, and he's tearing off the red and gold wrappings with one of his flick-knives and pulling out the presents as greedily as a spoilt child, the presents he got for Christmas from all his rich clients....

Should we go up and pay him a visit? he asks.

What for? she asks.

To eliminate him, he proposes.

We don't have a weapon, she says.

I have my feet, he says.

He's a dangerous man, she says, with lots of guns and pistols and knives.

Then it will be an interesting fight, he says. Shall we go up?

Some other time, she says, mesmerized by the movement of his fingers writhing of their own accord like the snakes on the head of the Gorgon Medusa.

Don't you want to kill him? he asks.

Some other time, she repeats. Let's not spoil this pure night.

Whatever you want, he says.

I want to forget him, she says. To close my eyes and open them and discover that Tony was only a bad dream.

That will happen soon, he says, very soon.

On the day it happens I'll be a free person, she vows in a whisper opposite the clear cold sky, I'll never let anyone control me and use me again. For the first time I'll do as I wish with my life.

I'll help you get to that day, he says.

You've already helped me, she says. Until now I never had the courage to even dream about it, and now I'm standing here and saying it out loud: I want to be a free person.

And what do you want to do now? he asks.

To run with you, she says. To run with you in all the streets of this city. To run with you in Central Park. And on Washington Bridge. When I run with you I'm not afraid of anyone.

Then let's run, he says.

We'll run, she says, but first give me a hug.

He wraps his thick arms around her thin body—

26

Why are you sighing? asks Mona.

That's so good, he says.

What's so good? She demands suspiciously.

The air. He yawns a jaw-breaking yawn and breathes in a lungful of air, down to the pit of his stomach.

He lies on the deck of the boat rocking on the water, lacing his fingers behind his neck and contemplating the stardust covering the night sky. Snowflakes of stars. A bright snow of stars floats in the black of Melissa's window as she lies with him in a hot bath. All relaxed after the long run in the freezing night air. Her long flexible body nestles on his body like a lizard basking on a source of warmth.

How come you weren't afraid to go into that place? she wonders.

What place? he asks.

The belly of the mountain, she says, the abandoned copper mine.

How do you know it was a copper mine?

By the color of the water, she says, and pushes the foam away with her hands and looks at the blue water fragrant with scented bath oils.

What water? He doesn't understand.

The water in the underground lake. The color of Bordeaux soup. It has to be a copper mine.

You're an expert on chemistry too?

No, but I've read a few things about copper.

Why copper? he asks in surprise.

I was curious to know why it's regarded as Aphrodite's metal.

I didn't know copper was Aphrodite's metal, he confesses.

It's obvious, she says, copper is a soft, malleable metal. It's a good conductor of energy, of heat and of electricity.

What's that got to do with Aphrodite? he demands an explanation, and she goes on playing with his fingers, and speaks so softly, in such an inner voice, that he doesn't know if he's hearing her voice or her thoughts.

Don't tell me you didn't know that Venus was connected to that mine, she says. It was one of the threads that drew you in.

How exactly? He doesn't understand, and she plays with the roots of his fingers and explains:

There's a story that Venus hid a small and precious treasure somewhere, in some secret alcove in an abandoned copper mine. And whoever succeeds in laying his hands on the treasure, and also in getting out of the labyrinth of underground tunnels alive, will win the love of everybody he meets.

It's enough for me if the ones I love return my love, he says.

You already have their love, she says.

So why should I enter that abandoned mine? he asks.

Because Venus caught a certain solitary adventurer red-handed trying to steal the treasure—she goes on brushing her fingertips lightly over the area destined for the slashing of veins, next to his wrist, and her touch sends currents through him that cloud the no-man's-land between his thoughts and her thoughts, which he isn't sure if he's reading or hearing:

This poor guy didn't know that the minute he crossed the threshold of the tunnel leading to the belly of the mountain, he activated a very delicate, sophisticated system programmed to lock all the entrances after a period of time set in advance. This trap was set by Hephaestus, who as you know was Venus's cuckolded husband. He was a metalworker, and he created the trap in order to catch his wife's lovers. In any case, Venus caught our unfortunate thief and imprisoned him somewhere deep down in one of the dark mine pits. The kidnapped prisoner lived on a daily ration of Siren milk which was hardly enough to keep his body and soul together.

I still don't understand what really prompted me to enter that dangerous place.

And he asks himself if this Sybil will be able to conjure up a vision capable of shedding light on the most obscure affair of his life, an affair in which he went to the rescue of the lover of the only woman he ever loved. The one who is now with a light sure hand steering the sailing boat over the dark sea which is beginning to show signs of turbulence.

One day you get a message, says Melissa, who seems more and more like a strange reincarnation of that prophetess of dubious identity whose prophecies the cunning Josephus Flavius took so seriously.

Who do I get the message from? he asks.

Someone leaves it in your mailbox.

And this message tells me—he begins, and she finishes:

That someone is imprisoned in the depths of an abandoned copper mine, and he's waiting to be rescued.

He looks at her with growing interest. Is this long-limbed spider a wily CIA agent? Have they put her on his case? Is she trying to weave a web around him in order to trap him and program him to execute the character she calls 'Tony Fritshke'? Or perhaps she is trying to extract information from him about the methods of the organization to which he belonged in those distant years of the previous century, in the days when his band of 'Cunning Cooks' were busy systematically liquidating the gang of 'Butchers from the City of Hangmen'—which is what they called the murderers they eliminated one by one, to the last but one of them. Impossible, he says to himself. No one could have known that he would walk down precisely that avenue, and go into precisely that Irish pub...unless someone had programmed him to make those moves as well...Interesting, Shakespeare whispers to him. Now you have to find out the truth about this Segestria Perfida. Don't fall into her net. Don't be seduced into going to bed with her. Keep a clear head. It looks as if you're going to need it.

But the country boy with the delicate soul rebels against the wild romanticist from Stratford, who is threatening to drive him insane. This girl isn't an agent of any espionage agency. She's simply a poor innocent girl who was the victim of an alcoholic mother, and fell into the claws of vicious pimps, who exploited her to death, but how in the hell did she get onto the story of the pursuit in the copper mine? Did you provide her with the information? Impossible. But she knows the story. This kid knows everything there is to know about you. Everything? Let's see what she knows.

Who is the man imprisoned in the depths of the mine and waiting to be rescued, he asks.

It doesn't say specifically, says the Sybil.

It sounds like a poor joke, or a hoax.

But something about the message continues to trouble you and haunt you.

Why? he demands. Why should it trouble me?

Because from the minute this information gets into your system, it begins to grow and echo inside you.

Why? he repeats insistently.

Something in the phrasing makes it special, personal. Only you can get this message and decipher it, it's so personal—she astonishes him with the accuracy of her words.

And at the same time it's ostensibly completely impersonal—he tries to lay a mine for her.

There's something very strange and obscure about it, she bypasses the mine.

Who can he be, this person waiting for me at the bottom of the pit? He scrutinizes her with an eagle eye.

You have to examine the message again, she says.

Yes, I decide to examine the message again, he agrees, careful not to add a crumb of information to what she provides.

But when you examine it, suddenly it seems to you that certain words which appeared in the message on the first examination, have changed into different words.

That's impossible! He makes an effort not to shout.

Perhaps your memory is playing tricks on you?

Perhaps.

And perhaps the message really has changed, in some mysterious way.

How can I tell?

You repeat the present version to yourself, and then you look at it again.

I don't believe it! A few of the words have changed again.

How do you explain it?

Maybe it's a kind of message that changes from reading to reading, he suggests.

Perhaps you have an ambivalent attitude towards this message, she says, and this makes you read it differently each time. In other words: perhaps it's you who changes from one reading to the next.

Perhaps the message changes without any relation to whether I change or don't change?

Perhaps it has a kind of built-in inner clock, she suggests carefully, that makes it change whether anybody's reading it or not?

Perhaps it's simply growing old? he suggests.

If it's growing old, is it getting clearer or more blurred? she asks.

Maybe one day it will die and stop troubling me, he says hopefully.

The message, or the man imprisoned in the pit? She takes him by surprise.

You know, when I try to characterize the changes in the message, I realize that from reading to reading it really is becoming more blurred.

But the cry for help that came from it in the first reading is still echoing inside you, without any relation to the blurring of the message, she says.

Letters are missing from the words, whole words are missing...

Suddenly you understand that if you don't act, if you don't set out immediately to journey to the belly of the mountain, soon nothing will remain of the original message, only some dim unpleasant memory, that will go on haunting you and never let go of you until the day you die. You understand that the longer you hesitate, the longer you go on trying to understand the message, the more obscure it will become, and something tells you that if you hesitate a little longer, or if you try to read the message one more time—the whole thing will turn into nonsense.

So why should I go on breaking my head over this fucking message?

Because one thing is becoming clearer and clearer: you have received a cry for help.

If it really is a cry for help, then why not an open, direct appeal? Why is the message so strange and indirect?

The man who sent the signal apparently knew that on its way to you the message would have to pass through very unfriendly regions. He apparently assumed that the message would have to get past all kinds of extremely hostile censors.

And perhaps the whole thing's a setup? Perhaps the message was sent by some hostile force, trying to con me into a trap and lead me to perdition? He confronts her with the sixty million dollar question.

One thing is clear, she states, you will never be able to forgive yourself if you listen to this cowardly voice, inciting you to forget the whole thing and go on living as if the cry never reached you. At the same time as your brain is telling you to keep a cool head and try to discover first of all who sent the call, you sense in the depths of your heart that someone is trapped there in the bowels of the mountain, someone who needs you very much and whose life now depends only on your courage.

But my gut-feeling warns me against this dangerous adventure, he admits.

And at the same time your strong legs are already waiting impatiently to set out.

You mean, my short legs.

Strong, she repeats emphatically, I've seen all kinds of legs in my life, but never legs as strong as yours.

And so out of proportion, insists Hanina, admit it: completely out of proportion to the rest of my body.

What's true is true, she admits and passes an amused glance over his naked body facing her in the bathtub, your proportions are quite special.

Strange and ugly, he insists.

Beauty is in the eye of the beholder, as you know, she says, but he holds his ground:

There's nothing beautiful about me. And I'm not trying to fish for compliments. Look at my neck.

27

Melissa tilts her head with a lascivious smile, puts out a long-fingered hand and strokes his neck with a delight unlike anything he has ever known, and says that before she says anything about his bull neck it is only fitting that she devote a few words as well to the back which carries this neck, and therefore she asks him to kindly turn over onto his stomach.

Why don't we get out of the bath? he suggests.

After drying his body with a hair dryer, which looks like a huge revolver, she runs the balls of her fingers over the width of his back, and then its length, and now she is ready to admit that his back really is long in relation to his short legs, which accounts for the fact that, in conjunction with his Modigliani neck, he nevertheless reaches a height of five foot ten inches—she accurately estimates at the end of the measurements taken by her outspread fingers in their agile crabwise scuttle from the top of his head to the tips of his toes.

Admit it, this body is composed of parts stolen from all the races walking the face of the earth, he laughs, and she agrees with him, and is even prepared to specify:

A Mongolian skull, Tartar cheekbones, a Norman chin, a male Nefertiti neck, a Latin back, African hips, the backside of a matador and legs that I don't know where you got them from.

This body can tell you a tale of the journey of survival of the race that brought me into the world, he says.

She laughs: This bizarre combination misled my friend, who brought you trousers too long for your legs. I admit that I've never seen anything like them before.

Just say chimpanzee legs, he tries to make it easier for her.

You like putting yourself down more than you deserve, she protests.

Throw me a banana, he requests and lies on his naked back with his legs in the air.

She throws him a banana, and before she knows what's happening he sends out a leg and catches the banana in mid-flight with the long toes of his left foot, and peels it with the help of his right big toe in three rapid movements, and again with the help of the toes of his left foot he breaks the banana in two, and while his right foot throws one half to Melissa, his left foot flings the other half into the air so that it falls straight into his mouth.

Melissa can't believe her eyes. Amused and laughing in all her stringy nakedness she throws him an apple, and he catches it with his foot. She throws him another apple, which he catches with his other foot, and when she throws him a third apple, the secret nameless friend begins to juggle the three apples with his feet before her astonished eyes, until she springs from her place intending to land on this mischievous foot-juggler lying on his back on the floor, but before she realizes what's happening to her his feet begin to turn her in the air like a giant fan, and she laughs and laughs, stop it, you lunatic! You're killing me! I'm dying! But he swivels his strong legs, those legs that will still be spoken of in connection with the development of the new Olympic sport of infinite distance running, and then his feet throw her up into the air and catch her very gently like the hands of a father catching his baby daughter, as if she were a pillow full of feathers and not a long-limbed woman, and Melissa indeed laughs out loud like a little child, until Hanina slows down and lowers her gently to his body, and she lies on top of him exhausted, choking and sobbing with laughter—

28

You're sighing like an old Jewish woman again, mocks Mona. Once in a while it helps to let out a good Jewish *krechts*, he says.

Once in a while? she retorts— this is your third or fourth *krechts* since we set sail.

Don't despise the Jewish *krechts*, he says. More than the Jewish people preserved the *krechts*, the *krechts* preserved the Jewish people.

All right, all right, she dismisses the subject in disgust, but he stands his ground:

In certain situations all you can do is let out a *krechts*. He lies on his back, raises his legs in the air, bends his knees to his stomach, turns the soles of his feet to the sky, and lets out another sigh, which ends with 'Ai, Mona, Mona…'

Is there something you want to say to me?

Come and lie down on my feet, he proposes.

What else do you want me to do?

Nothing, I'll do all the rest.

What will you do? she expresses mistrust in his intentions.

Don't ask questions, he requests, just lie down on my feet.

Have you got any more ideas?

Come on, he coaxes her, I'll do something to you that nobody else has ever done before.

We've exhausted the subject, she pronounces.

Please, he sighs deeply, please.

Sit up and hold this rope tight, she orders him, and don't do anything I don't tell you to do.

He raises himself to a sitting position, and she throws him a thick rope, attached with a ring to the bottom of the boat. A damp rag of darkness covers the universe. Even the tip of the spotless white sail is swallowed up in the dense darkness of the last hour of night before the dawn. He turns his head back to see how far they are from the shore, but there is no trace of the shore. No spot of light flickers in the gloom. The green lamp pulsing its pale light like a heart on the point of the prow is the only light in the immense darkness. The bow cuts a white line over the dark water, which rises and falls like the breathing belly of a giant animal, and they are borne on this belly, which suddenly lifts them high in the air and immediately slips away and disappears beneath them, and the little boat plunges into the chasm like an airplane entering an air pocket, and for a minute he stops breathing and his guts rise into his throat, and before he can recover from his astonishment the breathing belly flings them up into the air again, and again they slide down into the dark chasm, and the bow of the boat rises like a roller-coaster and their little nutshell is slammed down to the bottom of the pit of water gaping in front of it.

What's happening? he asks anxiously.

Nothing, she dismisses him. Hold tight to the rope. We'll be out of it soon.

She maneuvers the sail with her strong hands, pulling ropes whose operations he doesn't understand, moving swiftly from side to side and casting the weight of her body first to one side and then the other, leaning over the sides of the sloop.

You're something, he starts to say to her but at that moment the little boat rises to the pinnacle of the Ferris wheel, and when it begins its swift slide down, the upper valve of his stomach opens, and all the Kentucky whiskey in his guts rises into his mouth in a wave of fermented corn. He barely manages to lean over the side of the boat before a murky jet bursts out of his mouth, and then another and another, and his stomach convulses in painful spasms, and it seems as if in a moment his guts will turn inside out, and as he crouches there leaning over the railing, a great spray of water from the bows washes over his face, and in the fog that descends on him for a moment he sees

29

A skinny body like a wet rag, folded in on itself, on the stone quay next to the water churning and rushing under the wooden bridge in Lucerne, and he sends a last look at that head, which made murderous plans and also executed them in vile ways, and reads the place and the time running in little letters at the bottom of the picture, only a moment before that head had turned when they called its name, to make sure there was no mistake in the identity, and the man still had time to send his hand under the flap of his jacket, but the kick of death hit him on the chin, and he rose and fell back with a popping sound, and now he hears the Alsatian's voice whispering in his heavy French accent, *ça va pied-mort, ça suffit*, it's okay, death-foot, it's enough, and he leans over the man and puts his hand in his pockets and takes out a wallet stuffed with bank notes, and airline tickets, and a silver Lebel 7.65 French pistol, which he makes haste to slip into his black leather bag, and then they push the body over the edge of the quay, and the raging current snatches it up greedily and whirls it round and takes it on a long journey to the depths of the cold winter night, and the Alsatian asks him to give his regards to Lorelei before the waters of the Rhine carry him out into the ocean, and at that moment the Alsatian didn't know that his body too would be given up to the water of another river, which would carry him to another ocean, two dead men in the tens of thousands of dead in one war which according to his calculation had already been going on for eighty years, ever since they had smashed in the faces of Josef Louisdor and Josef Haim Brenner with a hoe, but all the seas were one sea, and all the dead were one dead, and only the living were distinguished from one another as long as they were alive, each living person and his world closed in on him, and where was this thought leading, he tries to think—

30

What's going on with you and Moran? Mona's voice cuts the thread of his thoughts with an unexpected question.

He sits up and turns his face dripping with salt water to her.

What? he asks, not believing that he heard the question correctly.

Is there something going on between you? she asks.

He sees her dimly through the veil of salt burning his eyes.

Don't lie, she says. I saw how you were drowning in her eyes.

I was drowning in her eyes? he repeats in surprise.

I know that horny look of yours, she states.

Moran doesn't turn me on, he says.

It's a pity you didn't see yourself looking at her.

I don't remember looking at her in any special way, he says.

And how you looked, she says, hypnotized as a snake by a snake charmer.

You're imagining things, he says.

Listen, Nini, she says, if you're fucking her—go ahead and fuck her, but don't bullshit me.

I'm not fucking her, he states firmly, and adds in a feebler tone: And I don't want to fuck her either.

You look at her like a drunk at a bottle, she says, you don't hear what's being said to you, you don't function, you're simply out of it.

It's not because of her, he says.

Oh no?

Moran to me is as transparent as the rays of a glorious sun, he is astonished at the image that comes out of Shakespeare's mouth.

Is that so? she says. I wonder who they illuminate, the rays of this glorious sun.

You won't believe me if I tell you, he says.

Go on, let it out, she says.

The granddaughter of the assistant hangman at Nuremberg.

What? she says. Say that again.

At Nuremberg they executed the Nazi leaders? he asks. So?

The hangman was an American, he says.

Maybe he was, she concurs. What's that got to do with it?

He had an assistant who cut the hole in the floor.

What hole?

That the hanged man falls through the minute they open the trapdoor he's standing on.

What is this nonsense, she wrinkles her brow.

This assistant hangman married a black girl, he explains, and I met his granddaughter in New York. A shop assistant at Yves St Laurent, no, at Ralph Lauren, no.....

Make up your mind, Yves St Laurent or Ralph Lauren?

Maybe Ralph Klein or Stephen Klein, he says.

Ralph Klein was a basketball coach, Mona says scornfully. Maybe you mean Calvin Klein, or Stephane Kellian.

Perhaps, he says. I don't remember what shop I met her in.

A-ha, she nods her head. An interesting story. Now let's have the truth.

That's the truth, he says.

Listen, Nini, she says, and the way she says 'Nini' already sounds like a rebuke. Listen, Nini! I'm fed up with your adolescent fantasies about cocoa colored Barbies.

Melissa isn't exactly a Barbie, he says, but she cuts him short.

Melissa! She spits the name out in contempt. Are you sure it's not Verbena? Or maybe Chamomile? Melissa! Couldn't you invent a more idiotic name?

It's true, he fights a rear-guard battle in a lost war.

Melissa! She laughs. How about Earl Grey, or Orange Pekoe?

I knew you wouldn't believe me. He apologizes for his failure to persuade her.

If you don't tell me the truth now, the whole truth and nothing but the truth, she threatens, I'm sailing back into the heart of the storm, and it isn't only your stinking whiskey you'll throw up, but your spleen and your gall bladder as well, and you know I'm not joking.

No, no, pleads Nini the frightened child, full of guilt for being born as a child of the second generation, and for the very fact of his existence in place of his two dead half-brothers, don't take us back into the storm, I'll tell you the truth.

Go ahead, says his mother, I'm listening.

I met her in Florence, he says. You won't believe me, but it's the truth: she's an American policewoman who was disguised as a nun.

Go on, she says, I'm listening.

From Vermont, he goes on cautiously with the story that Yadanuga didn't believe.

Pretty? she asks.

Not on first sight, he says. Not stunning. Not glamorous.

Don't try to soften the blow.

I'm not. It's the truth. She isn't gorgeous.

Tall? she inquires.

Small, he lies.

How old? she demands.

Thirty-two, he invents a number.

What was she doing in Florence?

She was at a conference on computer crime.

Why was she disguised as a nun?

It gave her protection from men.

Is she an expert on computers?

Exactly, he says. The subject of computer crime—

Are you in love? She interrupts him.

Well, he hesitates.

Why did you come back? Why didn't you stay with her?

I don't know, he confesses.

So why are you giving me a lecture on computer crime? You think I'm interested in what she does?

No, he hesitates.

I ask you why you didn't stay with her, and you tell me, I don't know?

That's the situation, he says. That's exactly what happened.

What exactly happened?

Nothing. A week passed, and....

You fought?

No.
You didn't get tired of her in a week.
No.
For that you need a little longer.
Right.
Did she make a scene?
No, not at all.
Because you don't like scenes.
Right.
If she made a scene, I'd understand.
I wouldn't have stayed with her for a single minute.
I know. I know you.
When you're right you're right.
So what happened? In a week you hardly have time to begin to admire one another. It's still the time when the food tastes more and more delicious, the wine has more of a kick, the fucking is only beginning to get better...

There wasn't any fucking, he hurries to slip one true fact into the fantasy he's weaving, but this poor truth is rejected with contempt:

Don't give me that bullshit! What happened to make you get up and leave after a week?

If I'd stayed there I would have murdered someone, he confesses.

Mona stands up in the boat. With great care she folds the sail, takes off her life-jacket, throws off her shirt, and unfastens the hooks of her bra, freeing her breasts which burst joyfully into the night air, shaking themselves like two wet puppies; she wriggles out of her trousers, drops her panties, jumps onto the prow and sets her strong feet on either side of it, and before he has time to admire the beauty of her muscular buttocks she dives into the water of the bay and distances herself from the boat with a few strong crawl strokes, smooth and supple and elegant as a dolphin, and is swallowed up in the darkness.

Mona? he calls hesitantly. Mona?!

No answer. For a moment he wonders whether to strip and jump into the sea after her, but the water is too wet, and the night is too cold, and even if he jumps into the water, how will he find her in the darkness? And anyway, Mona is a professional swimmer, who had swum for the national youth team in her time, she was a master of all the styles of swimming, whereas he was an amateur with no style at all. If it was a question of running, he consoles himself, you would overtake her even if she had a start of two kilometers, but when it comes to swimming you haven't got a chance to come close to her. He strains his eyes and scans the sea around him, but the darkness of the water merges with the darkness of the air very near to the boat, and beyond the point where the two darknesses merge it's impossible to see anything. There's nothing for it but to wait in the hope that she'll return.

There's no danger that she'll drown herself like Jack London, who she admires so much, the thought crosses his mind, she isn't the suicidal type. But suddenly the possibility occurs to him that she might simply swim ashore and leave him alone in the boat in the middle of the sea. She's capable of it. But on the other hand, she wouldn't go ashore naked, even though she is capable of that too. But the keys of the Land Rover are still on the boat, in her trouser pocket, he reassures himself

31

And he lies down on his back again, on the soft sand of the shore of the Atlantic Ocean, opposite the Breakers Hotel in

Palm Beach, with Melissa lounging next to him, sliding her slender foot over his legs covered with frizzy black hair, and saying to him:

You ask why you went into that dangerous mine?

Yes, he says, I hoped that you would solve the riddle for me, but up to now you haven't solved anything for me.

All the way to Florida I thought about it, she says, and it seems to me that I've found the answer.

Let's hear it, he says.

You're a leg-man, she says.

What's a 'leg-man'? he asks.

There are four human types who are permitted to enter the labyrinths of Venus, which are carved into the bowels of the copper mountains. Let's start with the brainy type, she suggests. The brain-man seeks to solve every problem by means of logical thought. He will never give way to spontaneous impulses. He'll always try to obtain all the information on any given subject before he makes a decision. He'll also try to predict the probable consequences of the next step before he takes it. This type is the ideal chess player. Before he sets out he always draws himself as accurate as possible a map of the surest route to his goal, and calculates the precise length of every part of the road, and the time needed to cross it.

What's all this got to do with the labyrinth of Venus? he asks, even though he hasn't got the faintest idea of what this labyrinth may be—he allows himself to flow with the words.

The connection is simple, she explains. The minute the brainy type enters the labyrinth—the spirit of the labyrinth gets who he is and programs the labyrinth to react to his brainy characteristics.

The spirit of the labyrinth? he stops the stream of her words, what's that?

Have you ever driven a car with a smart gearbox, that in the first seconds of the journey gets the driving style of the driver and behaves accordingly?

Yes, he says, holding the wheel of the dark green Citroen MX, making its way through a dense oak wood on a mountain road winding along the ancient Limes Germanicus, somewhere in the state of Hessen—

How did it behave?

Like a woman in love, he answers. She loved every crazy thing I did.

You asshole, she scolds him and jolts him out of that distant summer evening, I asked you how the car behaved, and not some woman you're dreaming about now.

I was talking about the car, he laughs, why did you think I was talking about a woman?

So how did the car respond to you?

Like a sport, he says.

So why are you surprised that a labyrinth of tunnels in an abandoned copper mine is able to recognize the type of person who enters the belly of the mountain?

Go on, says Shakespeare and notes to himself that this conversation is so silly that it has to lead somewhere. He learnt long ago from personal experience that clever, logical conversations put the imagination to sleep and fail to produce interesting ideas, whereas idle talk, ostensibly banal and pointless, in the end awakens the imagination from its slumbers. Therefore he relinquishes responsibility and abandons himself to the vicissitudes of the strange conversation, ready to flow in whatever direction it takes him. And as if she reads his thoughts she says:

The brainy type will stop at every junction in the tunnels and seek information that will help him to decide which way to go.

Who can he get such information from? asks Shakespeare.

He will appeal to the brainy types who preceded him on the journey.

And how will the spirit of the labyrinth respond to him?

It will give him a very strict timetable, every deviation from which will lead immediately to the closing of the gates, and then the savior will turn into another captive in the belly of the mountain, and he himself will be in need of a savior to come and rescue him.

The second type is the man of feeling? he guesses, and thinks of Jonas, and a wave of painful longing for his dead friend suddenly overcomes him.

Yes, she confirms, this type is the heart-man. He is very open and sensitive to others. He feels the other, he is moved by him, he feels with him, and he operates according to the commands of his heart. He inflames the feelings of his mate too and leads her to behave according to her feelings, and the two of them release a lot of energy, and he expresses himself poetically.

Like Shaninas de los Rugashivas, he suggests.

Who's that? she asks.

A Brazilian poet, he hears Shakespeare beginning to develop a character. During the day he worked as a gray clerk in the electric corporation, and at night he would put on a green suit and a fedora hat, and go out to enjoy himself in the bars of Copa-Roja, he invents the name of a quarter. He wrote amazing erotic poetry. I saw fat women melting like butter in the sun when they longingly recited his poems.

What do you say, she says, I'll look for his poems.

Now go on, he requests.

What were we talking about? she asks.

The heart-man.

The heart-man, yes, she remembers, the heart-man activates the soul of the labyrinth, but the labyrinths of Venus have two souls, one good one, creative and friendly, and one evil, destructive and dangerous. While the good soul will love the heart-man and try to help him with singing and music to accompany him on his way through the abandoned mine, the evil soul will try to seduce him with its sweetness and lead him astray in the tunnels, so that he will never reach the prisoner sitting and waiting to be saved. He will be lost in one of the dark chasms.

We've spoken of the brain-man and the heart-man, he sums up. Who's the third type?

The guts-man, she pronounces confidently. He is activated by dark drives, animal instincts and gut-feelings.

I have a friend like that, he says to her and thinks of Yadanuga. Tell me about him. Maybe I'll understand at last why he did what he did to me.

Here goes, she says. The guts-man doesn't believe in words, he is almost deaf to verbal messages. Nor does he believe in poetic outbursts or emotional outpourings. On the other hand he responds to signs, omens, smells and colors. He believes only in his gut feelings, and he is alert to every tiny movement to which the brainy and emotional types are oblivious. When he enters the labyrinth, the labyrinth immediately adapts itself to him and speaks to him in the language of smells, shapes, murmurs and whispers. This man is sure that he is closer to the true reality than the men of brains and emotions, but this confidence often leads him to make bad decisions and to enter places where the brain-man and the heart-man would not risk setting foot.

Interesting, he says, all this is very interesting. But let's hear now about the characteristics of the leg-man, he urges her.

The leg-man, or the homopod, she informs him, is a man who has lost his faith in what the brain, heart and guts can tell him.

So what remains for him?

Only legs remain for him, she says. Long and thin like mine, or short and sturdy like yours. He doesn't trust anything except for his legs.

And his shoes, he says.

Shoes? she repeats in surprise

Have you ever heard of a language called Yiddish? he replies with a question.

The language of the Hasids in Queens, she says.

That's what's left of it, he corrects her.

What's it got to do with the legs-man? she asks.

It was his language, he says, and sees his father. Some people think that Yiddish was the language of the heart and the guts, but this is a superficial view of this language, he pronounces. The people who lived in this language believed only in their legs, and their shoes. His motto was: *Ich un meine shich*, which means—

Me and my shoes, she guesses.

You understand what it means?

Sure, she says. As long as my shoes are okay, everything's okay.

Not everything, he says, but the main thing. The ability to move wherever your legs can take you, when the earth begins to burn. But what did you want to tell me about the leg-man, or what did you call him?

The homopod proceeds only along the difficult path of trial and error, she says. Even if somebody tells him that a certain tunnel leads to a dead end, he won't believe it until he discovers it for himself. He has to do the wrong thing in order to discover that it's wrong. Only by making mistakes and erasing them will he arrive at the right results, but then he will know the truth in a way that cannot be denied.

If I understand you correctly, the leg-man doesn't believe in signs, words, or the experience of others, he is astonished to discover and formulate for the first time with complete clarity his own attitude towards the world.

Right, she confirms, he has to walk on his own legs to the places that he wants to know.

And that means taking risks, he reflects out loud.

Risks and great difficulties, she agrees, and he is also ready to suffer the difficult or unpleasant consequences of his mistakes.

He isn't afraid or deterred by failure, he suggests.

On the contrary, she reinforces him, failure for him is a necessary condition of success.

And how does this affect the spirit of the labyrinth? he asks.

The labyrinth won't volunteer any information about what awaits him, not in signs, not in words and not in clues of any other kind, but at the same time the labyrinth will allow him to retrace his steps whenever he realizes his mistake, on condition that he doesn't make the same mistake twice.

A road you learn with your feet you don't forget easily, he says.

And therefore repeating a mistake is something the homopod cannot forgive, she says.

The leg-man isn't too clever before the event, he smiles sadly.

No, she agrees, but on the other hand, the leg-man, who perhaps we should call the 'journey-man', crosses greater distances than all the other types together, and nobody knows all the wrong roads like he does. Those feet have crossed countries and continents, and I'd like to hear the story they told the earth, she says and strokes his legs cast in steel. But it's beginning to get cold outside. Why don't we go up to the room?

They get up, shake the sand from the big towels they took from the hotel room. She drapes her skinny body in the white towel, and he drapes her shoulders in his towel too.

What about you, she asks him, aren't you cold?

I'm never cold, he laughs at himself, I have the coat of a seal.

Of a walrus, she laughs and strokes his hairy back, let me get the sand off your fur.

32

Should we play a game? he suggests as they stand under the hot water in the shower.

What game?

I'll ask questions and you answer quickly, without thinking.

Go ahead, she says, fire away.

Why do I enter the belly of the mountain?

To rescue a friend.

Which friend?

You're a team.

What kind of a team?

An action team, she answers.

How many of us are there in the team?

Four? She throws out a guess.

And what happened to the friend?

They abducted him.

Who abducted him?

The enemy.

Why?

He's being held as a hostage? She guesses again.

Do I enter the belly of the mountain alone?

Yes.

Where are the other two? He asks in excitement.

Standing guard outside, she states with growing confidence.

Who decides that I'm going in?

You volunteer.

I announce that I'm volunteering?

No, she says. You say to them: You keep guard outside, I'm going in.

Do they argue with me?

No, she states confidently. You're the foxhound of the team.

Am I afraid?

No, you don't feel anything.

How's that possible?

You're a leg-man. The brain and heart are neutralized. Only the legs work.

And the hostage?

What about him?

He knows I'm coming?

He's waiting for you, she says.

What makes him wait for me precisely?

He's a guts-man, she says as they emerge from the shower, and she rubs his body with a fresh soft towel.

That's right, he says and takes the big towel from her and starts to dry her body.

Oh, she sighs at the touch of his hands, your hands are so good.

How do you know that he's a guts-man? he demands an explanation.

He's the closest to you in the team, she states with absolute confidence again.

How do you know?! This is driving him crazy.

That's why you volunteered. And the others didn't argue with you.

Go on! he prompts her.

He prays to you.

I'm on my way.

In the dark.

I have an eye that sees.

The infrared?

Aha.

He doesn't see you.

No.

But he feels the heat.

So I'm close.

You're close.

Should I go on?

Yes.

Or rest for a minute?

Go on!

How does that feel?

Hot!

And now?

Hotter!

Am I getting close?

Yes!

Hey!

What?

Slowly! She shouts in a whisper and clings to him, trembling all over.

33

Suddenly, beyond the bend, the tunnel opens up like a funnel into a large alcove, and all at once he finds himself face to face with a man sitting on a rock. A pair of eyes glittering opposite him in the greenish light of the infrared binoculars attached to his eyes. The man stands up, presumably feeling the heat of the glow directed onto his face, and he raises a submachine gun, with a large flashlight mounted under its barrel. His thumb gropes for the switch of the flashlight above the magazine housing. Time almost stands still. Tenths of a second last as long as minutes. The brain is paralyzed. The heart is empty. The guts are silent. Only the legs act. The left leg, which is his springing leg, bends and pushes off powerfully from the ground, his body rises and describes an arc in the air, and his right leg bends backwards and flies forward in a kick that hits the barrel of the submachine gun. A burst of bullets sprays the roof of the tunnel, and he goes on walking on air—like in the dreams when he leaps into the air and moves his legs and floats above the houses of the village and the orchards and the cypress trees and pine forests of the Judean hills—and his left leg completes the move and hits the man in the stomach with all its power, accompanied by a roar that empties the air from his lungs:

34

The scream of an animal in the jungle bursts from her depths.

Melissa! He holds her and shakes her violently.

Melissa! He grips her shoulders and raises her to him.

And another cry. He cups her head gently in his hands, and she hangs onto his shoulders like a drowning woman, digs into the flesh with her nails, trembling all over, her foot stamping the air in search of a grip, and he reaches back with his left hand and seizes hold of her foot, and her toes spread out and curl round the five fingers of his hand, which twine between them, and she pushes her foot hard against his hand and whispers, don't move, don't move, it's so good, I want it to last forever, and they remain clasped in their embrace until evening falls, crossing together the unbearable moment when the body can no longer contain the soul—

35

I knew you were a killer, she says to him when her soul returns from the void. I knew the minute you came through the glass door from the street and I turned round and read you.

How did you know? he asks her and strokes her head which is resting on his chest.

I saw the eye in the middle of your forehead.

Where exactly? he asks.

She turns her head, peers at him through her weeping slits, which are now shooting sparks like cat's eyes lit up in the dark, and touches her finger to the center of his forehead, just above the bridge of his nose.

Here, she says, can you feel that you have an eye over here?

Yes, he laughs, of course I can.

I'm not joking, she says, I'm deadly serious.

She begins talking obsessively, like a person who has just been confronted by death. He lets her get it off her chest without interrupting the stream of words.

The great majority of people look at the world through two eyes located on the two sides of their faces, she says, leading to a lax, diffuse view of the world. This gaze, which I call 'the human gaze' because I haven't yet found a more accurate name for it, is a gaze which skims over things and doesn't penetrate them. It can be compared to diffuse lighting. The first time I noticed this characteristic of the human gaze was when I went to work as a sales assistant at a big branch of H & M. I liked to stand to one side and observe the customers coming in to survey the clothes. You can see the women, yes, mainly the women, taking in the whole store with one superficial glance, and then going through the hangers, flipping through them with their fingers and skimming over them with their eyes in a half-interested half-bored gaze, not seeing what they're seeing. I would watch them at the moment when they lost interest and went out into the street again, and went on seeing the street too with the same vague, unfocused gaze with which they looked at the clothes in the shop. And then I discovered that in the subway too, and even in the cinema and the theatre, people don't really look at what they are apparently seeing. Afterwards I worked for a while as a waitress in a big restaurant selling Asian food, and I checked to see if my discovery was valid there too, and I have to say that the same thing happened in restaurants too. People don't really see what they're eating. They order their dishes, and as soon as they identify in a general way that they have received their noodles with seafood, or whatever, they don't really look at the food in front of them. And then I saw that they don't actually look at their companions either, or at least they don't actually see them. Otherwise how can you explain the fact that so many women are prepared to spend their lives with creatures as lacking in charm as the vast majority of men in the world. And vice versa. I remember that couples would come into the restaurant, sit down, and I would bring them the menu, and in the first tenth of a second that I encountered their eyes or their faces, I would say to myself: What a revolting mug, how come she doesn't see what I see, how come she doesn't get up and run for her life at this very minute. Or those women who are incapable of seeing beauty in anything, because they look at the world with a gaze that is disgusted by the very materiality of all material, beginning with the paper that the menu is printed on, and the fork that they pick up with loathing as if it was a toilet brush, and ending with the delicious dish of fresh shrimps and calamari, glistening in their delicate coating of melted butter and garlic, and bringing a look of such disgust to their faces that it seems as if they are about to throw up on the table, and they pick up the toilet brush with lame fingers and touch the horrible thing floating on the plate in front of them with horror, and the man sitting opposite this woman looks at her with a lifeless look that doesn't see anything. Because if that man had a third eye in the middle of his forehead he would stab her with his steak knife and get up and get out of there. But there are very few executioners in this world, and you are one of them, she concludes.

How do you know? he demands.

I only have to look at you, she says, it's written on your forehead. The gaze of your two eyes combines into a single laser beam, which measures distances to the thousandth of a millimeter.

There's no such thing.

Yes there is, she says. Maybe you don't know, but that's what you do. You measure distances all the time. You simply can't do anything else. It's self-evident: it's not enough that you're a killer, you're also the leg-man to beat all legmen, and the combination of the two is lethal.

And you saw all this the minute I walked into the store to buy a suit? he asks.

Yes, she confirms. I saw that and a lot more as well.

What else did you see? he asks curiously.

I saw that you don't love any of the gifts that nature gave you.

What do I have that anyone could love? he laughs.

All of you, she says.

Really! he protests. In a minute you'll say that it's possible to love my fingers?

Why not? she takes his hand in her delicate hand.

There you are! he says. Look at my fingers.

What's wrong with your fingers?

They're German Bockwurst, not fingers, he says.

Let me taste, she says and puts a finger in her mouth and licks it with her warm moist tongue and grunts in pleasure.

Look, he insists, my fingers are almost the same size.

Of course, she says, are you surprised? It's the hand of a murderer. She strokes his hand with provocative sensuality.

You know, he confesses, when I was a boy I couldn't stand the fact that my fingers were the same length. I would look at my rectangular hand, and sometimes I would be tempted to take my mother's chopper and chop off a bit of my pinkie.

Now I understand where circumcision comes from, she says. You Jews are incapable of accepting yourselves the way God created you: you have to improve on his work.

I hated my fingers so much that I used to keep them in my pockets all the time, he says. And if I had to take them out, I would immediately make them into a fist to hide my shame. That's what got me into trouble with fighting.

Why shame? She doesn't understand.

Walking round in the world with hands like these is like walking around naked, he says.

Is it bad to walk around naked?

With legs like mine?

We're already spoken about legs, she says. What else don't you like about yourself?

This Mongolian skull, skewered on a cucumber.

You call this a cucumber? She strokes his neck. This is the neck of a Belgian horse, of a ox, it's a tree trunk!

You should have seen the neck I received from nature, he laughs. You know how many hours of working out, lifting weights and stretching springs with my head have been invested in this neck?

What kind of a child were you? she asks.

Can't you see what kind of a child this man was?

Not this man—you, she stresses. What kind of a child were *you*.

The kind of child—he begins, but she interrupts him:

No, don't talk about him. Talk about yourself. Say: I was a child...

Perhaps there's a child buried in me, he says.

Why is it so hard for you to talk about the child you were?

Why is it hard for me? he reflects aloud. Because there's nothing left in me of that lost child. I close my eyes and I can't even see him.

Take your time, she says. We're not in a hurry.

There's no chance that this man will succeed in meeting the child he was.

You're talking about yourself in the third person again, she says.

I'm not talking about myself, he says. I'm talking about some man and some child I have no connection with, and they have no connection with each other either.

Good, she compromises, who's further away from you now, the man or the child?

The child, he says.

So tell me about him.

Why are you so interested in him? he asks.

I'll tell you when the time comes. Now we're talking about the child. Tell me about the child.

36

The child was drawn more to the company of women than of men. He liked attaching himself to his mother's friends who came and sat on the porch to knit and gossip. The child played on the floor next to them and breathed in the smells that came from them. The child liked these smells. A strange mixture of sweat, talcum powder, scented soap and eau de cologne. This intoxicating mixture was accompanied by another smell, whose origins the child could not identify. A smell which definitely distinguished them from the men, who exuded only sweat, cigarette smoke and crude soap. At the end of summer this smell also came from the guava trees.

The child liked to listen to the women, who talked about fabrics and pregnancies and concentration camps and illnesses and troubles and medicines and cunning recipes for making chopped liver from eggplants and apple compote from courgettes, and whispered about a neighbor who didn't cook for her husband, and another neighbor whose husband waited on her like a queen while she spent all day lying on the sofa in a dressing gown applying hot and cold compresses to her forehead and reading journals, and a third neighbor whose husband beat her at night.

The men's conversations, on the other hand, the child found very boring. He discovered that the men used only a few words, and repeated them in short sentences, which were spoken in monotonous, uninteresting tones, and they only talked about pipes and irrigation systems, and fertilizer and politics and exterminating pests. But the women used many words, and threaded them into endless chains when they talked about what they went through in the camps, how they made little dolls from bread they chewed up and didn't eat, and how they gathered at night round the lavatory seat that served them as a stage and put on plays by candlelight in their miniature puppet theatre for the rest of the women prisoners, and from there they went on simply and naturally to gossip about a man and a woman who had been seen together too often lately, and not only had they been seen together, but he had even been seen going into her house when her husband wasn't at home, a second woman would interrupt the first, and he sits there for hours, a third would add, and the first would giggle and say who knows if all he does is sit, and a fourth would remark that tea and cookies wasn't all she gave him, and the conversation would heat up, and the voices would merge with each other, and stifled laughter would punctuate the speech which was sometimes loud as the chorus of birds in the morning and sometimes soft as the wind whispering in the dry fields at the end of summer—

You're a great storyteller, she says to him, I listen to you and it seems to me that I'm hearing a passage from a book.

From a movie, he corrects her.

What? she asks in surprise.

We're characters in a movie script by an amateur barman and a novice, completely irresponsible scriptwriter, who hasn't yet decided where to take us, he says to her.

And suddenly he lets out a deep sigh, and she asks him why, and without realizing it he starts taking about himself in the first person:

37

Once I wrote. I was then eleven and a half, and I was in love with a girl from my class, and I wrote a serial story for her, which I would read to her at recess, and all the girls in the class would gather round and listen.

While the boys played ball outside? she guesses.

Yes, he remembers. She would sit opposite me, this little girl I was in love with, cupping her sweet face in her hand, looking at me with her brown eyes, with the fingers of her other hand playing with her golden hair.

What was the story about? she asks and he answers:

It was a story about a young woman who escapes with her baby to the forest through the sewage canals, after her husband was murdered in front of her eyes at the entrance to their house, next to their photography studio in Szpitalna street, which was called after the municipal hospital at the end of the street.

Through the sewage canals? she wonders.

Yes, he confirms. Under the town is a network of sewage canals and catacombs and tunnels dating from the Middle Ages, and she waits for nightfall, and all the time her husband's body is lying in a pool of blood in the street, in front of their house, and when night comes, she wraps her baby in a blanket, and walks like a shadow along the walls until she reaches a convent, and the Polish abbess of the convent takes her down to a secret tunnel and gives her a flashlight and tells her go straight down the main tunnel until she meets the people who have been living underground for two years, and they will help her, and on the way she encounters an underground burial chamber full of open coffins, containing the skeletons of adults and children. And she passes through the skeletons with her baby and walks on. And in the next chapter she meets the people who have been living in the sewage canals since the outbreak of the war. Whole families who have been living under the ground for over two years.

How do they live there? she wonders.

They lead perfectly normal lives, he says. Friends visit friends, one family has dinner with another family. There are also solitary people who have lost everyone, and they exist there without God and without hope—he quotes the voices of the women he heard so many years ago speaking in Yiddish on their porch, '*un a Got un a hofnung*', but there are also young men and young women there who fall in love and get married and bring children into the world in the sewage tunnels. And on one summer night when the moon is full the moonlight filters into the tunnels through the iron grille, and a pair of young lovers go to seclude themselves in the moonlight in the pit under the grille, and they begin to kiss and embrace and they forget themselves, and they begin to utter sounds, and the soldiers who are passing in the street right above them, hear the voices rising from under the ground, and they realize that there are people there, and they go down into the pit and throw grenades, but the boy and girl succeed in escaping and disappearing into one of the sewage canals.

And what happens to the woman with the baby? she asks curiously.

She doesn't stay down there. She succeeds in reaching the forest, and joins a group of partisans. They go out to blow up trains and she cooks for them and washes their clothes. But her baby sickens with diphtheria, and there are no medicines in the forest, and the baby dies in her arms and she buries her in the forest, she digs a little grave for her in the loose soil, and covers her with rotting leaves, and there aren't even any stones there to put up a little headstone for her.

And what happens afterwards? Tell me, she requests.

The war ends, he says. People emerge from the forest, start going back to their towns and villages to look for relatives and acquaintances, to see what remains of their homes, their neighborhoods, their towns. The roads are full of survivors....

But what about the woman? she asks.

The woman joins a convoy of refugees, and they have to cross a bridge, and next to the bridge are soldiers who search the men, order them to take off their shirts, and there's an officer there who examines each of the men, and anyone who has a skull tattooed under his armpit is taken aside and given a bullet in the head and thrown into the river.

But what about the woman? she insists.

The woman returns to her town, and finds neither the house nor the street. Everything is in ruins. And then she joins another convoy of refugees, and they reach a DP camp, and young soldiers come and put her on an army truck and take her to the port, and put her on a little ship, together with hundreds of refugees like her, and they set sail for the Land of Israel, and when they're in the open sea a British plane flies over them, and when they approach the shore two warships come and British soldiers jump onto their little ship, and they pelt the soldiers with potatoes, but it doesn't help them, and the British soldiers put them on their ships and take them to Cyprus, and there they are imprisoned in camps again, and in the camp she meets a man who lost his wife and two children in the war, and the relations between them are far from simple, because she is torn between longings for her husband, who was the love of her youth and was murdered before her eyes, and the man she meets in the camp, who is also a person whose life has been broken, and it isn't easy for them together, and they don't talk much, because each of them is burdened with a terrible past, and only sometimes, when they sit outside in the evening, in the cool breeze, she speaks a little of what she has been through, in short sentences, hesitantly, afraid that perhaps she is talking about herself too much, knowing only a little about what he went though, and that little too is terrible, and therefore she is afraid of burdening him with the weight of her past, and he is a shy, reserved man, a short, sturdy man, withdrawn into himself and very sparing of words. His silences embarrass her, but since she knows what lies behind these silences, she is silent too, and thus they sit there in the evening on a tree stump next to the fence of the camp, two broken people, full of memories and pain, and are silent together, until they feel cold, and then they get up and part with a handshake which she initiates. Not even a kiss on the cheek.

In the meantime the United Nations decides on the partition of Palestine between the Jews and the Arabs, and the Arabs refuse to accept the decision and declare war on the Jewish population and one evening he comes and tells her that he has found a way to escape from the camp and stow away on a Greek ship sailing to Eretz-Israel, and he is going there to fight. And again they sit on their tree stump next to the fence of the camp, two shy people who can't find the words to dissolve the lumps stuck in their throats, sit until they feel cold and get up, and she accompanies him to his tent and parts from him with a handshake which she initiates, and the next day he sails for Eretz-Israel to join the Jewish army.

In the first weeks she doesn't hear from him, but one day a short letter arrives. He writes that the war is fierce, dozens of young men are being killed, his unit is fighting in the Judean hills, and they gave him a German MG machine-gun with a little swastika engraved on it, and he is fighting like a lion, because he is sick and tired of all the bastards pursuing him and wanting only to kill him, we'll win because we have no choice. We have a country, and if you want it you will have a home of your own at last.

And when she recounts these things her eyes fill with tears, and tears stream from the eyes of the other women too sitting on the porch with her and knitting.

This is my mother's story, he says.

Tell me about her, she asks.

38

She leaves Cyprus with the last group of prisoners. She disembarks from the ship at the port of Haifa, a small harbor town in the North of Eretz-Israel, a small, solitary woman, with a little bundle holding everything she has left in the world. And who does she see there in the quay, but a small man in a soldier's uniform, standing and looking anxiously at the people coming down the gangway of the ship. She recognizes him before he sees her. She waves at him. Now he sees her. Recognizes her. It seems to her that he even smiles, this reserved man.

She runs towards him. Embraces him. Laughs and cries. He too is moved, but he doesn't cry, her iron man. This is what she calls him in her language when she talks to her neighbors from the farming village on the porch. '*Mein aizener man*', or simply '*der aizen*'. And the nickname sticks, so that he too, the son, calls his father by it when he comes home from school, and later from the army: 'Mom, is the Iron at home?' and she answers naturally: 'No, Huneleh, the Iron is in the fields.' Or: 'Today the Iron is lifting crates in the packing plant. Let me give you a thermos with tea for him, take it to him, he'll be pleased.'

And after the army, when the son is attached to the special unit whose teams are sent all over the world to hunt down airplane hijackers and terrorists and murderers of all kinds and close accounts with them, and he calls home after the operation, and her anxious voice answers: Huneleh! Are you well? Are you all right? and he hears the sigh of relief breaking out of the depths of her soul tortured by terrible memories—he hurries to ask her: how's the Iron? And she replies: the Iron is the same as always, yesterday he went to cut the grass in the plantation. Maybe you can persuade him to take a little more care of himself, and he says: let me talk to him for a minute, and he hears her telling him that Huneleh wants to say something to him, and he hears the Iron grumble: what did you say to him already? And he hears her justifying herself: nothing, I swear, he just wants to say hello. And then the Iron's sandals clatter on the floor, and he hears his voice, strong and firm as always, as if the disease which is spreading throughout his body has nothing to do with him and exists only in the morbid imaginations of the doctors, who despaired of his life three years ago and gave him no more than two months, maybe three, to live, and when he hears the strong 'Hello?' he hesitates for a second before saying: Dad? How are you? and the Iron almost rebukes him for even asking the question, and raises the same metallic voice that organized the uprising of the body burners, most of whose participants were killed before they succeeded in getting away from the camp, and only he and five of his comrades succeeded in escaping their pursuers and reaching the forest: I'm fine! announces the Iron, are you all right?—I'm fine, Dad, but I hear that you're going off the rails a bit.—Nonsense! The Iron cuts him short, if I'd listened to the doctors I'd have been rotting in the ground a long time ago. And in order to leave no room for argument, the Iron immediately changes the subject: Did you do the job? And after he receives confirmation, he sums up: very good. One bastard less.

And if you knew him, you would have heard in his voice the reserved pride in his son, who is doing exactly what he himself would have liked to do.

And that's what turned you into a professional killer? she asks.

No, he says. It was the feminine side of my character again.

How come, she wonders, you'll have to explain that to me.

It was the look in my mother's eyes, when she came across strangers.

Tell me about it, she asks and curls up in his arms and nestles into his chest.

It's hard for me to talk about it, he whispers.

Try, she urges.

39

She had this look...he begins after a long silence, but the lump sticks in his throat. He had never spoken these words. He had never spoken of his mother's eyes, which are looking at him now out of the void, and he feels that if he says one more word he will burst into the tears that have been seething inside him ever since he can remember himself and which he has never allowed himself to weep.

What kind of look did she have? She won't let go.

He makes a gesture with his hand for her to wait a minute. That in a minute he will open is mouth and speak. He swallows his saliva, but the lump is still stuck there. And suddenly he can't contain it any longer. He gets up from the carpet and walks naked through the luxurious hotel room, takes a glass from the magnificent bar and pours into it the golden liquid from the green bottle of Laphroaig which he bought at the liquor store crowded with New Year's Eve revelers, and goes over to the big window where the vast ocean stretches silver in the moonlight painting in phosphorescent green and white the strip of sand along which they ran that afternoon. He takes a hefty gulp of the fierce liquid suffused with the smells of iodine and carbolic acid, and leans his forehead on the freezing windowpane, and she comes and stands behind him, leaning her slender body against his, and he feels her pubic hair on his buttocks, the plums of her breasts tickling his back, her arms enfolding him and her hands stroking his chest and stomach, and the words start coming out of his mouth, carefully feeling their way round the picture he sees before his eyes.

40

It was a shamed look, as if she was ashamed of not being able to prevent what they did to her, ashamed that they took her parents one morning, with other old people, and put them on a truck and drove them to the forest and stripped them naked and stunned her father with blows to the head, like stunning a pig before the slaughter, and afterwards they shot them. And she was ashamed for her husband who stepped empty-handed out of their little photography studio to wipe the display window clean of the eggs people had thrown at it, and a drunken soldier kicked him to his knees, and put a pistol to the nape of his neck and shot him and spat and walked away to join the band of soldiers on the other side of the street, who were standing and drinking schnapps from a bottle passed from hand to hand, and laughing loudly. And she was ashamed of not being able to save her little baby from death by suffocation from diphtheria, and Dr. Gott-lieb's explanations didn't help, the devoted country doctor who sat one day on their porch overlooking the Judean hills and while sipping steaming tea and fanning himself with his handkerchief tried to persuade her in a gentle voice that in those years, before the discovery of antibiotics, and all the more so in the conditions of life in the forest, there was almost no hope of saving a baby from the Corynebacterium diphtheria bacillus. And the attempts by the good doctor to console her, and even the giving of a name and identity to that bacillus, only increased the disgrace of her failure to perform her role as a mother. And this suppressed shame, which settles inside a person and has nowhere to go, was reflected in her eyes and in all her body language whenever she met strange people for the first time. She would shrink into herself like a wounded body round its wound, as if try-ing to make herself invisible, her whole being one mute plea not to be noticed, not to be looked at, not to be seen in the disgrace of her survival.

Her iron man couldn't stand this weakness and didn't know how to deal with it. Sometimes, when she froze in the middle of plucking a duck, which he brought her from the yard after chopping off its head, or in the middle of gut-ting a fish, and she would support her waist with the hand holding the knife, and a deep, uncontrollable groan would break out of her depths, the Iron would respond with a kind of dull growl, that seemed to emerge from the blazing belly of a volcano about to erupt, and this mute dialogue between her groan and his growl was enough to make her pull herself together and return to the small acts of daily life, the activities in which she drowned her sorrow and her shame in the days when she cooked for the partisans too, or when she prepared sandwiches from thick slices of black bread smeared with butter and filled with rissoles cut in half lengthways for her iron man, before he took his Tommy gun and set out with a few other men from the village to prepare an ambush on the bank of the wadi for the infiltrators coming from the other side of the border to murder farmers in the fields, like they murdered Yatzker, when he went to move irrigation pipes at night, or Tibor Tomas and his beautiful wife Ilona—who were shot by infiltrators through the window when they were asleep in their beds.

41

No, he leans his forehead against the windowpane, no, he repeats to the ocean waves breaking in front of him, it wasn't the wish to continue the Iron's war that turned him into a killer. No no. His father had already done his bit when he took part in the uprising of the body burners, and afterwards, when he raced a jeep on the southern front, and when he was made the security-coordinator of the new border village—which clung to the mountainside in its little houses, two tiny rooms and a kitchenette and bathroom, forty-five square meters in all—and organized the guarding of the fields and orchards. And when the disease that had spread throughout his body was about to defeat him seven years after the doctors had given him three more months to live, and he felt his strength leaving him, and the pain was growing worse and soon it would be unbearable and he would need stronger and stronger doses of morphine, until the drug paralyzed his respiratory system and he died of suffocation in his bed—he rose before dawn and took his big Parabellum, which was his service revolver in the War of Independence and in all the years of his reserve duty as the commander of a reconnaissance unit, and went out to the well-tended yard, where he had planted every tree and bush, and sat on a bench he had made with his own hands under the sapling which had grown into a huge, spreading tree, and set the barrel of the gun to his right temple, and put an end to his iron life with the same iron hand which had raised it from the ruins.

No, he says to her and licks the salt from the stalk of her fragile hand, which is stroking his wet cheeks, it wasn't him who made me kill the soft, dreamy little girl I used to be—and this is the first time in his life that he has dared to utter these words, 'the soft, dreamy little girl I used to be', and now the fountain of tears wells up unimpeded from the hole drilled by his own words in the hard layer of ice which has covered it for so many years; and which her emaciated body, and her caressing hands, and something else, something hidden which he does not yet know how to name, has suddenly melted. Yes, he says, it was my mother, her shamed existence, the disgrace of the innocent victim—this is what threatened to crush me from within, and made me bury the poetess inside me alive, stifle her gentle, hesitant words, and become a man of action.

Come, she says, give me your face, and he turns to face her. She takes his head in her long slender fingers and licks the salt from his cheeks. Her tongue penetrates the corners of his eyes and licks the tear ducts, and this gentle tickling maddens his senses, but he lets her do as she wishes with him, and she lifts her long thin legs and coils them round his waist, and he whispers to her:

You're as light as the wind, as if you have no body.

You make me weightless, she whispers, let's go to bed.

And he leans forward, lowers them both to the thick carpet, and they lie there in each other's arms for a long time, almost without moving, afraid of disturbing the closeness growing ever greater between them.

42

And suddenly her hands grip the sides of the boat, and she leaps up from the sea like a dolphin opposite the coast of Florida, naked and dripping, and her wet skin glitters in the pale light of dawn turning the Eastern sky pink before his eyes. So the boat had not stayed still, but had evidently been turning slowly on its axis all the time she was away, an eternity or only a few minutes. Mona's body cast in bronze cuts a dark silhouette against the sky. She stands naked with her legs apart, her strong feet steady on the edges of the boat, on either side of the prow, and washes her body with water from a plastic container, another three like it strapped to the stern. And after she has rinsed the salt water from her body she wipes it with a round stick, a habit she brought back with her from her visit to Japan. Ever since she has not touched a towel, and he is surprised to see that she keeps such a wiping-stick on her boat as well, and the thought crosses his mind that this woman has built herself an entire world connected to the sea, where there is no room for him. His gaze climbs from her feet to her calves, her sturdy thighs, the curves of her hips rounding to her narrow waist and rising to her supple back, and his eyes are arrested by her breasts which are still the same as they were when he met her and fell in love with her, the liaison officer in the special unit he joined after he was discharged from the commando, and he looks at her muscular arms, which press the Japanese wiping stick to her neck and lead it with brisk movements to the erect pink nipples of her breasts, wiping away every drop of moisture—and as she performs this wiping action with the precision of a ritual act, she says to him:

Look, I'm not really interested in who and what she is, and if she's a mulatto or a Chinese woman. But it's obvious to me what's happened to you. You started having an affair with someone, and suddenly you got scared, because you felt you were beginning to fall in love with her. And you're afraid of falling in love. You don't know what to do with it. So you took to your heels and ran away. Now you're not there, but you're not here either. You're stuck in some no-man's-land. Floating like an embryo in limbo. Ever since you came back, I can feel that you're not the same person. You don't listen. You don't concentrate on what you're doing. And you hardly talk. You don't communicate. If it only concerned your life with me, I wouldn't like it but I'd put up with it. But the trouble is that it expresses itself in your running the business as well. And it's happening in these hard times, when hundreds of businesses are being wiped out every day, and our own business is on the verge of bankruptcy. And there's a rare opportunity to make a pile of money if we win the competition, and exactly at this moment, when you should be leading the company, you're suddenly not there, and you let your art director fight with the graphic artist and the idea-woman, and pardon me for putting it bluntly, but even though Mackie is your friend from days gone by, you have to face the fact that apart from his well known obstinacy, there isn't a drop of creativity left in him, and he can sense it, he's not a fool, but apparently it's difficult for people to admit failure, and even more difficult for them to acknowledge that their time is past. So instead he fights Golan and Moran, who came up with a brilliant idea if you ask me, and if we go with their idea we have a good chance of winning, and you know exactly what that means financially speaking. It could be the difference between bankruptcy and bringing in millions, for years to come. But I can see that even now, when I'm talking to you, you're staring at me without hearing a word I'm saying. The words fly past your ears like missiles that missed their target and explode in the air. So I'm telling you to pick up your heels and go to your model or nun or American policewoman, and I'll take charge of things here and run the business. I'll direct the project and I'll make the decisions. And if you come back one day with a clear head, and I'm still here, and the company will still exist, I'll be happy to let you take charge again, because I have plans of my own too. I'm planning to sell this boat and buy a two-master and take out a skipper's license for the Atlantic Ocean, and then to extend it to the Pacific as well. So I don't intend spending my life running the company, but at the moment there's no other alternative. If you have something to say, say it, she commands him and pulls on her sweater that swallows her magnificent breasts.

Do you intend on buying the two-master on your own? he asks the sweater which is still covering her face.

That's what's bothering you now? Her head emerges from the deep neckline of the red sweater.

A two-master that can cross the Atlantic Ocean is no small matter, he says.

What do you say, she says mockingly, and her hands pull the hem of the sweater over her hips. Don't worry, I won't buy it alone. I have partners who're interested in joining up with me.

Again he realizes the extent to which her life at sea has over the years become an unknown continent to him. He is not surprised that there are partners interested in joining this amazing woman, a winning combination of sex and power, and the thought crosses his mind that she could command a navy missile boat, or at least a coast guard gunboat.

Good, she pulls on her walnut leather pants. My understanding is that we agree. We're going ashore, we're calling a meeting, and I'm announcing the changes in the directorship of the company.

43

She drives the Land Rover through the empty streets of the city, still wrapped in sweet early morning slumbers, in a kind of hallucinatory slow motion, as if she is driving a hearse in a dream. Absorbed in her thoughts, planning and scheming—he says to himself as she reaches for the cigarette lighter and pushes it down with a jab of her thumb. Now she raises her hand to a strange new gadget attached to the dashboard. He follows her finger with interest as it lightly touches a glowing yellow button, and the filter of a cigarette pops out of the jaws of the gadget, which turns out to be a cigarette case. She extracts the cigarette with a brisk movement and plants it between her lips. At the same moment the red-hot lighter pops up and her hand, which comes to meet it with perfect synchronization, plucks it from its hole and sets its glowing coil to the tip of the cigarette.

He sends out his hand and touches the yellow button. A new cigarette is ejected from the jaws of the device.

Have you started smoking again? she asks in surprise.

No, he says in an amused tone of voice, I was just curious to see how this *mechutl* works.

She gives him a disgusted look, and her upper lip curls disdainfully. She hates this Yiddish word '*mechutl*' which he has attached to her sophisticated high-tech gadget. She sees this shabby word stuck to her Japanese toy as a bit of greasy old dirt congealed on the handle of a skillet bent out of shape with use. Her right hand goes out to the humiliated luxury item, and it seems to him that she is about to stroke it, to cleanse it of the verbal filth adhering to it and restore its trampled honor. But he is mistaken. Her finger simply touches the blue button next to its yellow twin with demonstrative indifference, and the shamefaced cigarette, which has remained stuck ludicrously in the opening, is swallowed back into its container with a dry click.

What an *uber-chuchemit pitchefke*! he says. Where did you get it?

A present, she snaps.

Who from?

From Golan and Moran.

What for?

My birthday.

Oy, he remembers, when was it?

When you were abroad, she says dryly, and adds: I was actually expecting you to call.

How could I have forgotten? he exclaims and immediately regrets it when she picks up the ball and slams it back at him with the crushing retort:

You were busy with your model.

Policewoman, he corrects her, adhering for some reason to his nonsensical story.

Model, policewoman, I don't care if she's a brain surgeon.

Why a brain surgeon of all things?

Why a policewoman if it comes to that, she retorts dryly.

He has no answer to this. Instead of drawing up some pointless remark from the emptiness gaping inside him like the great black shaft of an abandoned mine, he puts out his finger and presses the yellow button. The next cigarette appears. He presses the blue button, and the cigarette disappears into the maw of the device.

Leave it alone, she says.

Why, he protests and takes another turn on the gadget, actually it's a cute little toy.

Leave it alone, she commands and switches on the radio. A singer wails, 'To give your heart and soul / to give....'

He switches it off. She switches it on. The singer goes on moaning.

What do you want to listen to this rubbish for? he protests.

It's the news in a minute, she says.

Until the news could we do without it? he asks, and switches off the radio.

I want to listen to it, she switches it on again.

The singer goes on whining.

It's horrible, he says.

I like it, she declares.

Since when do you like this saccharine kitsch?

It's not saccharine kitsch, she says. It has true feeling.

You call this true feeling? He says scornfully and starts imitating the crooner in a tremulous, whining voice: 'To give your kidneys and your liver / to give / when you have nothing left / to give....'

Stop it, she commands, let me listen.

He falls silent and looks at her. She smokes her cigarette and hums the song in a strange, unfamiliar abandonment. Her fingers drum on the steering wheel in time to the changing beat of the tune.

Listen to the way he groans, he says to her. Never mind the words. Soul, soul.

You're disturbing me, she snaps.

Something about her has changed. Look at her swooning over this idiotic song. She never liked these songs. Suddenly she likes them. Interesting. As if she's reading his thoughts, she suddenly says:

I'm sick of those anemic Ashkenazi songs. Without heart and balls. He at least isn't afraid of expressing emotion. He isn't afraid of sounding sentimental. He doesn't care what anybody thinks. He says what's in his heart. What's in his guts. Open. Large as life.

'Heart', 'guts'. Suddenly she's talking about heart and guts. Words she never liked, words she mocked people for using. Mona the brainy. Suddenly she's using them herself with a kind of frank enjoyment. Wallowing in them. Brandishing them. Like a child emerging from the latency period and suddenly discovering afresh the pleasures of sex which he enjoyed without inhibitions as an infant. Like a religious Jew becoming free and eating pork for the first time in his life. What's happening to her?

44

If you play the emotional type, says Melissa, you'll meet sirens who'll lead you astray, and you'll have to deal with them according to their deceitful-emotional nature. But if you choose to play the role of the leg-man, the gods will fell trees, or roll rocks into your path to bar your way, and you'll have to exert all your strength to push them aside. On the other hand, if you choose to play the guts-man, you'll come across obstacles that will require all your courage and daring to overcome. And if you choose the role of the brain-man, you'll need to solve riddles and answer questions in order to neutralize the sphinx threatening to paralyze you.

So what is it? he questions the interior of the Land Rover.

What? Mona replies to this meaningless question.

Rocks? Sirens? Or is it someone who.....

What on earth are you talking about?

The news cuts into both the wailing of the singer and the senseless dialogue. The weary voice of an announcer informs them that the time is six a.m., and three soldiers have been killed by a terrorist attack on their post, and that the terrorist was eliminated by a force that returned fire, and that two terrorists were killed in work accidents in Nablus and Yabrod, and another two terrorists were killed when they tried to cross the fence next to Rafah, and two terrorists were wounded next to Ramallah—and without thinking he starts singing in French 'And all for nothing' by Yves Montand.

Stop singing, Mona commands him.

It was Danny's song, he says.

What are you talking about? she says dismissively. Danny never sang French songs.

You don't know what you're talking about, he retorts indignantly, Danny only sang French songs.

Danny sings French songs? she mocks. Apparently you don't know your son.

I wasn't talking about our son, he says.

So what Danny were you talking about?

Danny Altwasser, the Alsatian.

Ah, she says. So say Daniel, not Danny.

For me he was Danny, he says.

What made you think of him all of a sudden, she demands crossly.

Everything was for nothing, he says.

What was for nothing? she asks.

The people who were killed, our people who were killed. For nothing, it was all for nothing.

The city had not yet awoken from its slumbers. The houses smelled of sleep. And there's another man, he says to Melissa, the eyes-man. He's the invisible man. The omnipotent character who populated the world of childhood fantasies. Going into rooms without anyone knowing he's there. Moving objects on tables. Shaking lamps. Suddenly making a picture fall from the wall. Invading bedrooms. Pulling the blanket from a naked couple. Drawing the curtains in the room of a sick man for whom this is his last dawn on earth. Pausing for a moment next to cradles giving off the scent of babies. Accompanying the sons wandering the world, one somewhere in Nepal, another somewhere in Bolivia.

45

The sons, he says to himself, trying to test the extent of his closeness to them, but the words 'the sons' only serve to substantiate the infinite distance between them. He hears their names, Danny and Yoni, and sees his dead comrades, the Alsatian and Jonas. The one wrapped in white cloth soaking up the muddy water of the river, carried away on the slow current, and the other dying in his arms from a bullet from Adonis' pistol, that hit him in the chest. The dagger thrown by Yadanuga in the direction of the murderer hit him in the arm and made him drop the pistol and pick up his heels and run. And when he raises his head from the dying Jonas, and sees the murderer disappearing into the distance he shouts at Yadanuga:

Take care of Jonas!

And sets out in pursuit of the man who according to all the signs is Tino the Syrian, and after an hour of running in the desert the fugitive begins to tire, and the distance between them narrows, and when he comes within range he reaches for his pistol and discovers to his dismay that it isn't there, and in the nightmarishly long second in which he remembers that he put it down when he ripped Jonas' shirt to examine his wound, the fugitive was suddenly hidden behind a fold in the ground and he disappeared from view as if the earth had swallowed him, and the wadi was filled by shadows and the gathering dusk covered everything in darkness, and it was impossible to see anything at all.

46

What are you doing? she asks.

Sending an SMS.

Who to?

Danny, he says.

Isn't it night there now?

No, he says, it's afternoon there now.

His fingers tap out the message, and he sends it on its way and says:

And to Yoni.

What's the time there? she asks.

Ten o'clock at night, he says.

What did you write them? she asks.

V r ok how r u

Sure, ok, she says.

What do you want me to start telling them? he asks.

Nothing, she says.

He tries to see their faces, but they evade him.

Try to see them, he orders himself.

I can't, he answers.

Make an effort, he demands.

They're on two different continents. Which of them should I concentrate on?

Which of them can you see?

Neither of them, he admits in despair. I can't see my sons. I can't see their eyes. I can't see them.

47

She presses the button to activate the computerized sound system. The menu of options comes up on the screen. She moves the cursor, chooses a track, types. Dense, jazzy lyrics

in English, half sung half declaimed at a fast tempo, blare
forth from the Land Rover's state of the art sound system.
Something out of date, that was once new and sophisticated.
It sounded like an English band from the end of the seventies. Try to identify the band, he orders himself. A strange
name surfaces in his memory: The Specials. Where did that
name come from. It isn't clear. It's connected to the picture
of a journey on an autostrada on a rainy windswept night.
Only heavy trucks on the road. And there are three of them
in the car. Yadanuga driving. You're sitting next to him,
ready to take over as soon as he gets tired. Jonas is sleeping on the back seat. They're on their way back from an
execution. In order to keep awake they occupy themselves
with choosing a suitable name for a movie inspired by their
operation. 'Artificial respiration' suggests Yadanuga. 'Deso-
lation' you throw out a counter proposal. Yadanuga plays
with the buttons of the radio and a station comes up and
they're deep in the seventies, with the legendary Sex Pistols
punk parody of 'I did it my way', and he hears himself reflect aloud:

McLarn?

What McLarn? demands Mona in astonishment.

There's a clothes shop called that, isn't there?

If you mean Malcolm McLarn, she says, he once had a
shop in partnership with Vivian Westwood.

Do you remember the address? he asks.

What do you need the address for? she asks in bewilderment, that shop hasn't existed for ages.

Oh, no? he says doubtfully.

If I remember rightly, Malcolm McLarn left the fashion
business after he became the manager of the Sex Pistols.

Then it's apparently not McLarn, he concludes.

I don't know what you're talking about, she says.

She goes on driving in silence.

Is that The Specials? he asks about the song still coming over on the sound system.

Don't you recognize it? I'm surprised at you—'This town is turning into a ghost town'.

Right, he says, I recognize it now.

Your cell phone, she says in response to the electronic beep. He looks at the screen.

There's an answer from Danny, he says.

What does he write? She asks.

i m ok, he reads from the screen.

Good, she says.

Here comes Yoni's answer too.

What does he write?

Letters and numbers appear on the screen: c u b 4 2 b shvat i m ok.

He deciphers and translates:

'See you before Tu b'Shavt, I'm okay.'

Oh! she exclaims. So he's coming home!

Are you glad? he asks.

Aren't you? she says in surprise.

I don't know, he says, and for the first time he admits that he doesn't know if he wants his sons to return to the country.

48

At midday she assembles them all in the office. They have heard something. They sit in suspense. Moran scribbles symmetrical shapes on the paper in front of her. Her scribbles are always symmetrical. An arrowhead pointing from left to right, and opposite it an arrowhead pointing from right to left. A vertical line drawn under the left arrowhead, immediately followed by a vertical line under the right arrowhead. Golan for his part plays with his palm computer. Always absorbed in some screen or other. Take the screen away from him and he's blind in the dark. He touches the bottom of the screen rapidly with the electronic pencil in his hand, and the mini-computer squeaks and squeals like a little animal. Yadanuga on the other hand carves wood. In situations of suspense he always carves pieces of wood from branches he saws off all kinds of trees. Long waiting periods have given birth to sticks with detailed carvings, while short ones produced sketchy and sometimes unfinished carvings. Every surveillance gave birth to a carved stick. The surveillance of Busidi produced a stick with ocean waves, and wooded mountains soaring above them, on the Northern coast of Scotland. And the liquidation of the octet was immortalized in a view of the French Riviera, where the murderers enjoyed their last days and nights on earth, before they were taken out in a villa in the middle of a pine forest, on a hill overlooking Nice, the opposite of which is Sin, which gave rise to the passwords Sinbad the Sailor and Binbad the Bailor to convey the setting out on the mission and the homing in on the villa, and afterwards they called in Tinbad the Tailor, to report that the bastards had been sewn up, and Zinbad the Zailor, to confirm that the operation had been successfully completed and the quartet was in a safe place.

And while he is sunk in memories, wondering if all this has actually taken place in reality or if it all exists only in his imagination, and perhaps memory is only a form of imagination—he hears Mona's voice announcing the change in directorship of the firm.

Hanina is taking a long leave, she says, and will be out of the country for an unspecified period of time. As of this moment I am taking his place as director of the firm, and of the pill campaign in particular. The firm is going with

Moran and Golan's idea. From this moment the efforts of the whole team will be directed towards executing that idea.

And when they all get up to leave, Yadanuga touches him with the tip of the stick in his hand—a fresh branch of the hushhash tree, whose thorns have been removed and whose bark has been carved with sexual symbols. He leans towards him and says:

I'll be waiting for you on the motorbike.

49

They speed north. The powerful motor roars between their legs. If, of all his collection of motorbikes, Yadanuga has chosen the old Harley Davidson—which was used by the traffic cops in the fifties of the previous century to put the fear of God into the roads of the country—it was a sign that he was in a fighting mood. Any doubts were laid to rest by his wild driving of the terrifying vehicle, which testified that he was ready for war. As if taking part in a skiing competition on the alps, he slaloms between the cars crowding to exit the city, and without slowing down one iota he tilts the bike sideways on the curves until their knees almost shave the road, and with the same sure hand he straightens it up again, and they leave behind them the long rows of cars blowing their horns in the traffic jams, and here they are at the dunes, and the nature reserve of carobs and mastic trees, and in a swift, daring move Yadanuga turns the bike sharply to the left, charges through a gap in the dividing wall between the traffic going in different directions on the expressway, cuts across the lanes with one bold leap, and already they are racing along the dirt track winding down to the sea. Two prostitutes in G-strings rise to greet them from white plastic chairs in the shade of a spreading carob

tree, displaying their bodies and waving their hands, showing their disappointment when the motorbike passes them
without stopping, and only Shakespeare waves back at them
from the passenger seat and blows them a kiss with warm
regards from Melissa. They pass a white Fiat parked by
the roadside, through whose open back door they can see a
woman lying on the back seat, her left leg thrown over the
backrest of the front seat, her right leg on the shelf between
the back seat and the back window, and the bare backside
of a man with his trousers down rises and sinks like a piston
between her parted legs, and Hanina remarks to himself that
nothing has changed in this nature reserve since the seventies
of the previous century, when they used to drive down this
dirt track to the beach in order to put in hours of training
climbing up and down the cliffs.

Yadanuga, who apparently knows every old track and
every new path here, navigates the motorbike down the little
canyon towards the beach, and stops a few feet from the
water line. He silences the monstrous engine, takes off his
big leather gloves.

You know what I want.

To fight, says Hanina.

Get undressed, says Yadanuga and takes off his shoes
and socks.

Hanina too removes his shoes and socks, and they ar-
range the shoes and socks next to the motorbike. Yadanuga
takes off his heavy biker's leather jacket, and Hanina removes his windbreaker with its synthetic fleece lining, which
he had purchased in a cheap Chinese store on 14th Street,
when he went out for a morning walk with Melissa and
there was an icy wind blowing. Now Yadanuga takes off his
sweater and tricot undershirt, and Hanina takes off his thick,
turtleneck Irish sweater and gray flannel undershirt, and the
two of them fold the garments and place them neatly on top

of their shoes. They confront each other in their trousers, the upper halves of their bodies bare. Yadanuga opens his belt and Hanina follows suit. They take off their trousers with thoughtful, serious expressions on their faces, like two monks in some Indian sect preparing for a ritual salute to the setting sun, which is painting the gray winter sky a blazing red. Now they stand facing each other clothed only in their underpants.

Should we run first? asks Yadanuga.

If you like, says Hanina.

So let's run, determines Yadanuga.

Let's run, agrees Hanina.

They start running along the deserted beach, shoulder to shoulder, paying attention to each other's breathing, inhaling together, exhaling together, silent together. The wet sand is firm beneath their feet. Without opening their mouths they run like this to the place where the cliff enters the sea and jagged rocks rise from the water erupting between them. Wordlessly they turn round and run back towards the lone motorbike stationed on the shore, as if to stand guard over the clothes stacked neatly at its feet. When they approach the bike Yadanuga stops and starts dancing on the spot, swinging his arms and loosening his muscles. Hanina follows suit and dances opposite him. They watch each other closely. And then Yadanuga's right hand shoots out and his fist hits Hanina's left shoulder. The blow is hard and painful, and is immediately countered by a left-handed punch to Yadanuga's chest. Again Yadanuga sends his fist to Hanina's left shoulder. And although Hanina could have evaded the blow, he leaves his body where it is and absorbs it, but counters with another jab to his opponent's chest. Without agreeing in advance, these blows appear to mark the permitted limits which both of them respect. Neither of them tries to hit the other's face, or go below the line of the diaphragm. But the blows raining down on their shoulders and chest, with increasing frequency, are painful enough, and their effect accumulates. Both of their shoulders and chests turn red, their breathing becomes heavy, and when Hanina feels that the pain is beginning to get to him, and he wonders whether he should start evading his opponent's blows, Yadanuga opens his arms, and they embrace puffing and panting, patting each other's shoulders, and it isn't clear which of them smiled first and which of them responded with a light, almost inaudible snort, and which replied with a more well-defined titter, but the laughter which has apparently been building up for some time in both of them can no longer be contained, and suddenly they both burst out laughing loudly, and at the same time Yadanuga smacks Hanina on his bum, and Hanina gives Yadanuga a kick on his, and when Yadanuga wants to kick him back Hanina evades him, and again, as if at a prearranged signal, they fold their arms on their chests and break into a cockfight, hopping and skipping on one leg, circling each other like a couple of billy goats, jabbing at each other with their elbows, hopping backwards and charging again, like a pair of schoolboys rather than men with gray in their hair, and all this time they don't stop laughing, pushing each other and laughing, thrusting back and laughing, until they both fall onto the wet sand and lie there, abandoning their hot bodies to the velvety touch of the cool sand, and together they stand up and go to the motorbike, and Yadanuga asks Hanina if he has sand on his back, and they clean the sand off each other, and when they're getting dressed Yadanuga says:

I've got a lot to say to you.

Go ahead, says Hanina.

Over fish and wine? suggests Yadanuga.

Why not.

50

You always scared me, Shakespeare. And not only me. Jonas too. Jonas had a huge, open heart. Nothing scared him. Except for things that he couldn't feel. And he once said to me: Yadanuga, can you imagine a song without words, without a tune, without a beat? Or a melody without sounds? Or a painting without color or line? That's Shakespeare for me. A language without writing, a shape that changes when you look at it. Matter that evaporates the minute you try to take hold of it. If I had to define him in one word, I would say that he's not. And if in four words, I'd say that I don't feel him. I don't feel what's cooking inside him, and what he's going to do in another second. For me our friend Shakespeare is a labyrinth that changes the minute you enter it, and if you don't get out at once, you'll never escape. That's what Jonas said to me.

And the Alsatian. He had a cool head. A mind as sharp as a razor. If anything scared him he would analyze it in his Talmudic brain. Arrive at the heart of the danger. At the brain behind the machine. And he would take that apart too. Indicate with the precision of a laser beam the point that had to be hit in order to neutralize the system. What can I say, the soul of a demolition man. And you succeeded in scaring even him. You know how he defined you? A differential equation with infinite unknowns.

They never told you. And now they can't tell you. But you scared them. Yes, yes. After all the years we worked together, after everything we went through, I can tell you one thing. I don't know you any better today than I knew you the first time we met. Yes, yes. Maybe even the opposite. You can laugh, but the more time passes, the less I know you. Not that you've changed. The truth is that you don't change. Not at all. At the base is the same thing that scared me so much the first time I met you. And with the years it scares me more. Yes, yes.

What is it exactly? There's no word for it. I can try to describe it for you. Here you are sitting in front of me. Listening to me with interest. Or as if you're interested. Even that I can't say for certain. You hear what I'm saying to you. And what do you do? How do you react? You go on crushing the pincers of that lobster. Extracting its flesh. Sucking its marrow. Calmly. With concentration. As if cleaning out the shell of that fucking lobster is the most important thing at this moment. No less important than the things I'm saying to you. Yes, yes. As if I was talking to you about the taste of the new Beaujolais. I tell you that the best friends you ever had were afraid of you—and you go on polishing off the lobster.

Friends? Maybe the word friends isn't relevant. Were we your friends? Is there anyone in the world who's your friend? It takes some nerve on my part to say this to you. If I'm sitting here now and talking to you, and my body isn't decomposing in some dark alcove at the end of a maze of tunnels in an abandoned copper mine in the Austrian alps, it's thanks only to you. Yes, yes. Thanks to your quiet madness. So what gives me the right to even ask you if you're my friend?

Let me tell you something.

Jonas was sentimental. We both know that. When he drank he became even more sentimental. Once we were sitting and drinking. We sat and drank the whole night long. He was quite drunk. He had a fit of sentimentality. He said to me: Yadanuga. Yadanuga, he said to me. You should know, Yadanuga, you're still alive thanks to Shakespeare. That's what he said to me. Jonas was a real mensch. Straight as a ruler.

If it had been up to me and the Alsatian alone, he said—and he was crying when he said it, but he said it, yes, yes—if it had been up to me and the Alsatian alone you would have given up the ghost long ago in the belly of that accursed mountain in the Tyrolean alps. No one would have dreamt of giving them what they demanded in exchange for letting you go. And you would have remained there, Yadanuga. There was no proof that they were holding you inside that mine. Apart from the things you succeeded in dropping on the way.

I asked the Alsatian. He said it was true. I doubted the whole thing, he said to me. I went along with it against my better judgment, he said to me. Against what my brain told me. Yes, yes. You should know, Yadanuga, that I went along with it only because I gave in to Shakespeare and his madness, he said to me. He told me that when you got the maps from the German engineer, and when he saw how many tunnels and subterranean halls there were, he said that there was no point in even thinking about going into the mine. There was no chance of coming out of there alive. According to the German, some of the tunnels and halls and pits didn't even appear on the maps. For three hundred years nobody had set foot in there. Since the eighteenth century. Your decision to enter the mine seemed suicidal to the Alsatian. If you want to understand Shakespeare, he said to me, you have to take into account that all his life is a rush towards death. He confessed to me. And you know how hard it was for the Alsatian to confess. But he confessed to me that he said to Jonas: Say goodbye to Shakespeare before he enters the belly of the mountain. You won't see him again. Yes, yes.

When I sat there in the absolute darkness, in the absolute silence that reigned there, broken only when the guards changed shifts—the only thing that kept me alive was the gut feeling that you were on your way to me, and that as long as you were alive you wouldn't give up. But what that feeling was based on I can't tell you. Because if you allow me to tell you the truth, Shakespeare, however painful it may be—I never felt you. I could understand the Alsatian, even if it was difficult. He would explain himself with his complicated Talmudic logic, and in the end you could understand him. With Jonas it was easier, because I could feel him. I always knew where his heart was. I always had a sense of what he would do and what he wouldn't do. I could feel where his boundaries were. And therefore I knew that neither the Alsatian nor Jonas would suddenly appear before me in the belly of the mountain. But with you I haven't got any gut feeling. I feel you like an empty space. And that's scary. Awfully scary. You know what? When you left me to take care of Jonas when he lay dying, and threw off your coat and set off in pursuit of the surgeon, and I suddenly realized that you were pursuing him empty-handed—I was sure I would never see you alive again. Only a lunatic like you would be capable of throwing off everything to be lighter for the chase! I imagined that you did it without thinking, but without feeling too, without an sense of the situation. Otherwise, I can't understand how anyone sets out empty-handed in pursuit of a crack shot, who's presumably carrying another revolver in addition to the one that flew out of his hand when my dagger missed his heart and hit his hand. I thought I'd never see you again, until you loomed up out of the dark and said: I nearly killed him, but at the last minute the sonofabitch disappeared into the darkness.

Do you remember the words Jonas said to you before you entered the mine? You don't remember? I'm not surprised. Your memory too is a riddle to me. You remember the most insignificant details of the most trivial things in the world. But what your friend says to you when he shakes your hand and parts from you, and what you say to him in reply—that you forget. Yes, yes. So let me remind you.

When Jonas told me what he said to you, and what you replied, cold shivers ran down my spine. I see that terrible moment when he told me. As if it's happening now. You shout at me: Look after Jonas! And before I can understand what's happening, you're already running into the distance and leaving me alone with Jonas dying in my arms next to the Sheikh's tomb in that oasis—

Sheikh Muamar, says Shakespeare.

And suddenly he opens his eyes and asks: Where's Shakespeare?

Chasing Tino, I say.

Good, he says, He'll finish off the bastard who killed me.

Yes, I say, he'll finish him off.

When he comes back, tell him that I understood what he said then to the Alsatian.

What did he say to him? I ask, and Jonas whispers:

We have eyes, but we have no tongue.

When did he say that? I try to keep him awake.

Before he entered the tunnel, he whispers with the last of his strength.

What tunnel? I ask him, even though I know what he's talking about.

The tunnel in the copper mine.

Do you remember what else happened there? I ask him and hold his head, trying to keep the conversation going, not to let him sink.

Yes, I remember, he whispers. The Alsatian told me to say goodbye to him because I would never see him again.

And how did you say goodbye to him? I go on drawing out the conversation.

I went up to him, shook his hand, and said to him: Thanks, Bill, it's been beautiful.

And what did he answer? I ask him.

Let's synchronize our watches. I have one-zero-six. That's what the sonofabitch answered me.

Do you remember what happened afterwards? I go on drawing the conversation out.

Afterwards the Alsatian checked the infrared binoculars and flashlight, and said to him: Keep your eyes open. That's all you have. The radio won't work inside the mountain. And Shakespeare replied: We have eyes, but we have no tongue. I never understood what he meant, Jonas whispers with his eyes closed, and now I understand.

What did he mean? I ask him.

And I'll never forget that moment to the day I die. Jonas opened his big childlike eyes to the clean desert sky and said in a clear voice:

We have eyes to see the beauty, but not the tongue to describe it. Tell him thanks for everything, and that it was beautiful.

It was beautiful—those were his last words.

There was beauty in him, that guy. Beauty you and I don't have, Bill. We're corrupt. I'm telling you what your friend's last words were, and you go on cracking that lobster and cleaning out its shell. Go ahead. Bon appetit.

Thanks.

You're welcome. The Alsatian himself told me that he gave in to you and agreed to let you go into the mine, just because Jonas said that even if there was no proof that I was imprisoned inside the mountain, if in the end it turned out that you were right, he would never forgive himself to his dying day.

And when you showed up with me in the end—he thought he was hallucinating. But you didn't surprise me. All the time in there I relied only on you. I had the feeling that if the signs I left outside reached you, you would come in and get me out of there. Not because you love me.

Or because I'm your friend. In your deepest place, you're indifferent. Indifferent to your friends, indifferent to the world. I don't know if you're indifferent to yourself as well or not. I'm not asking you. I don't expect any answers from you. According to what I see at the moment, you're not exactly indifferent to the fish you're about to eat. Otherwise you wouldn't be examining its flesh so attentively. You wouldn't be squeezing the lemon over it so precisely, you wouldn't be sprinkling the crushed garlic over it with such concentration.

But to me you're indifferent. Yes. Today I received the final proof. You simply threw me to the dogs. You abandoned me completely to Mona. And Mona, forgive me for saying so, is all teeth and claws. You know exactly what score she has to settle with me. Still from the days of the unit. I'm going to say things now that will hurt you. But I have to say them. Mona loved me. You know it. And I was indifferent to her. That was the situation. Mona lives by her instincts. She doesn't act from her head or from her heart. She acts from her guts. We both know that. She waited years to do what she did to me. To hit me in a painful, sensitive place. The weakness of an aging man versus the strength of a young man.

That's what the struggle is about. You think I really care so much that this pair of yuppies are prostituting our profession? As if anyone could prostitute it any further. There's no taboo that hasn't been broken long ago. They've already used real pictures of executions. And what is this unrestrained use of children, if not contempt for childhood. You look at the children made use of by advertising. You see the old expressions on the faces of the little smartypants parroting the words the cynical copywriters put in their mouths, and you want to vomit. And both of us have already used children more than once. And when we demeaned children in our advertising, I loathed myself. But I did it. And I loathe the pornographic use that Golanchick and Moranchick are making of children and old people in their advertising of this fucking pill. But this isn't what makes me so mad. I'm not a pious virgin. I'm an old whore. Like you. What makes me mad—or rather, who makes me mad is you. You saw what was happening. You saw Mona's game. You saw how she built the conflict between me and those two little pishers. With a Mona Lisa smile she did everything to bring me to the moment when she could get rid of me with a kick in the balls. Tell me that I'm no longer relevant. That I need to admit it, step aside. The next stage will come when she tells me that an advertising agency isn't a geriatric institution. Yes, yes. That's what she'll say.

You're the only person who could have delivered her a knockout. Told her: Madam, Mackie's a friend of mine, and you're not going to walk all over him. Nobody touches my friend. You could have done it easily, without risking a fingernail. All you had to do was open your mouth and say: We're going with Mackie's idea. End of story. But this time, the minute I needed you, you weren't there.

What happened to you since you went into the mountain and risked your life to rescue me? Now I'm asking for help, and you're abandoning me and you don't care. What kind of a person have you become? What kind of a person are you, Bill?

51

Listen, Yadanuga, Shakespeare raises his eyes from the fish and sees the evening descending on the sea and the blood rapidly draining from the slaughtered clouds, leaving piles of gray rags in the celestial rubbish dump. Against this background, on the other side of their table, strewn with plundered *mezze* saucers, and pieces of pita bread, and broken lobster shells, and the decapitated heads of little red mullets, and chips bloody with crushed tomatoes, the face of the bearded man opposite him appears to him like the landscape of a disaster zone, and he feels a powerful urge to put out his hand and stroke this sad face with love and great pity, and to kiss the puzzled eyes staring at him as if at some undecipherable riddle, and he hears Shakespeare speak from his mouth.

You ask me a little question: what kind of a person am I. We've been friends ever since I remember myself, but we've never talked the way you talked to me now. I never asked you who you really are, and you've never asked me what kind of a person I am.

If it bothers you—Yadanuga begins to say, but Shakespeare cuts him short:

No, no, on the contrary. After all these years, and after everything we've done together, it's time we sat together like this, quietly, over a bottle of whiskey, and talked about ourselves, even if it isn't easy for us. And perhaps precisely because it's so hard for us. To tell the truth, I don't even know how to begin to answer you. And from where. From what. So forgive me if things come out in a muddle. In bits and pieces. When I try to think about myself, I can only think in fragments, splinters, broken bits and pieces. I can only give you fragments. Take them however you can, and put them in any order you like.

I won't put your words in order, Shakespeare, says Yadanuga. There comes a moment when a man is a broken vessel, and any well-constructed story is a complete lie. Give me fragments of truth and don't sell me a well-told lie with a beginning, a middle and an end.

Excellent, says Shakespeare. That will make it a lot easier for me, because I haven't been a good story for a long time. And the more time passes, the more of a story full of contradictions and dead zones I become. There's a dark side of the moon too, where I've never been, and I can't tell you what happens there and what comes from there. The lit side of a man is the side that other men see. Your lit side is the side that I see now.

I'm with you on this motorbike, says Yadanuga. Step on the gas and don't stop.

Okay, says Shakespeare. So what kind of a person am I. Let's see. Maybe I'm a person with an artificial aspiration to the meaningless. Now that I hear these words coming out of my mouth, I ask myself where they came from. But let's put that question aside. Let's tackle the statement itself, as if it contains some truth. The very fact that it came out of my mouth shows that something in there, on the upper cortex of the right lobe of the brain, arranged those words one after the other: a person with an artificial aspiration to the meaningless. How do I know that it comes from the upper cortex of the right lobe of the brain? Because I can feel that this spot is now activated. I can feel the heat and weight of some mass there. But let's get back to the statement itself. Let's see what words it draws behind it. And I'm giving you notice that from now on I take no responsibility for the words that come out of my mouth. I'm a person with an artificial aspiration to the meaningless, because it has more life than a life that aspires to the meaningful. What do you say to that?

That's what I always liked about you, admits Yadanuga. That you were an invention.

All four of us were an invention, corrects Shakespeare. We operated in the wild territory of pure, immoral, asocial, unnatural, inhuman action: we executed. We didn't murder. Murder is a natural, human act. Every murder has a motive. Committing a murder is surrendering to nature. Execution is something else entirely. It's an artificial act, without any motive on the part of the executor. Remember how we operated when we operated well: we executed people without instinct or urge. Our act was a simple, pure, vulgar act, calculated as a game. And this I received and learned from you, Yadanuga.

You learned that from me? protests Yadanuga. I learned it from you!

No, no, Yadanuga. Of the two of us, you were always the natural player, and I was the one who had to acquire every new ability with tremendous effort. By learning. By practicing. Through exhaustive training. When we were kids, you were the gifted athlete. The champion sprinter, high and long jumper. Not to mention ball games. You grasped every new game on the spot. And I trailed behind you clumsily and awkwardly. Everything you did easily, gracefully, thanks to the perfectly proportioned, athletic body you received from nature—I had to torture myself to acquire.

But why did you do it? wonders Yadanuga. You had other gifts. You had imagination and inventiveness that none of the rest of us had. To this day I don't understand where you got the name Yadanuga for me from.

From the same place that you got Shakespeare for me.

Good, that was completely natural, says Yadanuga. You always saw things that nobody else saw. You had amazing powers of observation, and that was a gift from nature.

Yes, that's true, says Shakespeare. I wasn't born for action. I was born to be an observer, and if I'd accepted myself as I was—that's what I would have been all my life. But the minute I realized that that was what nature intended for me, I rebelled. Ever since then what people call 'nature' doesn't interest me. Only the artificial attracts me. I never wanted to be only an onlooker and observer of the world. Today I know that from my early childhood nothing fascinated me like the magic of action. The magic of the body. And that's exactly what I tried to do all my life. To turn disadvantage into perfection.

Look how strange it is, says Yadanuga, when we were young, I was sure you would be a poet. In the end you became the most physical of all of us.

And perhaps the activity of the poet, in its origins, isn't linguistic but physical, Shakespeare muses aloud.

You know what, says Yadanuga, when I think about babies, I understand what you're talking about.

I was actually thinking about play-actors, says Shakespeare.

You're not only talking about the theater, clarifies Yadanuga.

Certainly not, says Shakespeare. I'm talking about every act of play. A man who plays is a poet of the body. Poetry interests me only when it leaves a space that demands to be filled by play-acting. By the presence of the body. By a physical act. That's what's so fascinating about sound and movement, that it's impossible to separate them from a body acting here and now. On the other hand, written words can be separated from physical existence, and that's the danger of words.

Because that's what makes it possible to construct with the help of words a story that's all a lie? Yadanuga reads Shakespeare's next thought.

Yes, says Shakespeare, Thomas Mann thought that music was dangerous, because it is liable to arouse men to irrational action, but the truth is that there is no power on earth that motivates men to acts of violence more than a false story well told.

Are you thinking of the story of the exodus from Egypt and the giving of the Torah and the promise of the land and the conquest and settlement? asks Yadanuga.

And the story of impregnation by the Holy Ghost and the birth of a man who's the son of God, and his crucifixion, offers Shakespeare, and Yadanuga continues the same train of thought with quotations from the Koran, which both of them learnt by heart in Arabic, in an Iraqi accent, with the help of Jonas:

And the story about 'the hereafter, to which the righteous believers are to aspire to pass speedily, and only the sinners will never aspire to death, for fear of the punishment awaiting them for their sins, for Allah knows the sinners, and therefore you will find them more eager for life than any other man, and even more than the idolaters, and every one of them hopes to live for a thousand years!'

'And after you have become believers', laughs Shakespeare, 'many of the people of the Book, out of envy, wish to return you from your belief to unbelief....'

'Because they have recognized your truth'! Yadanuga adds quotation to quotation, and Shakespeare concludes:

'Do not call those killed for the sake of Allah dead, for they are alive! And you Jews, who were given the Book, believe in the revelation that has been sent down to us now, which confirms what was previously in your hands, before we smash your faces to a pulp'!

Ah, Jonas, Jonas, sighs Yadanuga, where are you now?

Nowhere, says Shakespeare. If the dead were anywhere, they wouldn't be dead.

I see him, says Yadanuga, his gaze lost in the dark of the cyberspace of his brain. I see Jonas with his enormous nose, and his hard, heavy hand that could break five tiles at once.

We see the dead like we see stars that haven't existed for millions of light years. The light they radiated before they were extinguished goes on reaching us as if they still existed, even though they died long ago, says Shakespeare. And those who remembered their dead, and saw them in their imagination, invented the beautiful story of the world to come, where they go on existing.

Interesting that every new false story rests on a false story that preceded it, like a man without a leg on a man without an arm, and the two of them lean on a deaf man, and woe to whoever makes fun of the pretension of these cripples to represent the true, the just, the good and the beautiful, muses Yadanuga, and concludes: there really is nothing more dangerous and violent and murderous than a false story well told.

Which is why I say that the act of a true poet is not in words, but in what is left unsaid. Which has to be filled by a physical presence and by action.

All this is well and good, Yadanuga rouses himself from the philosophical discussion into which the two of them have unintentionally been drawn, but I asked you who you are, and once again you succeeded in slipping away and disappearing among all these words.

That's what I am, says Shakespeare.

What exactly? demands Yadanuga.

An escape from direct confrontation with any form of violence, laughs Shakespeare, an escape that I've elevated to an art.

The question I asked you, 'Who are you?' is a form of violence? wonders Yadanuga.

You remember the test we took before we were accepted into the unit? Shakespeare replies with a question.

We took all kinds of tests, says Yadanuga. Which one precisely do you mean?

The decisive test, says Shakespeare.

Heart-lungs stress test?

Yes, says Shakespeare, and he elaborates: accelerated heartbeat in a situation of excitement, of fear, of exertion, and mainly—the combination of all three factors in a situation of extreme stress.

What about it? asks Yadanuga.

Do you remember your results?

No, says Yadanuga, how could I remember?

Your heart beat rose from forty five at rest to sixty-three in excitement-fear-exertion.

How can you remember details like that? demands Yadanuga in astonishment.

Because at that stage, after hard, back-breaking exercise and training, I succeeded in attaining only fifty beats at rest and sixty seven under stress. You know what my heart beat is now, sitting and talking to you?

No, says Yadanuga, what is it?

Thirty two beats a minute, says Shakespeare, and he adds: When we fought on the beach, after running, I reached forty.

You still train, Yadanuga half asks half states.

Yes, admits Shakespeare. I want to achieve total control over my heartbeat, up to complete cessation.

You're insane, states Yadanuga. Dangerously insane. Our war is over, and you haven't accepted it. You continue developing yourself as a lethal weapon.

Not at all, protests Shakespeare. It has nothing to do with weapons. There are fakirs in India who can stop their heats beating for fifteen seconds and even twenty, and they're not in the least warlike.

So why do you do it? inquires Yadanuga. Are your sins so terrible that you want to live a thousand years, like Mohammed says in the Sura of the Cow?

No, says Shakespeare. My sins don't bother me. Like all the tellers of perfect tall tales, Mohammed was very well acquainted with human nature. He knew that it was nature that made men fear death, and nature that made him submissive and in need of love, protection and security. This fear is what makes people crowd together and create societies. Have you ever asked yourself what society is based on? Common interests? guesses Yadanuga.

No, my friend, says Shakespeare. Society is based on imitation. Human socialization is a process which is entirely based on the act of imitation. That's why the lives of people who live in societies is an imitation of life. And that's why they love stories which are an imitation of an imitation of life so much. The natural fear of death drives people to run away from life to the imitation of life. Because only he who lives can die—anyone who isn't alive can't die. And therefore, anyone who devotes his whole life to the imitation of life, and avoids living life as it is in the original before any imitation, is ostensibly protected from death.

What exactly do you call the imitation of life? Yadanuga demands a clarification, and Shakespeare clarifies:

All socialized human behavior. Everything that you do in the framework of a community, tribe, nation, religion, army, state, system.

Tell me one thing, if any, that you did outside those frameworks, demands Yadanuga.

I want to escape from any imitation that precedes the original, declares Shakespeare, and immediately regrets the declaration, and adds: I aspire to the performance of an act that is pure action, an act that can't be made into a story.

What I'm hearing from you now contradicts everything I knew about you, states Yadanuga.

What you're hearing from me now contradicts everything I myself knew about me before I opened my mouth to answer your question about who I am, admits Shakespeare, and the truth is that I'm not committed to everything I just said. If we go on talking I may say things that will contradict what I said up to now, and in another minute or two

I may do things that will have no connection to what I am about to say.

In other words: what was is nothing, and what will be is also nothing, Yadanuga begins to develop an idea, and Shakespeare hastens to complete it:

And this union of the nothing that was and the nothing that will be permits you to do anything at all in the present.

That can lead to crime or madness, warns Yadanuga.

Precisely the opposite, says Shakespeare. Crime is always an imitation. There is no original crime. After the first murder, every murder is only an imitation of it and of all the others that will come after it. Every rape is an imitation of all the rapes that preceded it, and every theft is an imitation of the thefts that came before it. The very urge to commit a crime comes from the aspiration to imitate a previous personal example. Take the suicide bombers. Every suicide imitates the ones who preceded him in every particular. He wears the same clothes, binds his head in exactly the same green band, and parrots the words and sentences that scores of suicides have already recited before him. The suicide bomber is entirely an imitation of an imitation, and he himself serves as a role-model for children and youths who aspire to imitate his act. Crime is perhaps the most striking example of an act which is all imitation without anything original about it, and therefore it's no wonder that this act is so connected to the Sura of the Cow: If you are righteous, you must aspire to pass quickly to the next world. Because of its imitative nature, crime has a past and a future. On no account can it be born of the union of the nothing with the nothing. Only the unique union of the nothing with the nothing can give birth to an act that will not be an imitation or a duplication of any other act, and therefore it will also be an act with no meaning, an act that is all invention, all imagination, all body.

And it's an act like this that you're going to perform now? Yadanuga presses him.

Perhaps, says Shakespeare. The truth is that I don't know yet what I'm going to do now. I could get up this minute and travel to a place where I've never been, and which is nothing to me. Like for instance Oregon, or New Mexico, and meet someone there who may be Adonis and may not be Adonis, and clarify something with him quietly, or get into a confrontation with him because of a girl he calls Winnie, and who calls herself Melissa, or Timberlake, and some judge once called her Pipa, and I don't owe her anything, and I don't feel anything for her, and I don't have any urge or need to do anything for her, and at the same time I might kill or be killed for her.

You know what, Shakespeare, confesses Yadanuga, sometimes it seems to me that you make things up and exaggerate wildly, or else you're simply a compulsive liar.

You know what, Yadanuga, declares Shakespeare, if I lie I only do it in order to assert one indisputable truth, which is that it's impossible to determine what the truth is.

You want me to believe you that your story with this Melissa isn't a love story, but a story about nothing, but I'm telling you that it's a love story.

What's a love story? asks Shakespeare.

52

It's a story about what happens between two people who love each other, says Timberlake as she leans forward over the table, on the terrace of a seafood restaurant on the banks of the Indian River. In the river dolphins frolic, leaping in silver sinusoidal arcs against the background of the sunset and the evening enveloping the coconut palms on the east coast of the Buena Vista Park, and her tongue, which has licked so much, very delicately licks the salt from the corners of his eyes, and her tearful eyes laugh at him:

So they call you Shakespeare, your executioner friends?

Yes, he laughs, and sometimes even Bill.

Tell me the truth, Bill, she says and wraps his hand in her fingers, why do you do it? I don't understand anything anymore. You rescue me from Tony's claws. You risk your life for me. Because he won't accept it, he'll try to murder you to get me back in his control. And now you give me a Christmas holiday like nothing I've ever had in my fucking life before. You take me to Palm Beach to spend New Year's Eve at Breakers Hotel, and you do the most wonderful thing for me, which I can't even believe is happening: you don't try to fuck me. I lie in bed next to you at night and I feel your big warm body responding when I touch you.

If you didn't let me touch you, I would understand that I was involved with someone so in love with himself that he can't stand anybody else touching him. I already had a hunk like that once. He was a model for underpants and swimwear, and he was also one of a group of men who did a striptease act for audiences of hysterical women. He paid me good money. He would take off his clothes and walk round the room naked, like you, but unlike you, he would open all the closet doors with mirrors, and set them at an angle that allowed him to see himself in all of them at once, and he would contemplate his perfect body, and make me look at him too and tell him how gorgeous he was and how I was dying to fuck him. It was all an act of course, because all that magnificent body with its flat stomach and its big prick gave rise in me to nothing but boredom. He would stand in front of the mirror and talk about himself, look what beautiful hands I have, and I would have to repeat after him like a parrot: What beautiful hands you have. Look what an adorable bum I have. Your bum is really adorable. And so it would go on, sometimes for half an hour, and we would go into minute details, about his neck and his lips and his nipples and his prick, I repeated whatever he said like a broken record, until he came just from talking about how gorgeous he was. And when he came he would stand in front of the mirror with his hands spread out at his sides, without touching himself, like Jesus Christ, and he only needed me as a witness. And sometimes, when I tried to touch him, just out of curiosity, he would lose his temper and yell at me not to dare to come near him. I've already seen more than a few ugly things in my short life, but believe me that I've never seen anything so pathetic as that underwear model with his love for his perfect body.

Why am I telling you this? Because you let me touch you, and I can feel that it gives you pleasure. You can't hide it from me. I can see what happens to your body. And you can feel too that at these moments I'm *ready* to fuck you, sometimes it even seems to me for a moment that I *almost want* to do it with you. We could have done it easily. But you don't do it with me. Maybe you're waiting for *me* to do it to you? For me to rape you? I could have done it a few times already. Everything was ready. All I had to do was sit on top of you and slide you into me. But I don't want to do anything to you that you don't want, just as you apparently don't want to do anything to me that I don't want, and it's the first time in my fucked up life that somebody considers my wishes. Every time I stroked you and got it up, I said to myself: In a second he'll grab hold of you and open your legs and fuck you, but you're made of stuff I've never come across before.

Okay, I'm not pretty, I know. But you're not exactly gorgeous either. You say so yourself. But sometimes it seems to me that from the two not beautiful people we are, something far more beautiful could emerge than what comes out of all kinds of beautiful people. And perhaps what's happening between us is precisely that beautiful thing?

You simply give me rest. The most wonderful rest I've ever had in my life. But why do you do all this for me? I don't dare to think that you love me. I lie next to you naked. I stroke you. And I feel good. I feel so good. You've taught me something. For the first time in my life I'm restraining myself. And it's so good. It's so wonderful to feel it and not to do anything with it. Just to lie there, body touching body, and not to do anything. How long can we go on like this, before we do it? All you have to do is take me in your strong hands and lift me up, and my legs will open of their own accord, and you'll only have to lower me gently and put me on top of you. Why don't you do it to me? How do you succeed in restraining yourself? Is it a sign that you don't love me? Or perhaps I'm wrong. Perhaps I don't know what love is at all. There is such a thing as love, isn't there?

What is love? What happens to us when we're in bed, is that love? When you lie naked on your back, quiet as the Indian River, with a dolphin smile, and I fawn on you and splash in your dolphin river and chatter like a myna bird. Do you love me? If you love me you hide it from me very well. In any case, up to now you've never said it to me, I love you. And I actually like that. Because in the fucking world where I've been living up to now, that's the first thing that every fucking guy says to every fucking woman when he wants to fuck her without paying the price. After they've paid they don't say anything anymore. They get dressed and go.

Maybe you're a saint? No. You're not. You're an executioner. And I'm not going only by what you told me about yourself. I'm talking about what I can feel in you. You're not the saintly type, not at all. You're totally down to earth, a man of flesh and blood, and I'll bet a lot of sperm as well. Sometimes I feel like doing it to you just to prove that what I feel is true. One day, or one night, I'll do it. I'll give you a hard-on like you've never had before, you know by now that I can do it, and neither of us will be able to restrain ourselves any longer and we'll fall on each other and fuck and fuck and fuck. Sometimes I'm dying to do it to you. Because you're destroying the picture of the world I built up over years of suffering. Shakespeare! If you love me, don't hide it from me. Please. You can tell me that you love me. If you tell me now that you love me, I'll believe that you're saying it differently from all the men I've come across up to now. You're the first one that I'll believe. And if you don't love me, tell me that you don't love me, and I'll accept it without being hurt. I promise. But if you don't love me, why are you doing all this for me? What kind of a person are you? What's going on between us? What kind of a story is it?

53

It's a story about nothing, he says and lets the astringent bitterness of the whiskey turn little by little into a kind of smoky sweetness in his mouth.

There's no such thing as a story about nothing, protests Yadanuga.

And what do you call the world? asks Shakespeare.

The world is a story about nothing? says Yadanuga, concerned for his friend.

Go on, tell me what it's about, this story of a universe that expands and contracts, and pulsates and stretches, and twists and turns and coils around itself like a rope, and un-ravels, and comes apart, and expands again towards infinity, and is compressed again and collapses into itself, until it turns into a black hole which vomits itself with all the planets that explode and turn into floating dust in the interstellar space—what is this tale told by an idiot full of sound and fury, if not a story about nothing?

I'll tell you what, says Yadanuga as if in a sudden flash of illumination, you, with your story about nothing, have succeeded in evading the question I asked you again: Who are you, Shakespeare, what kind of a person have you become, to abandon me to the mercy of Mona and her lust for revenge.

You're avoiding the question that I asked you, says Shakespeare. You're avoiding the question of whether the whole story of our *life* isn't a story about nothing.

The story of *our* life is a story about nothing? Yadanuga demands indignantly. Tell me, Shakespeare, do you hear what you're saying?

Shakespeare hears. He hears too everything left unsaid in Yadanuga's question. He hears the stress on the word 'our', while he himself, in the question he posed in the same words, put the emphasis on the word 'life'. He knows that Yadanuga is thinking now about the Alsatian and about Jonas. The body of one of them they had been obliged to abandon to the water of a river in India. The body of the other they had buried in the sands of the Libyan desert, before setting out on the dangerous trek to the collection point on the coast, dressed as nomads of one of the tribes in the vast ocean of sand. Presumably Yadanuga was thinking now that the Alsatian, even though he had never said so explicitly, lived his life in the shadow of the fact that his parents had been forced to flee Alsace with the invasion of the German army, and had spent the entire war in hiding in an apartment in St. Denis, which had been put at their disposal by the mother of an engineer who worked before the war

with the father of Daniel Altwasser in the Ministry in charge
of roads and bridges, until they fell victim to informants,
and before they were expelled to Drancy towards the end
of the war, managed to entrust their one-year-old child to
the mother of this engineer, a devout Catholic, who brought
him up as a Jew, and took care to tell him everything she
had heard about his parents from her son, who was active in
the Resistance, and was caught by the Gestapo and tortured
and executed. And when the Alsatian volunteered for the
unit after the murder of the athletes at the Munich Olym-
pics, he was closing a circle.

And Jonas's story, he hears Yadanuga wondering aloud,
is that a story about nothing?

Jonas, whose parents had been deprived of their Iraqi
citizenship in 1947, and whose property had been confis-
cated, and who had lived for three years as persecuted
displaced persons in their own country, before they found
their way to a collection point in 1950, and were packed
into the hold of a dilapidated plane together with another
two hundred Iraqi Jews, who had also been turned over-
night into homeless destitute refugees in their motherland,
and even though Jonas too had never explained his joining
the unit as a closing of the circle, it was hard for Shakespeare not to think of the sentence, 'If you wrong us, shall
we not revenge?'

And the figures of his dead friends send him back in a
storm to that distant winter day, when they huddled round
a kerosene stove in a cold room on a windswept jetty in the
navy base, trying to restore a little warmth to their frozen
bones after a training exercise that had almost ended in disaster. Their little rubber dinghy had overturned in the middle of the stormy sea, and the mighty waves had crashed on
their heads, and Jonas had reached the overturned boat first
and seized hold of the rope and made for Yadanuga, and

together they made for the Alsatian, and then the three of them began to search for him. He saw them in the distance, but they didn't see him, and whenever a wave lifted him high for a second he waved at them, hoping they would see him through the salt water blinding their eyes, and by the time they finally spotted him, the currents had already swept him far away, and he said to himself that it was all over, that even if they tried to reach him they wouldn't make it, the raging sea would tire them out before they could cover the increasing distance between them, but they didn't give up, they didn't stop straining forward for a second, holding onto the rope encircling the boat, and when he saw them making such an effort, he was inspired with a new strength, and he too began swimming towards them, and after what seemed like an eternity a great wave came and lifted him up, and he saw them at the foot of the breaking mountain of water and he stretched his arms out in front of him, surfing the crest of the wave and tumbling down to the depths in the thunder crashing around him, thrown every which way until there was no knowing what was up and what was down, and then, all of a sudden, a firm hand gripped his hand flailing in the water, and this strong hand dragged him forcefully to the side of the overturned boat and put the rope in his hand, and his hand clutched the rope, and when he opened his stinging eyes he saw through the mist of the spray the faces of his friends at his side, and he was flooded with love, but the waves breaking over them and covering them with foam made it impossible to open his mouth and say anything, and there was no need to say anything either, and only Jonas, who was the strongest of them all, didn't stop urging them on, swim, guys, keep on swimming, don't give up guys, we haven't reached the shore yet, and it was Jonas's powerful voice that inspired them with a strength whose origins were unknown, until their feet touched the ground, and together with the overturned boat they reached the shore, and as soon as they were a few steps away from the water their knees gave way beneath them and they collapsed onto the wet sand, and lay there unable to lift a finger, breathing the cold air into their stinging lungs, and that was the first and last time in his life that he knew the meaning of utter exhaustion, and Jonas recovered first and rose to his feet and said that they had to get up and go before they froze to death, and to this day he can feel branded on his palm the touch of the strong hand that gripped him and pulled him up and helped him to his feet, the hand of Jonas with his huge body, whose life had drained out of him in the desert because of a little nine millimeter bullet. Adonis was their last target, before the chapter of the assassinations was concluded and the unit was disbanded and they took off their uniforms and it was the end of one story and the beginning—

54

The story of our lives is a story about nothing? He sees before him Yadanuga's childlike face and his astonished eyes.

Why are you fighting those two children, Moran and Golan? Shakespeare wonders. Why is it so important to you to have your idea about the campaign for that fucking love pill accepted?

Are you kidding? asks Yadanuga. You think we're talking about a disinterested fight for justice here? Don't you know how much money the copyright for the idea that wins the competition is worth?

I know exactly how much money it's worth, says Shakespeare.

So why are you surprised? asks Yadanuga.

I'm surprised at you, that you're fighting for the right to make a living from prostitution.

Prostitution? You call it prostitution? demands Yadanuga.

What do you call it? asks Shakespeare.

We're selling a product, says Yadanuga, just like anybody else selling a product on the global market.

Did you ever know love? Shakespeare nips his lecture on market economics in the bud.

Who didn't know love once? Yadanuga replies with a question, which he himself goes on to answer: anyone who had a mother knew love once.

You're evading the issue, Yadanuga, says Shakespeare. You know what I'm talking about.

No, says Yadanuga, why don't you tell me exactly what you're talking about.

You had a few love affairs in your life, says Shakespeare.

I did, Yadanuga acknowledges.

And whenever you started a new affair, didn't you ask the new woman to judge if you'd never known love before her?

It never occurred to me to request such a thing! protests Yadanuga.

Not in words, says Shakespeare. In actions.

Excuse me? Yadanuga makes a face. You're talking to me in riddles. Why don't you explain what you're talking about?

In the lips she offered you, didn't you plant a kiss that asked the new woman to judge if you'd already known love? And in the way you caressed her body—and let's not go into any more details, think about whatever you like—didn't you ask your new lover to judge if you'd already known love? And didn't your body declare to her body that this was all you were looking for in her? In other words, the great love that you'd already known, and that was lost forever, and that you seek in very new love.

What's all this got to do with the subject? Yadanuga demands an explanation and Shakespeare provides it willingly:

This lost love that you're seeking, Yadanuga, is sought by everyone on earth. Okay, maybe not everyone, but at least all those who when their story is told, all that should be asked of those who judge them is that they be judged by whether they once knew love.

Go on, says Yadanuga, maybe in the end I'll understand what you're talking about.

Imagine a crowd of ants running around stunned and confused after a storm, not understanding where the grains of wheat that they were holding in their pincers, carrying them back to their nest, have disappeared to, suddenly blown away by the storm. Do you see the picture?

I see it, says Yadanuga, and Shakespeare continues:

Those crowds of ants are the people running around stunned on the ground of the world, not understanding how it happened that this love, that they were already holding fast and were about to carry to the nest of eternal happiness, has been suddenly torn from them by the storm and blown away on the wind and disappeared. And they run around and look for it under every skirt and every pair of pants, and they are ready to buy every potion and every book and pill and perfume and powder with the word 'love' written on its label, especially if they are promised that in the pages of that book they will find a clue to the riddle of the disappearance of love from their lives, or that this pill will restore the capacity for love which they may have lost and that is why they have lost the love they knew when they knew love. Go to the cinemas, go to the theatres, go to the concert halls, go to the pubs and rock clubs, look at the boys and girls with the cell phones whose screens shine with a blue synthetic light in the darkness of the halls, and look at them when they tap out with trembling fingers, in the middle of the movie or the play, the cry for help that they are sending into cyberspace, 'i miss u', 'i miss u 2'; 'i love u', 'i love u 2'. Look at these young people, hooked on their electronic talk boxes like junkies on their drug, poor people who already at this stage of their lives are broadcasting the despairing cry: 'When all is told, ask her to judge whether you never knew love.' Now close your eyes and think about how we're advertising this product, the cellular telephone. Think how we sell it. Not as a magic means to hold onto love so that it won't run away? And how do we sell books, panties, orange juice, if not as the pursuit of fleeing love? And how do we sell shaving cream or deodorants, if not as a magic potion to hold onto the love we knew, or at least as bait to lure a new love, so that we can ask it to judge whether we once knew love....

And you arrived at all this—begins Yadanuga, and Shakespeare continues the sentence:

When I was tempted to look for my lost love in a New York call girl, and met the personification of human misfortune.

What lost love were you looking for in a whore? Yadanuga asks with the trace of a sneer.

You dared to ask the question, Shakespeare smiles, and you will have to hear the answer.

Why have to? I'll be very interested to hear it, says Yadanuga.

Good, says Shakespeare, do you want it with an anesthetic or without it?

I suppose I should ask for anesthetic? guesses Yadanuga.

55

Waitress! calls Shakespeare, and when she signals that she's heard him and she'll be with them in a minute, he says quickly to Yadanuga:

You see that waitress?

What about her? asks Yadanuga in surprise.

You know who's going to marry her?

No, says Yadanuga.

You, says Shakespeare.

Interesting, says Yadanuga, I haven't heard about it yet.

Neither has she, says Shakespeare, but it going to happen.

How do you know? demands Yadanuga.

It's what's written for you.

Where, in heaven?

No, says Shakespeare, in the scene that's being written at this very moment. Would you like to read it?

Yes, says Yadanuga.

And at that moment precisely she stands at their table, tall and slender, her belly exposed, with a friendly smile on her slightly freckled face and a mane of honey colored hair.

Yes? she says briskly, holding a pen and notebook, ready to take their order.

Do you know what your name is? asks Shakespeare.

No, she smiles in surprise. What's my name?

Talitha, Shakespeare informs her.

Okay, she is ready to continue playing the game whose rules are not yet clear to her. I'm Talitha, and where am I from?

From a farm, suggests Shakespeare.

And what am I doing in the big city? she asks for more information.

You're studying acting, says Shakespeare.

Amazing! she says. What's your friend's name? She turns to Yadanuga.

Shakespeare, he replies.

Okay, she says, Shakespeare...what play are we in?

Choose, says Shakespeare, *Othello* or *A Midsummer Night's Dream*.

Wow! says the waitress. *Othello* isn't a good story, right?

It isn't an easy story, Shakespeare corrects her.

Then I choose to be in *A Midsummer Night's Dream*, the waitress laughs.

In that case, says Shakespeare, my friend requires the appropriate potion.

Brandy? Whiskey? she inquires.

A double shot of ten year old Lagavulin, says Shakespeare.

Bring one for Shakespeare too, orders Yadanuga.

When the waitress is out of hearing, Othello begins:

56

Do you remember when they sent me to Norway alone, to take a course in Nordic skiing?

When was that? Yadanuga repeats the question. Was it when they sent you to eliminate 'the doctor'?

It was less than a month before Mona and I got married, says Othello in a low voice, and leans over the little table separating them, bringing his face close to that of his friend, who draws back a little and casts his eyes down and to the side—like Judas in Leonardo's last supper, Hanina sees the picture in his mind's eye, sorry now that he opened his mouth, but already it's impossible to stop the words gushing out and peeling layers of dead skin from an ostensibly long-healed wound.

When they defined the target, and it became clear that it was a suicide mission, and therefore they would only risk one man, I knew that I had to volunteer, says Hanina.

You were much better than the rest of us in long distance running and mountaineering, says Yadanuga.

Yes, Hanina agrees. When I volunteered for the mission, Mona and I took a vow, that if I came back alive, we would get married. And I left.

And in the end you got the better of him, says Yadanuga, even though 'the doctor' was a master of Nordic skiing.

Yes, says Shakespeare, he was an excellent teacher. I joined a group he was instructing, and after a week I asked for private lessons. I think he suspected me. He was clever as a devil, and mean as a gatekeeper in hell. He gave me tasks to perform that were clearly designed to kill me. He would send me to ski down narrow courses on steep slopes at the edge of deep chasms. It was clear to me that any wrong move would end in certain death. After I completed these dangerous runs I would stand still, open my eyes and look around me, unable to believe that I was still in this world, and then he would come down after me, laughing all the way like the devil he was. One day, before one of these suicide missions, I put two metal pegs with a transparent fisherman's line between them in my pocket, and I succeeded in stopping for a minute at the deadliest curve and sticking the pegs into the snow. He came down the slope at terrific speed, laughing his usual demonic laugh. I managed to see his face, and the next second he was flying and turning over in the air like a shot bird.

And what happened after that? asks Yadanuga.

First of all let's talk about what happened before that, says Hanina, when you stayed behind with Mona.

You know what happened, says Yadanuga. Mona told you.

I want to hear it from you, says Hanina.

It's ancient history, says Yadanuga. It happened so many years ago.

But we've never talked about it, insists Hanina.

It's hard for me to talk about it, says Yadanuga.

I can imagine, says Hanina. But you asked me what kind of a person I am—so I ask you: what kind of a person are you, Yadanuga?

Look, says Yadanuga, we were children of twenty-something, and we played dangerous games. Mona loved us both, and we both loved her. There was a strong attraction between us. She attracted me no less than I attracted her. You knew that. But you volunteered for the suicide mission in Norway anyway. You knew exactly what you were doing when you left the two of us alone together.

I had no choice, says Hanina.

Yes you did, retorts Yadanuga. You could have insisted that they send Mona to wait for you in a hotel in Oslo.

I suggested it to her, says Hanina. But she wanted to stay in Israel.

You could have demanded that she come with you, says Yadanuga.

No, says Shakespeare, I've never demanded anything of other people, and I hope that I never will.

Why not?

Because that's who I am, says Shakespeare. And a minute later he adds: What people give you against their will there's no point in accepting.

You demanded that I talk, and I talked against my will, says Yadanuga.

And you know what, I didn't accept any of it, says Shakespeare. 'We were children' and 'You knew exactly what you were doing'? Give me a break.

What do you want? You want me to go into detail? Tell you exactly how it happened? What we did? What we said before, and what we didn't say afterwards?

Why not? says Shakespeare. God's in the details.

Okay, says Yadanuga. We were summoned for a briefing. As far as I remember, it was something like eleven in the morning. When I arrived at the briefing room Mona came out to meet me and said that they were busy conducting an investigation into the failure of operation 'Delicate Balance', and that it would take until at least until three o'clock in the afternoon. We have a minimum of four hours, she said, and then I suggested taking a stroll in the avenue. It was a fine winter day. Blue skies, a low but warm sun. We walked along the avenue between the fields next to the camp, hand in hand. We went on walking like this, holding hands, for about a quarter of an hour, or more, without saying a word. We simply couldn't talk, because we were both choked with lust. Our feet led us of their own accord to a hole in the fence of the camp, next to Mona's room. We went into her room, and the next minute we were naked and in each other's arms, and that's it.

That's it what? demands Shakespeare.

It was a lousy fuck, what can I tell you, one of the worst fucks of my life, confesses Yadanuga. I'm not saying this to make it easier for you. We were both too hot. We lusted for each other too much, and I came before I realized what was happening.

But after that there was a second time and third time, says Shakespeare.

There wasn't a third time, says Yadanuga.

So there are two versions, says Shakespeare.

There wasn't a second time either, says Yadanuga.

What happened, asks Shakespeare, did you have a guilty conscience?

That too, says Yadanuga.

What else? demands Shakespeare.

We were incompatible, says Yadanuga.

You were in such a hurry to jump to conclusions? inquires Shakespeare. The first time isn't usually the best.

It happened because of you too, says Yadanuga.

How because of me? demands Shakespeare.

You were in Norway, alone, on a mission that bordered on suicide. We didn't know if you were dead or alive. This excited us, but at the same time it also ruined any chance of something good coming out of it.

I'm sorry for ruining things for you, apologizes Shakespeare.

Don't play the innocent, Shakespeare, says Yadanuga, you knew very well what you were doing when you left us alone together.

So now it seems that I did it on purpose, says Shakespeare.

I didn't say that, protests Yadanuga. But we both loved her, and you got her.

Let me tell you a secret, Yadanuga: when I volunteered for the mission in Norway, I abandoned the field, and I took into account the possibility that if I came back alive the two of you would inform me that you'd decided to get married.

But exactly the opposite happened, says Yadanuga, and what happened between me and Mona was a one-off, unsuccessful and insignificant.

Maybe insignificant for you, says Shakespeare.

Yadanuga is silent, and Shakespeare goes on:

When it was all over and I emerged safe and sound from the passport control at Schipol, Mona was waiting for me there in jeans and a white sweater, and she came to meet with outstretched arms and we embraced, and she clung to me wildly, with a passionate devotion I'd never seen in her before, but at the same time her body told me: judge for yourself if I've never known love.

And after that you got married, says Yadanuga.

Yes, says Shakespeare. We drove straight from the airport to Amsterdam and got married.

Why did you do it? Because you swore an oath?

No, says Shakespeare, because we were children, and we didn't know what we were doing.

And without knowing what he was doing at that moment, the leg-man's lips began to softly sing an old lullaby:

Go to sleep my baby, mommy's clever lad,
Sleep now in your cradle as soundly as you can,
Hard work and tears await you in plenty
Before you turn into a man...

57

I know that tune, says the waitress as she sets the glasses with the golden liquid, saturated with the smells of peat and smoke before them, and Yadanuga announces ceremoniously:

You've been accepted into the unit!

Thank you, says the waitress, without asking what unit, and what exactly she did to be accepted. Suddenly an intimacy has come into being between them, which makes such questions redundant, because it is clear that what is at stake here is not any kind of unit, but simply a wish for closeness. And accordingly she sets a bowl of ice cubes with a pair of stainless steel tongs carefully down on the table, and says:

My grandmother on my mother's side used to sing that song to me when I was a baby.

What do you say, exclaims Shakespeare, where did your grandmother come from?

A place you've probably never heard of, she smiles, straightening up and showing her tanned stomach. I'm not sure how to pronounce the name. Karshimiz or Karzimish.

You must mean Kazimierz, suggests Shakespeare.

Right! exclaims the waitress. How did you know?

I was there once, he says, but what's the ice for?

If you want to put it in the whiskey, says the waitress as if stating the obvious.

You don't dilute this whiskey with ice, Shakespeare explains to her. In Scotland they would have you put to death for merely suggesting such a thing.

How? inquires the waitress enthusiastically. By burning, or drowning in some loch?

By hanging, Shakespeare informs her. Burning and drowning were taken off the menu in the seventeenth century.

Is it true that those condemned to death get an erection and ejaculate when they hang them? The young waitress teases the two broad-shouldered heavy-jawed men.

Yes it is, confirms Shakespeare, and if you were the hangman's wife, you would have the right to collect the sperm ejaculated by the hanged man.

Wow! cries the excited waitress. But what would I do with it?

You would divide it up into small portions, and the night after the hanging you would sell it for a good price to barren women who have a hard time getting pregnant.

Whoa! exclaims the waitress gaily. Do you know any eligible hangmen?

Allow me to introduce you to my friend, says Shakespeare.

So you're both eligible hangmen? The waitress teases.

Sorry, not me, admits Shakespeare.

You're just trying to get out of it! the waitress accuses him, but Yadanuga comes to his friend's defense:

He's seriously involved at the moment.

I don't believe it, says the waitress. He looks like a confirmed bachelor.

Sorry, says Shakespeare, the truth is that I have unfinished business with the daughter of a family of hangmen.

Whoa! the waitress responds with demonstrative disbelief.

The granddaughter of a hangman from Nuremberg, says Shakespeare.

All in the family, jokes the waitress.

Hangmen marry only the daughters of hangmen, Shakespeare explains.

Obviously, says the waitress. Who'd want to have anything to do with a hangman?

So we don't have a chance with you, concludes Yadanuga sadly.

Who told you I wasn't a hangman's daughter? The waitress flirts with him.

You're a hangman's daughter? Yadanuga's spirits rise.

The daughter of a hangman son of a hangman, the waitress winks at him.

Then if you're looking for an eligible hangman, Yadanuga's your man! says Shakespeare and points to his friend with the gray lion's mane on top of the strong face where the eyes of a child peep out of the lines etched by time and cruel deeds.

Yadanuga, croons the waitress in a wet voice, what a great name! Where does it come from?

From his tender hand, Shakespeare points proudly to his friend. The man you see before you is a born samurai. A master of knives and swords unrivaled in the Middle East. When he received the command 'execute', he would finish the job before the man condemned to death knew what hit him.

Whoa! says the waitress. Can I join you after I get off work?

We'll keep a place for you, promises Shakespeare. Just tell us under what name, please?

Talitha, laughs Talitha, have you forgotten? You yourself gave me that name! And she hurries off to another table, where a bald man is beckoning her to bring him the bill.

Talitha, says Yadanuga, his eyes following her receding waist with frank yearning, where did you get that name from?

I don't know where the names come from, admits Shakespeare, and I don't want to know either. Just look at her, can't you see that she's as pure and innocent as a lamb?

If only I was fifteen years younger, laments Yadanuga.

You're already ten years younger, says Shakespeare.

Come on, says Yadanuga, don't exaggerate.

Did I say ten? Shakespeare corrects himself. Fifteen at least, if not twenty!

Okay, okay, Yadanuga makes haste to change the subject, why don't you go on from where you broke off?

Where were we? asks Shakespeare.

Where were we? wonders Yadanuga. To tell the truth I don't remember.

58

At that moment the cell phone in his pocket vibrates. Shakespeare quickly pulls it out. The caller is unidentified. He presses the green button and puts the phone to his ear. A stream of crude American curses trickles through the holes and drips poison into Hamlet's father's ear.

Do you want to talk to Winnie? asks Shakespeare. The stream of curses breaks off abruptly. For a moment there is complete silence in interstellar space, and then Tony's voice comes through again, shaky and faltering:

Let me talk to her...

Stay on the line, says Shakespeare. He holds the silver cell phone up and beckons Talitha with it, as if the call is for her. It appears that her radar, from the other end of the restaurant, is directed exclusively at the hangmen's table. Within seconds she is standing next to the table of her fellow members in the unit. Her laughing eyes are teasing.

Who is it? she asks Yadanuga.

I don't know, he says, ask Shakespeare.

You're a sales assistant in Stephan Kellian's clothes shop in New York, and a hooker in your spare time. Your name's Winnie, your voice sounds like Sarah Jessica Parker, and this is Tony, your pimp—who you escaped from—with me.

Give me the shit, says Talitha gleefully, eagerly embracing the role.

Shakespeare hands her Tony's silver heart, which trembles in her hand like a fish in a net.

Tony? I'm out of my mind with longing! I miss you so much! Where are you? Talitha-Winnie begins in a voice so sexy that the people at the nearby tables stop chewing, their gluttony joined by lasciviousness, and their hungry eyes devour their pretty waitress who has found her love.

I'm dying to suck your cock, she almost comes in Sarah Jessica parker's voice. I can't!...Because they won't let me... yes! The cut-throat dog brought a friend of his...what? I can't! I'm terrified of them...they're dangerous characters... hangman...yes! Hangmen! You don't know what hangmen are? Hangmen! I can't answer my cell phone. They took it away from me. Where am I?...She signals to Shakespeare to supply her with information. He writes on a paper napkin stained with olive oil, and Talitha Jessica Parker deciphers quickly and transmits in a voice full of longing:

I'm in Tucson, Arizona...in a motel, on Benson Highway and West Nebraska Street...I'm so sick of the topopo salad that they keep feeding me...So come! Come! She implores in a voice impossible to refuse. They're taking the phone away from me...I kiss you, you know where....

She hands the cell phone to Shakespeare, who says to Tony:

Are you done?

If you're half a man—come and meet me you fucking Jewboy!

It may happen sooner than you think, says Shakespeare and hangs up.

Poor guy! says Talitha compassionately. He misses me so much!

I'm not surprised, flatters Yadanuga. You're really dangerous. Your voice in inflammatory. Lethal. Capable of starting a world war.

Tell me, she turns to Yadanuga, is your friend really as crazy as he looks?

Even crazier, says Yadanuga.

Will he really go to meet him? She talks to Yadanuga about Shakespeare as if he isn't there.

His word, says Yadanuga, is like a bullet between the eyes.

I suppose the pimp will come armed, she says.

Then he'll have a problem, states Yadanuga without clarifying whose problem it will be, the pimp's or Shakespeare's.

Isn't he afraid of anything? She continues addressing herself to Yadanuga.

Are you afraid to be alive today? Yadanuga asks her.

No, what should I be afraid of? she asks in surprise.

For someone condemned to death, today is yesterday's fear, just as tomorrow is today's fear.

Who's condemned to death? she asks.

Anyone who's alive, he says.

Whoa! laughs Talitha.

Shakespeare smiles. He knows his friend. When Yadanuga starts talking in proverbs, it means he's trying to make an impression, or in other words: in a state of sexual arousal. I wonder what the next proverb will be, he says to himself and surrenders to the pleasure of the whiskey.

So he's going to America to act the role of the sheriff? she teases.

The role of the bat, he says.

Could you explain?

The bat is blind by day, but sees very well at night: like justice.

Whoa! she compliments him on the metaphor.

There are fruit bats, and there are vampires, Yadanuga takes advantage of his success to conclude on a fateful note: And Shakespeare is a vampire.

Shakespeare—is that from his parents?

It's from the unit, Yadanuga reveals a secret that nobody knows but her, and takes the trouble to elaborate on the meaning of the name as well: The guy made up plots that we lived, and some of us died of them, in the fifth act.

Wow, says Talitha. What act are we in now?

The fourth act, says Yadanuga. The complications are coming to a head.

Whoa, she expresses her curiosity, I'd love to stay until the end of the fifth act, but I have to get back to that table. I left them in the middle of their order.

We're here, Yadanuga reassures her, take your time.

You won't run away?

Don't worry, says Yadanuga and points to his half empty glass. Even if we wanted to, we couldn't take off without fuel. We're completely at your mercy.

I'll be back, she promises, my shift will be over soon.

When you join us, bring another three double shots of Lagavulin, requests Yadanuga, and after she leaves he becomes serious and turns to his friend:

Are you really going to look for him?

I have to.

Because of the girl?

I have to find out if this character is Adonis, says Shakespeare.

Shakespeare! Forget Adonis! Yadanuga begs him. You finished him off on that chase in the desert. Intelligence received reliable information. The unit closed his file. I had a gut-feeling that he was done for the minute you came back from the chase. I told you straight out—

Sorry, Shakespeare cuts him off, I don't trust the head of intelligence, or your gut-feelings. I'm a leg-man. I have to meet the man myself to be sure that it's not him.

And if it is him, what will you do? Kill him?

I don't know, says Shakespeare. First I have to meet him. Whatever happens will happen.

Yeah, yeah...says Yadanuga, who is already somewhere else. What a girl! Did you see the job she did on the phone? IQ of 160 minimum. How about that 'topopo salad' hey? What am I supposed to do with a girl like that?

Trust her, recommends Shakespeare. Let her take the lead.

How did we get here? Yadanuga tries to return to reality.

It all began from me abandoning you to Mona's mercies, Shakespeare offers him a starting point and leaves it to him to choose between the present abandonment and the one that took place a quarter of a century ago, when he set out on the suicide mission in the snowy mountains of Norway.

Yes, says Yadanuga. This time his tone is conciliatory, philosophical, suffused with a kind of aesthetic indifference, as if they were talking about the sexual habits of the lizard-fish.

Imagine that I took your side, suggests Shakespeare. That I forced Mona to accept your idea. You would have been satisfied. You wouldn't have invited me to come with you, we wouldn't have ridden on your motorbike to the prostitutes' beach, we wouldn't have run on the sand, we wouldn't have fought, we wouldn't have gone wild, we wouldn't have breathed the sea air, and our blood wouldn't have sent ions of iodine to our nervous system, and then we wouldn't have become hungry for fish and wine, we wouldn't have arrived at this restaurant, and you wouldn't have met your Talitha.

Interesting, Yadanuga maintains his philosophical tone and ignores the 'your Talitha', interesting how things happen in life.

On condition that we're there when they happen, puts in Shakespeare.

Yadanuga sips the golden liquid from which a sweet, pleasant smell, reminiscent of an English fruit cake, rises and spreads, gradually evaporating and developing into a bitter conclusion, like the insight which now enters his mind, that this noble single malt, with every sip, presents you with the taste of an entire life cycle, from the smoke of youth, through the ripe sweetness of middle age, where he is now, up to the rich bitterness of old age, which is approaching fast in order to put an end to the whole affair—and he wants to share this new insight with his companion, and he takes a deep breath, raises his glass, examines the reflection of the light in the golden liquid, and says in one breath:

I'm glad that we finally found the courage to talk about something we've never talked about in our whole lives.

It's not a question of courage, says Shakespeare.

Of what then? The wisdom of old age?

God forbid, says Shakespeare. Once we were silent, because we were foolish enough to think that we were wise. Today we are wise enough at least to know how foolish we were.

Were? Yadanuga grins. And what are we now?

We're not wise enough yet to know what fools we are now, Shakespeare agrees with his friend, but if we live a little longer perhaps one day we'll know that too.

And what in your opinion can we know in the place we're at today? asks Yadanuga, and Shakespeare replies:

Today we can know that every execution we carried out was tantamount to street theater.

Street theater? You'll have to explain yourself.

Our executions provided entertainment for the mob that adored us when we turned the television screen for its sake into the hangman's square. When the news arrived of another murderer whose mattress exploded underneath him in a hotel in Athens, or another terrorist who went up in smoke when he ignited his Renault 16 next to the Luxembourg Gardens, the mob would gather in the evening round the court of justice of our day, in other words the television screen, to celebrate the execution with beer and popcorn, and to applaud the anonymous hangmen who carried out the job professionally and skillfully. But beware, my friend: the very same mob will change its attitude and tear the hangman to pieces on the day he removes the electronic hood from his head and dares to show his human face on the television screen; on the day he informs the mob intoxicated by the blood of his decision to take early retirement from the hangman's job. And God help him if at the same time he takes the opportunity to express his doubts as to the power of the death sentence to deter future murderers. Because the mob is still a long way from reaching the conclusions reached by its hangmen.

What are you trying to say, wonders Yadanuga.

I don't know, Shakespeare admits. I simply went with the words and let them lead me where they would.

Are you trying to say that everything we did was just part of some bloody carnival?

If that's what you understood, then apparently that's what the words said, Shakespeare accepts the interpretation.

But you also say that there's no avoiding this bloody carnival, because the mob needs it.

Apparently, agrees Shakespeare. The carnival of blood is apparently a vital part of the play in which we played the part of the hangmen.

So what can the hangmen do at this stage? wonders Yadanuga.

59

Nothing, says Talitha, who joins their table bringing with her three double shots of Lagavulin, hangmen, like everybody else, can only play the roles assigned to them.

Until when? Yadanuga asks the young woman who sits down at his left hand with all the naturalness and intimacy that exists between two people accepting their mutual attraction.

Until the play is over, says Talitha and raises her glass and clinks it with Shakespeare's glass, and then with Yadanuga's, and toasts 'Lehayim', and sips the whiskey, her laughing eyes gazing intently and with undisguised delight into the childlike eyes of the man with the mane of gray hair.

What a stinking drink! She pulls a face. How can you bear to drink it?

With memories, says Yadanuga in a deep voice, with blood, sweat and tears.

It smells like the stuff used to disinfect chicken coops, states Talitha, wrinkling her nose.

Where do you know about chicken coops from? asks Yadanuga.

Have you forgotten that Shakespeare brought me from a farm? replies Talitha.

Let me smell, Yadanuga buries his nose in the golden wheat of her hair and confirms: right, from a farm. But which one?

A funny farm for old men, she laughs. Don't take it to heart, I'm only joking. The truth is that I have cousins in Ramot-Hashavim, who have a hatchery and a brooder house. When I was a child I used to spend my summer vacations there. Between one batch of chicks and the next they would disinfect the coop with something that smelled like this whiskey. Afterwards they would spread sawdust over the cement floor before bringing in the new batch of chicks. The air would fill with the soft cheeping of hundreds of chicks, who would gather under tin heaters in the shape of wide pyramids, where it was warm and cozy.

And what kind of taste do you have in your mouth now? inquires Yadanuga.

Actually a warm, sweet taste, like carobs, she sounds surprised.

In a minute the bitterness will hit you, Yadanuga prepares her for the development of the taste of the golden liquid from Scotland.

Whoa! confirms Talitha and grips Yadanuga's tender hand. Awesome! Really awesome!

And what do you really do, apart from waitressing? asks Yadanuga.

Exactly what Shakespeare said, she laughs, I'm an actress.

We saw the way you acted Winnie, says Shakespeare. Not bad at all.

The truth is that I'm not quite an actress yet. I'm studying acting. In my third year.

Do you have a steady job here? asks Yadanuga.

The truth is that this is my last day here. From tomorrow I'm in Eilat.

With friends? probes Yadanuga.

Alone, she says. But before things get complicated, I
have to confess that I'm not from a family of hangmen. My
parents are doctors, and my grandfather was a doctor too.

Dear oh dear, says Yadanuga, what are we going to do
now?

Just a minute, Shakespeare intervenes, what kind of
doctors?

My father specializes in back surgery, and my grandfather is an anatomist and a well known pathologist.

Excellent! exclaims Shakespeare.

What's so excellent about it? demands Talitha.

At this hesitant stage of the development of the relationship Shakespeare hurries to inform his astonished
listeners that the profession of modern surgery is closely
connected to that of the hangman. Since the Middle Ages,
and on the threshold of the modern age, when the hangmen also carried out the sentences of amputation of the
fingers, cutting off of the hands, and dislocation of the
shoulders of those convicted of petty crimes, they had to
be well versed in the anatomy of the skeleton, the muscles
and the blood vessels, for a hangman who inadvertently
caused the death of a person sentenced to have his hand
amputated, risked being severely punished himself by having his arm cut off, and there was a well known case of a
hangman from Klagenfurt, who was condemned to death
after having caused the death of a man sentenced to have
his arm amputated. And if this wasn't enough, it turned
out that doctors and anatomists kept in close touch with

hangmen, so that the latter would put at their disposal, for a fee, the bodies of those condemned to death who had no relatives to claim their bodies. But the close connections between the hangmen and the physicians didn't end there, for when the profession of hangman began to decline, and the execution of the death sentence was transferred from the gallows of the public square to the dungeons of the prison houses, hangmen were obliged to look for a new profession, and since the traditions of their calling had gained them a detailed knowledge of anatomy, many of them naturally turned to the profession of medicine, and ancient dynasties of hangmen produced dynasties no less illustrious of medical men, especially in the fields of anatomy, pathology and surgery. Thus the 'killer' became a 'healer', and from the philosophical point of view this is not surprising—for who is better qualified to rescue mortal men from the claws of death than the Angel of Death himself? And from where will the healers of the soul of a human society afflicted with the syndrome of the dance of death come, if not from the ranks of the hangmen carefully selected and trained by this same society to regale them with the rituals of the carnival of blood to which they have become addicted, the spectacles which have become one of the needs of the soul spoken of by the Jewish philosopher Simone Weil who sought death in the Spanish civil war— but who, in her ineptitude, one night walked straight into a cauldron of boiling oil in which some members of the International Brigade were frying chips on the Gerona front, and to her shame and disgrace forced her Yiddishe Mama to take a taxi from Paris to the Spanish front in order to collect her revolutionary daughter and take her back to the warm bosom of her bourgeois family in the sixteenth arrondissement, which annoyed her to such an extent that she became a fan of Hitler's out of spite. And she didn't rest until she killed herself in a fit of anorexia in the refuge which her mother imposed on her when the family fled to England for fear of the Nazis who invaded France, otherwise she would presumably have landed up in Auschwitz, where she would have marched happily into the gas chambers, just as she had marched into the cauldron of boiling oil, and thus fulfilled the dream of her executioners, who would have been delighted to see their victims becoming their own executioners, in order to prove the rule that the work of the wicked in always done by the righteous, and in certain cases even by the victims themselves—

Shakespeare! Yadanuga tries to stop the gush of words.

Leave him be! Talitha puts her hand on Yadanuga's hand, it's fascinating!

But what fascinates Shakespeare at that moment is the sensual touch of the surgeon's daughter's fingers on the back of the hairy joints of the fingers of his friend the hangman, and when he sees the dialog of the fingers continuing longer than necessary, he notes to himself that the hangman of hearts is performing his role faithfully—

60

His reflections are interrupted by the cell phone which is fluttering in his palm again like a butterfly, and Timberlake says to him in a voice trembling with terror:

Bill? Tony left me a terrible message on my voice mail.

What did he say to you? asks Shakespeare.

I can't repeat it, she sobs in a broken voice.

Calm down and tell me exactly what he said to you.

He said he would cut out my tongue with a box cutter, and he would sit next to me and watch the color draining from my face, and he promised me that while it was happening he would sing to me in his lyrical tenor, and I know that he means everything he says.

He can't do it, Shakespeare tries to calm her down, he doesn't know where you are.

I'm afraid that he does know, her voice trembles over the phone. I guess the deaf-mute must have seen me.

Where? asks Bill.

In front of the house, she says.

Did you go to the old apartment?

No, it happened next to the new apartment.

What happened exactly?

I got out of a taxi, and before I went into the building I suddenly saw someone in a car photographing me with a little video camera. When he saw me looking at him, he drove off. Bill, she pleads, this is a real body crying and shaking with fear over here, this is a real person calling for help, and not a ghost, Bill! I have no one in the world to protect me. Come and rescue me, Bill, before all that's left is my voice in your memory.

Listen carefully to what I'm telling you, Shakespeare calms the sobs shaking his cell phone. Dress like a man, go down to the street, don't stop the first cab that comes. If it stops, don't get in. Let a few cabs go past, and only then stop one. After changing cabs at least twice on the way, take a room in my hotel in the name on the document I gave you. Don't open the door to anyone. I'm getting on a plane in four hours' time, and at six a.m. I'll be landing at Kennedy. I'll arrive at the hotel between half past seven and eight. Should I go over that again?

No need, she says, I remember it all.

I'll see you tomorrow.

Have a nice flight, she says and hangs up.

Shakespeare clicks a number.

Hello, Tony? He says in a businesslike tone, if you want to see Winnie, and if you've got the balls, go to Shakespeare, New Mexico, and wait for my call. I'll contact you within twenty four hours and give you exact instructions where to go.

Son of a bitch, spits Tony's voice, I'll finish you.

I love listening to your voice, says Shakespeare. You have a lyrical tenor as soft as velvet. By the way, I'll be coming to meet you alone, and unarmed. I want to talk to you face to face. If you have the guts to come to the meeting empty-handed, you won't be sorry, he concludes the conversation and hangs up.

Have you got a plane ticket? asks Yadanuga.

I hope so, replies Shakespeare and dials the computerized ticket service, and clicks the number of the flight. He is asked to give his credit card number and expiry date, receives confirmation, and sighs: That's it, now I have—

61

Two more hours to kill, his legs tell him, waiting impatiently to go into action while his eyes see the black Hummer, wide as a toad, driving slowly down the slope on the other side of the canyon and approaching the deep ravine, whose steep walls are impassable by vehicular traffic. The Hummer stops on the verge of the escarpment, exactly where Hanina indicated, between the many-armed yucca plant and the pine tree, the bittersweet taste of whose nuts fills the mouth of the country lad from the hills of Jerusalem.

The man who gets out of the Hummer is wearing fashionable khaki pants, an imitation of army trousers with four side pockets and two back pockets, and a matching safari jacket. At the distance of one thousand, three hundred and thirty-two steps separating them at this moment it's hard to tell if he is indeed the man in the black cashmere suit from the Irish pub who had brought him on this journey, which would reach its end in one and a half or two hours. The voice that had answered him on the cell phone that morning, after Hanina had warned him that if he showed up with anyone else, the meeting would not take place, and he would never see Winnie again, was without a doubt the lyrical tenor that had been seared into his memory years before, when he had listened to it for hours in recorded conversations.

If so, this Tony is none other than Tino the Syrian, in other words, Adonis. Hanina endeavors to convince himself and get rid of any lingering doubt in his heart, but the heart has its reasons of which reason knows nothing, in the words of the philosopher who according to rumor cut his reflections up with scissors and mixed them up in a box, in order to avoid imposing a forced order on them, so that they would sit in the box in the same muddle as that which exists in our brain, where our thoughts are not arranged in any kind of order either, but rise up from the darkness and disappear back into it, and if you allow your brain to operate in its own way, you never know what thought will surface in the next second. For instance, that very possibly this man, who has just stepped out of the Hummer, has nothing at all to do with the Adonis who murdered Jonas, and if so, are you about to confront someone you didn't know from a bar of soap before your paths crossed on Christmas Eve in New York?

Hanina raises the miniature digital telescope he wears on a strap on his right wrist to his eyes.

The guy, who in the meantime has taken a few steps away from his vehicle, is holding an assault rifle, which looks from a distance like an AKS-74, equipped with tele-scopic sights and an unusually long barrel. Hanina notes that this rifle, when it has a regular barrel sixteen and a half inches long, can kill at a range of 1350 meters, one and a half times the distance separating them now. He trains the miniature telescope on the lower half of the man's body, and discovers that in addition to the assault rifle, he is also carrying a large revolver, in a holster attached to his right thigh. Strapped to his right calf, below the holster, a little above his pseudo military boots, is a black sheath, from which the handle of a hunting knife peeks out. The latest model field glasses hang round his neck. The man armed to the teeth from top to toe goes up to the edge of the canyon to see if he can drive down to the bed of the creek in his car. Hanina presses 9 for speed dial. The guy reaches for the pouch attached to his belt and takes out his cell phone. He puts it to his ear.

Welcome, says Hanina, but we said unarmed.

Climb out of your hole, the guy growls. Show yourself unarmed if you've got the balls.

Hanina emerges from his hiding place behind the yucca plant growing tall as a man on the south bank of the canyon, beneath which winds the dry river bed. He raises his empty hands and waves them, to show the guy he is unarmed.

Tony returns the cell phone to its pouch, and without waiting starts climbing down the steep canyon wall. From time to time he stops to inspect his opponent through his field glasses, as if trying to discover where he is hiding his weapons. Hanina reads his intentions and waves at him with his empty hands. When Tony reaches the bottom of the can-yon, Hanina begins moving towards the open ground of the level plain stretching out on the south side of the canyon, in order to keep a distance of eight hundred meters from his opponent and his automatic weapon with its sniper's sight.

Now that Hanina is on open ground, without even a fold in the earth to hide behind, Tony can see beyond the shadow of a doubt that his opponent isn't carrying a long-barreled rifle or even a submachine gun. He hesitates, as if trying to figure out what kind of trap has been set for him here, but after a minute of hesitation, he appears to make up his mind. In order to forestall any possible surprises Tony holds his rifle at the ready and begins to quickly cross the dry river bed, to close the distance from his unarmed opponent, who at most is carrying a revolver. Hanina too quickens his pace, with the aim of keeping a safe distance of eight hundred meters between them.

From time to time he turns his head to make sure that his opponent isn't stopping to take up a sniper's position. He knows that a skilled sniper equipped with a long-barreled AKS-74 is capable of killing his target at a distance of a thousand meters. But Tony-Adonis is in no hurry to shoot, and he has no reason to be. His eccentric opponent, who had chosen the codename Shylock, and entered the open territory, which constituted an ideal killing ground, empty-handed, now seemed an easy prey. Twelve minutes of fast walking and easy running brings him to the southern edge of the canyon. For a moment he disappears from Hanina's sight, giving him the opportunity to lengthen the distance between them by another two hundred meters, and then Tony's head comes into view.

He appears to be aware of the danger, jumps up quickly and starts running in rapid zigzags until he is at a distance of about a hundred paces from the edge of the canyon, and then drops to the ground and rolls behind a bush overlooking the yucca plant behind which Shylock had first appeared. He inspects the yucca plant through his field glasses, and after making sure that nobody is lying in wait for him there, he turns the glasses onto Shylock, who goes on receding

towards the flat horizon, a solitary figure against the background of the white sky.

Hanina's cell phone starts playing Jingle Bells. Hanina
accepts the call, and the voice of Tony-Tino-Adonis rises
from the instrument:

Hello Shylock. Have you got a cigarette? he asks.

Sorry, says Hanina, I don't smoke.

Pity, says Tony-Adonis. I forgot mine in the car. Maybe
you've got some gum?

I don't have any gum, says Hanina, but I do have some
candy.

What poison are they dipped in? inquires Tony.

Actually I have the kind that you like, says Hanina,
anisette-cinnamon flavor.

Great, says Tony. I see the whore told you what I like.
I'm coming to get them.

The moment Tony starts walking quickly towards him,
Hanina breaks into an easy run, taking care to keep a fixed
distance between himself and the Syrian.

Hey, Shylock, why are you running away? Tony asks
over the phone. You said you wanted to talk to me.

Put down the rifle, the revolver and the knife, and come
empty-handed, says Hanina, and I'll stop running.

It's a little dangerous round here without a weapon, says
Tony.

Really? Are there wild boars here?

What? the Syrian lets out a strangled cry, as if he has
been gored in the stomach.

I thought that after your accident you'd never go hunting again, says Hanina.

What accident? Tino-Adonis's voice tenses over the
phone.

In the Beqaa Valley of Lebanon, says Hanina. Wasn't
that enough for you?

I'll rip you to pieces, whispers the voice on the cell phone, I'll cut open your belly and eat your liver.

Come and do it to me, Tino-Tino-Tino, whispers Hanina in a sexy voice, come and eat my liver. Come and eat my spleen and heart and kidneys. Come and suck me, Tino. I like love that hurts.

The conversation is abruptly cut off. Tino raises his rifle, and Hanina breaks into a zigzagging run. He knows that at any minute he could be hit by a well-aimed shot from the superior firearm. His mind, heart and guts tell him that this is the minute to throw himself to the ground, but his legs have a logic of their own, and they refuse to listen to the chorus of these voices. They break into a joyful run, zigzagging here and there without any order or method. And when the shots don't come, he turns his head back and sees that his foe has overcome the urge to shoot from so great a distance, and instead is pursuing him in order to narrow the range. Presumably he considers a range of five hundred or four hundred meters more effective.

Excellent, whispers Hanina to the wind, run, boy, run!

He starts to run a little faster, but at the same time he is careful not to get too far ahead, so as not to cause the man pursuing him to despair. From time to time he even slows down to a walk, puts his hand on his stomach and bends down a little, to give his pursuer the impression that he losing his strength, which causes Tino to run faster, and when Hanina estimates that the distance between them is shortening dangerously, he resumes running and increases the distance again.

The chase lasts twenty to twenty-five minutes, and then another yucca plant looms up in front of Hanina, standing on the edge of a shallow dip in the ground. This is the moment to slow down to a walk, he says to himself. To tempt Tino into opening fire, in order to test his marksmanship after the exhausting pursuit. He casts a glance behind him. It's happening, he exults. He stretches his hand out in front of him, raising a finger to measure Tino's height. A little over eight hundred meters separate them. Tino drops to his knee and raises the rifle to his shoulder. Give him a second to aim, and another second for the bullet to arrive—he counts 21, 22, and throws himself to the ground behind the yucca, and a burst of seven or eight bullets flies over him and tears the desert silence to shreds. He crawls quickly away from the plant, and rolls down into the little dip in the ground that hides him from his enemy. The right thing at the right time, Shakespeare congratulates himself as a long burst of fire wreaks havoc with the yucca plant. Excellent. The guy is sure that he is still hiding behind the plant.

Go on wasting ammunition, my friend, he whispers to the desert air.

A second and a third burst explore different corners of the plant, tearing through the tongues of the long leaves and digging into the sides of a little hillock three hundred meters away. After three more long bursts silence descends. Hanina cautiously raises his head. Tino is changing the magazine. Before he has time to think, his legs pick him up and start running into the desert. He relies on them to do the right thing, widening the distance between him and the man out to kill him, making his fire ineffective. The bullets whistle past his left ear and he throws himself to the ground.

With lightning speed he whips an ampoule of blood from his pocket and smears it over his shoulder, on his white tee-shirt. He smears another ampoule on his trousers, in the area of the thigh, and stands up bloody with theatre-blood and limps over to a nearby rock, takes shelter behind it, and crawls quickly to the side, behind another rock. A quick glance in the direction of his enemy brings a smile to his lips. The guy is training his field glasses on the first rock.

Swallow the bait, go on, piece of fashionable shit that you've turned into, Hanina urges him, and he swallows it. He sprays the rock and its surroundings with bullets, changes the magazine again, and starts running towards the rocks.

Hanina takes off his shirt and trousers, crawls behind the first rock, which took most of the fire, pulls up handfuls of weeds that look to him like a local variety of wild alfalfa, stuffs his shirt and trousers with them, and arranges the result in the figure of a man curled up behind the rock. He wonders if it really is alfalfa, which actually originated in southwest Asia, in other words our own Middle East, and lent its Arabic name of *alfasfasah* to the Spanish corruption alfalfa, which was adopted in America too, whereas in England the plant is known by another name, let's see—Luce? No, that's *A Comedy of Errors*. Maybe Lucio? *Measure for Measure*? No no...and not Lucentio either, we're not in *The Taming of the Shrew*, maybe Lucetta? No, my dear Gentleman of Verona, let's see, let's see, Luciana? No you're in *A Comedy of Errors* again, not Lucullus, we're not in *Timon*, and not *Julius Caesar*, just a minute—Lucerne, Lucerne! That's the English name for alfalfa. I wonder where it came from. Perhaps the French *luzerne*, that comes from the Provencal *luzerno*, which means a glow-worm, which the French call *ver luisant*...maybe the Provencals gave this name to alfalfa because of the gleam of its seeds, and what's all this got to do with the city of Lucerne in Switzerland, where you kicked to death the partner of this man, who three years later, after the failed assassination attempt against the hunter of wild boars in Lebanon, murdered Jonas, and is now chasing you without knowing who it is that he's pursuing, or perhaps he does know and that's why he came armed to the teeth....

And while these thoughts chase each other in Shakespeare's head, he chooses a stone the size of a man's skull, covers it with his baseball cap, and whispers to it, 'Turn my heart to stone, stone, make me a man of stone with a heart of stone, or I won't be able to do what I have to do', and so saying he attaches it to the neck of his bloodstained tee-shirt. Then he breaks another ampoule of blood from the theatrical accessories store, smears it over his naked shoulder and thigh, and the minute the guy enters the dead zone, his fingers activate his state of the art stopwatch— automatically synchronized by means of a radio wave with the nuclear time-setting center near Grenoble—and sets it to send a warning signal after one hundred and twenty seconds, and his legs lift him from his place, wearing nothing but white underpants and marathon running shoes, and even before he can command them they take off at a rapid run on the path between the low hills leading in the direction of the sun now standing at an angle of forty-five degrees above the horizon line.

When the watch vibrates on his wrist to warn him that the two minutes are up, he stops and looks back. His eyes measure the distance to the rock from which he set off at a run: about eight hundred meters. His armed pursuer has not yet seen him, due to the fold in the ground rising to the height of a man. His legs demand another thirty seconds of fast running, and while his fingers are busy setting the stop-watch again he says: Take me, legs, you are the lifeline connecting me to the world. And again they set out at a fast run.

Thirty seconds of running for survival. He hears Shakespeare's voice commanding his tongue to run freely in his head. Not exactly freely—how would you translate 'this tongue that runs so roundly in thy head'?

Perhaps the right word would be 'smoothly'? He says to Shakespeare. And perhaps 'lightly' would be better.

'Smoothly' has a connotation of dishonesty, but 'lightly' is associated with 'light-headed', 'light-minded', with the giving of a light and frivolous answer to a weighty and hard question. Is that what you're doing now, Hananiah ben Hezekiah ben Gruen? Giving an answer as flighty as water to a grave question which you were asked and to which you had no reply?

What exactly was the question that you asked me in the way in which you lived your life, father?

If you answer it lightly and smoothly, with a tongue running freely and loosely in your head, that head deserves to be crushed and unyoked from the shoulders that have cast off the yoke of duty, Richard the Second warns him, while his legs carry him with a lightness that exceeds even the lightness of his tongue, running round in his head and saying to him:

A fine pair of legs you've raised, legs that feel at home everywhere on earth. Just let them run, and they're at home. On the banks of the Ganges, on the marble steps of an Indian temple, on *hamada* desert soil strewn with pebbles of Nubian sandstone in a North African enemy country—everywhere that you are hated, persecuted, pursued, you're at home, Shylock my friend, leg-man. Let your legs carry you in the wind, let them tell the earth the story of your father's run for life, your father who looked at your hand one morning and said that it had reached the required size, and took you to the hills above the young little village in the forests of the Jerusalem corridor, and gave you your first lesson on the big Parabellum, which he called 'Par' for short, a lesson that opened with words that issued heavily from the tongue in the gray head of the iron man:

A pistol is not a cannon. Not a weapon to aim from a distance and kill. A pistol is a weapon to save life. It is the continuation of your hand, of your finger. Use it only to save your life, or the life of another person who somebody is going to kill.

And if I see someone who wants to kill me from a distance?

Run, said the iron man. For that you have legs. If somebody attacks you, run.

And what about honor, Daddy?

Leave honor to fools. If somebody attacks you, cast off everything, including honor which will only get in your way, and run. If you can, leave all the honor to your pursuer, and he won't catch you easily. But if he does catch up with you, stop, turn to face him, and point your finger at him. How long does it take you? Less than a second. We said that the pistol is a continuation of your finger. Here, take the 'Par' and point at that tree trunk. Don't say to yourself, now I'm going to shoot it, because then you won't shoot in time and you'll miss. Just think about your left hand holding your right hand on the handle, and say to yourself, 'Left, left, left', and let your finger pull the trigger lightly. Let the shot surprise you, and then it will also surprise the person who wants to kill you. Now cock the pistol. You're running. You hear his footsteps behind you. He's coming closer. Stop and...

The stopwatch vibrates on his wrist. Thirty seconds of running and survival.

He stops and looks behind him. The guy is still out of sight. Has he given up and gone back? So soon? Impossible. Wait. Be patient. A little longer. Give him a few more seconds. His head appears behind the rise. He peers suspiciously right and left, he's careful, the cur. Because he's so busy looking around him, and perhaps because of the weariness that is beginning to show its signs, he fails to notice a little pothole and he stumbles and falls and the rifle slips from his grasp. But it isn't over yet. He rises quickly to his feet, wipes the dirt off his hands, rubs them on his trousers like a big fly wiping its feet. He picks up his gun, brushes the

sand off it and holds it ready to shoot. He looks at the rock
behind which three minutes ago you arranged your clothes
stuffed with alfalfa. He approaches it at a crouch. Apparently he's afraid that you're waiting for him there with a
pistol in your hand. Now he stops at a distance of fifty paces
from the rock. He hesitates. Raises the field glasses to his
eyes. Presumably sees the trousers smeared with blood. He
appears to be making up his mind. Then he begins to move
again, very cautiously. He flanks the rock from the south,
approaches his prey with feline steps. Despite the distance,
you can sense his excitement. He never imagined it would
be so easy.

Mister Adonis, you can't imagine yet how hard it's going
to be, you whisper to the desert air, and your legs break into
a limping run. The distance between you is now more than a
thousand meters. Soon he'll realize that his prey has escaped
him, and then he'll raise his eyes and look around him and
discover you limping away from him into the desert. He has
to see that you're limping. You have to entice him to go on
pursuing you. There is nothing that tempts a pursuer to continue his pursuit more than the weakness of his victim.

A burst of rifle fire pierces the silence, but you don't hear
the whistle of the bullets. You stop and look back. The guy,
who discovered his wounded enemy hidden behind the rock,
is standing at a distance of twenty or thirty meters shooting
at him mercilessly. Riddling the local wild alfalfa with one
burst after the other. Then he gets up the courage to approach the rock, and shoots the stuffed clothes again from
a distance of a few meters. Now he goes up and stands over
them. Pokes them with his shoe. Picks up the bloodstained
and bullet-riddled trousers, looks at them disbelievingly and
throws them furiously to the ground. Kicks the shirt and cap
in a rage, and immediately bends down and holds his foot as
if he has been wounded. The stone skull hidden inside the

baseball cap has done its work. Two and half seconds later
a roar of pain reaches your ears. Because of the distance
everything happens as in a movie whose soundtrack is lag-
ging behind the picture. Now a curse uttered two seconds
before in a foreign language reaches your ears. Something
that sounds like 'sakashanya-khashanya'. He goes on hopping round on one foot. He must have really hurt himself.
You can't help yourself. You press 9 again, and wait. The
guy raises his cell phone to his ear.

Sorry, you say, I didn't plan for you to kick the stone.

Get fucked!

There's no one to do it with.

Wait till I catch up with you, Shylock.

You're not my cup of tea, you say apologetically.

You'll rot in the desert, the guy promises.

One of us will, you correct him.

During the entire conversation he tries to locate you, but
for some reason he's looking in the wrong direction.

Look in the direction of the sun, idiot, you suggest.

He turns towards the sun. Shades his eyes with his hand
and discovers the naked figure hobbling at a distance of a
thousand two hundred meters. He raises the field glasses to
inspect his opponent, and sees the blood on his shoulder and
thigh. He overcomes the pain in his foot and breaks into a
rapid run, hoping to catch up quickly with the wounded
Shylock, who goes on running away from him like a duck
with a broken wing.

Excellent, whispers Shakespeare, everything is happening
almost exactly according to the script by Tyrell the Third.

Run, son of a horse, run as fast as you can, and you'll
run out of air faster than we thought.

Keep up the appearance of limping, Tyrell Shlush instructs the hero of his movie, but quicken your pace a little.
Maintain a distance of a thousand meters between you.

After five minutes running, the guy appears to be losing control of his breathing. He goes from running to walking and back to running again. A good sign. He's getting tired. Timber was right: from time to time he raised his left hand and felt his stomach. The heartburn must be burning his throat, the smell of dead meat rising from his upset stomach and filling his mouth. Now is the time to narrow the distance, in order to give him the illusion that he can come within effective range of you. You're entering the dangerous stage of the game. Narrowing the distance will give him hope, but it will also increase his chances of hitting you. If you start being afraid, your legs will start running faster than they should, and he will understand that he's lost and give up the chase. Despite the danger you have to let him come closer to you. This is a nerve-racking stage. You won't be able to stand it if you don't get out of yourself, says Tyrell. We'll shoot the next scene from a helicopter. Imagine that you're seeing the arena now from above.

Go higher. Higher, Tyrell instructs the pilot of the helicopter. That's it. Take the picture, he instructs the cameraman. Two people are moving over the ground below. Pursuer and pursued. Look at everything from this angle. Forget that he's the pursuer. And above all—forget that you're the pursued.

After another five minutes Shylock allows Adonis to narrow the distance to eight hundred meters, in the hope that he'll be tempted to shoot again. The chance he's taking justifies itself. The pursuer stops and aims. The pursued turns his head and discovers that his pursuer is unhappy with his position. He drops to one knee. The pursued lurches to the right and left, to make it difficult for the shooter to get him in his crosshairs. The shot doesn't come. He looks back and discovers the reason: his pursuer is wiping his forehead with the back of his hand. Apparently the sweat is dripping into his eyes and blinding him. The pursued goes on staggering from side to side like a drunk and advancing at a limp. He knows that at this distance only a crack sharpshooter has a chance of hitting a practiced runner like him, and this is the time to start running in a rapid zigzag, he tells himself, exactly half a second before another two bursts split the air a meter or two above his head. He turns to face the shooter and goes on running backwards. The guy aims his rifle from a completely ineffective range. The whistle of a single bullet pierces the air close to his right ear. The pursued falls to the ground. The shooter stands up. He busies himself with his weapon. He ejects the magazine and looks at it. The minute he changes the magazine, get up and start running, the script girl reads Tyrell's instructions.

But what's happening here?

Adonis doesn't change the magazine.

He throws down the rifle. Draws his pistol, cocks it and starts running towards Shylock, lying motionless on the ground.

Don't move, Tyrell instructs his hero. Let him run. Let him come to within two hundred and fifty meters from you. He's running fast, the fool, he's in a hurry to finish you off, to confirm the kill. Let him come a little closer. When I tell you to get up—start running, but as if you took a shot to the head.

How do you run when you took a shot to the head?

I don't know, says the beginning scriptwriter, you're the actor! Invent something! Four, three, two, one—go, Shylock!

The wounded man raises himself from the ground with difficulty, and sets off at a kind of staggering run.

Great! enthuses Tyrell. You're running like a drunk who polished off a bottle of lousy whiskey!

There's no such thing as lousy whiskey, stinking Markus reproves Tyrell the novice scriptwriter, there's only better whiskey.

I don't have the time to argue with you now, the beginning scriptwriter says nervously.

I'm not arguing with you, pronounces Markus, that's a fact.

Enough of the polemics, Hanina silences the antagonists quarreling inside him, you're interfering with my concentration.

He casts a glance behind him.

My acting really is perfect, or perhaps Adonis isn't thinking straight anymore, he notes to himself, because the guy has swallowed the bait of the severely wounded target, and he is running after him as fast as he can with his pistol drawn. You haven't got a choice, you have to put on speed, but not too much, Hanina says to himself. He draws his pursuer behind him for about another twenty minutes, allowing him to slowly narrow the distance between them to two hundred meters. Then he decides to risk letting Tony advance to a range of one hundred meters, on the assumption that he is already exhausted, and his chances of hitting his target at a run are close to zero. The closing of the gap excites the pursuer, who imagines that his prey is about to fall into his hands, and he gathers up the last of his strength and mobilizes for a final, decisive effort to overtake him. This is exactly what the pursued has been waiting for, he increases his speed and opens up the gap between them again, but takes care to do it gradually, so that it will take time for the pursuer to realize that the distance between him and his prey is not only not diminishing, but is even growing, albeit very gradually, a meter to a meter and a half for every minute of running.

They run for another twenty minutes before the pursuer realizes that the distance between them has increased again. This has to drive him crazy, says the pursued to himself. He has to ask himself how a man wounded in the shoulder and the head and limping from a shot in the thigh is able to out-run him. Soon he'll despair of the possibility of overtaking you, and then he'll presumably try to shoot again, but the longer the chase lasts, the less chance he'll have of steadying the pistol in his hand and hitting his target.

And indeed the shot doesn't take long in coming. A bullet whistles past the right ear of the pursued. The next bullet hits the ground a few meters in front of him. He turns his head to make sure that his pursuer doesn't disappear from sight. He sees him standing with his legs apart, aiming and shooting, and shooting, and shooting, but the distance between them has already put his target out of effective range. Nevertheless he doesn't take any chances and goes on running and zigzagging. The next shot misses by far. He turns to face the shooter and sees that he is having second thoughts and has decided to stop shooting. Apparently saving ammunition. Again the legs of the pursued take over from his mind, heart and guts, and they start running in a big circle round the pursuer. Now it is no longer clear who is pursuing and who is being pursued. And again, without he himself having made a decision, his legs begin to narrow the radius of the circle. His head tells him that perhaps he should save his strength and take a rest from the running, but his legs refuse to stop, and they know what they're do-ing. The owner of the pistol begins to sense the ring gradual-ly tightening around him and his nerves can't stand the pres-sure. He raises the pistol and shoots another bullet, which whistles behind the nape of the target, who pretends that he has been hit. He falls to the ground and writhes in the dirt.

As if he has learnt nothing from everything that has happened so far, the shooter rushes towards his victim. This time—he presumably says to himself—the shot went home.

In the time you still have left to live, says Shylock to his pursuer, I'm going to be your nightmare.

The leg-man's legs raise him from the ground in a sudden bound and break into a run. The pursuer stops for a minute, thunderstruck, unable to believe his eyes. He looks around him. Maybe he'll abandon this crazy chase and go back to his Hummer. But how to get back? Where did he come from? Where should he turn? Where is he? In the middle of the desert. No, he won't go back. A man armed with a pistol and a hunting knife doesn't run away from a man with empty hands. The short rest from the running has helped him too. He feels reinvigorated. He'll get him in the end. And even if they land up in hand to hand combat, he still has a dagger and he knows how to use it.

He's starting to run again. Now you have to be very careful not to make him despair, commands Tyrell Shlush.

I'll try, promises the double marathon runner, whose legs set out again.

The chase goes on for some time, until the pursuer realizes that he isn't catching up with his prey, and he slows down to a walk, and the movements of his body and arms show clearly that he is out of breath, and apparently the pain in his liver is getting worse, because his left hand goes frequently to the right side of his abdomen, while his right hand, holding the pistol, dangles at his side. This is the moment to begin closing the circle of death around him again, say the legs of the pursued, which have already set out on their circular route in ever decreasing radii.

The man with the pistol apparently understands that his fate is sealed. He comes to a standstill. Wonders whether to shoot or not. The legs of his quarry go into neutral, running very lightly on the spot, keeping the engine warm, ready to race again, which is exactly what they do the second the pistol is raised and a bullet whistles again behind the nape of the pursued, who casts a glance at the shooter, and suddenly has the impression that the latter is pressing the trigger again and again, and nothing happens. Has he run out of ammunition, or is he tricking you? The leg-man's mind has no answer to this question, but his legs are already running in ever smaller circles, tightening the noose round his pursuer, who suddenly picks up his heels and begins to flee in a straight line across the desert plateau strewn with fist-sized stones.

The tables are turned, say the legs of the pursued who has become the pursuer, growing lighter with every step. This is the moment to go back to being who I am—strange words sing in him:

I am Hanina ben Raya and Salek Rugashov from the Judean hills,
I am Hanina ben Raya and Salek—the man of legs!

Hanina's legs abandon the circle and set out in pursuit of the limping Tino-Adonis, who looks as if a wild boar has really gored him in the liver, but judging by the pace at which the leg-man's legs are moving, it seems that they are determined to drag the chase out as long as possible, until Adonis is utterly exhausted. And indeed, when Adonis looks back and discovers that the distance between him and his pursuer isn't decreasing, and may even be growing—hope of escaping his prey-turned-hunter springs up in him anew, and in the middle of his desperate flight his left hand goes to his pockets and examines them one after the other, and now the right hand transfers the pistol to the left, and once it is free it begins to rummage in the pockets on the right side of his stylish, pseudo-military trousers, and by now it is clear that Adonis is looking for a new magazine, and that he doesn't remember which pocket he put it in when he got out of the black Hummer, and it seems that the magazine is not to be found in any of the six trouser pockets, which are examined one by one as he runs, nor in his shirt pockets, which he is examining at this very minute, no, the spare magazine is nowhere to be found, and the question is whether the previous squeezing of the trigger was an act, to show that there were no more bullets left in the pistol, or whether this is in fact the case, and the question will be answered when the owner of the pistol reaches the end of his tether—which according to the way he looks now, will be in another twenty minutes, or half an hour at the most.

In the meantime they run.

Tino knows that he will remain alive as long as he runs, and as long as there is some distance between him and Shylock, the pursuer running after him in white underpants and yelling:

Wait till I get my hands on you, Anton, Adonas! I'll put out both your eyes and cut out your tongue with your hunting knife, and then I'll sit next to you and sing you arias by Donizetti until the blood drains out of your body.

These words have their effect. Adonas goes on running, in spite of his throat cracked with dryness, in spite of his burning lungs, sucking in air with a weird kind of screech, and letting it out with a sob, in spite of the redhot skewer piercing his liver. He knows that as soon as the man in underpants lays hands on him, the countdown will begin of the last seconds and fractions of seconds left to him in which to breathe the dry desert air. For a moment, without stopping, he tries to send his right hand to the haft of the dagger strapped to his calf, but the hand fails to get a grip, and he knows that he must not stop, and so he runs on.

As long as he has the strength, he runs. Stumbling and falling, he runs, his gaping mouth gasping for air like a fish on dry land, his throat emitting grunts and whistles like those of a boiling kettle.

Hanina runs two steps behind him—a distance sufficient for a spring and a kick, if Tino should suddenly stop and raise his pistol to shoot, or if he draws his knife.

But Tino doesn't stop.

On the contrary.

Suddenly he puts on speed. The cunning bastard. Has he been keeping his strength in reserve? Again he transfers the pistol to his left hand, and tries to take hold of the haft of the dagger with his right hand. Hanina has to keep him within range of a bound and a kick. He quickens his pace. He listens to the breathing of the man who wants to kill him. He thinks he can hear a kind of bubbling. Yes. No doubt of it. The bubbling of liquids. The guy has lost all control of his breathing. His lungs are bursting and filling with liquids. They're getting puffy. In a minute he'll stop running and start walking. Don't let him. Push him. He's started walking. Hanina's hand reaches out and pushes his shoulder.

Run! he roars in his ear. Run, you bastard, run!

The touch of the strange hand on his back momentarily instills new strength in Adonas, his feet begin to pound the ground again.

This is the moment to kick the pistol. Hanina leaps and his right leg shoots forward. The force of the kick throws the hand of the running man up into the air and the pistol flies through the air and lands behind the pair, who go on running.

I told you to come unarmed, whispers Hanina, but you didn't listen.

And again he pushes him, and again and again, refusing to let him slow down.

No, pal, you're not going to stop now, there's no more stopping, now we run, my friend, if you need a push from behind you'll get as many as you like, but stopping isn't an option, run, lover boy, run, until your heart bursts. This is your death run, pal. Have you ever heard of a death run? That's what we're doing now, friend. And he surprises himself and calls his enemy all kinds of pet names:

Run, my sweet. Run, my love. Run, my dear. Here's another push, here's another kick in the ass, go on, there's no stopping, darling, none, honey, none, pick up your feet, yes, go on, here's an uphill stretch, never mind, onwards and upwards—

Heave-ho! he yells savagely behind Adonas's back.

Imagine that this foot up your bum is the saddle of a horse! shouts Shakespeare in savage glee:

Imagine that you run on horseback up the hill,
If you don't wish
That I run it into you up to the hilt.

Run even if you're out of breath—he goes on pushing the man whose legs are buckling under him—even if your heart is a tom-tom drum and the blood in the veins of your neck is Niagara Falls!

And then the man suddenly stops in his tracks and spins around, and his hands reach out to hold onto some imaginary support, and they wave in the air like the legs of a slaughtered beast, and he loses his balance and his body spreads over the ground like a rag.

The leg-man's legs remember that stopping is forbidden, and they go on running on the spot round the body writhing and twitching on the ground, death-rattles and frothing blood gushing from its gaping wound of a mouth.

Hanina runs in a circle, thinking about the ruinous destruction raging now like an avalanche in the cells of the heart and brain of the vicious bastard whose back arches for a moment, as if he wants to get up in a last effort to hang onto the life draining out of him—and then he crumples and struggles no longer, and only his eyes open wide and gaze in terror at the man in the white underpants skipping lightly round him, and in the pain cutting through his chest with a red-hot blade, and the suffocation overtaking his swollen lungs, he tries to say something to this man

62

Who is bending over him and contemplating him curiously. Trying to decipher this clean-shaven face. To imagine a black beard covering most of the area of his cheeks. Is this the man? Is this face that he sees before him the result of plastic surgery, which changed the handsome face of Adonis beyond recognition? Is this face, distorted now in the terrible effort to breathe, a savage mask? The dying man's feet stamp the ground, wave in the air. His throat snorts. His hand shakes as it tries to reach his chest torn apart by pain. This is the man that only two hours ago was still running and shooting deadly bursts of fire from his state of the art assault rifle, and only a short time before was still aiming his pistol—now he lies here, purged of every killer instinct, struggling open-mouthed against suffocation, knowing with the vestiges of his consciousness that there is no one to help him.

And out of the fog descending on his senses he stares with frightened, astonished eyes at the hairy man bending over him and loosening the straps holding the sheath of the dagger to the calf of his right leg. And his eyes suddenly clear when he sees him draw the dagger from its sheath and examine its blade. Is he about to plunge it into his heart?

Hanina lays the dagger on the ground, a little distance from the dying man. He opens the buttons of his safari shirt, and pulls it out from under his body without touching him. His abdomen is exposed, full of scars. Hanina inspects them from close up. He counts three the size of a plum, and five smaller ones, the size of an olive. Scars typical of wounds from the shrapnel of a hunting gun, he says to himself.

Antonaus? He says out loud.

The dying man opens his eyes again.

Tino? Hanina tries the man's nickname.

Something stirs in the dying man's eyes, which focus on Hanina's eyes.

You deserve to die, Hanina says to him, and you know why, but I won't be your executor. I won't touch you with the tip of my finger and I won't help you to die. You'll do all the work of dying yourself. And I'll stay here by your side to make sure you finish the job.

In the meantime Hanina undoes the straps of the holster of the pistol hugging Tino's thigh, and then he unbuttons his trousers and pulls them of him. He sits up and examines the label and laughs.

Armani! he says. Who were you trying to impress here?

He pulls the trousers onto him, and they fit him as if they were made for him. He puts on the safari jacket and buttons it up at his leisure, button after button. He rummages in the pockets, takes out the cell phone, all kinds of papers which he inspects and puts back, and a pistol magazine. He examines it. It's loaded. On the side of the magazine there are two apertures. Next to the upper aperture the number 10 is engraved, and next to the lower one the number 15. The gilt body of a cartridge is visible through the lower aperture. So there are fifteen cartridges in the magazine. He waves it in front of the dying man's eyes and smiles at him sympathetically.

You were too eager, he says. When you set out to kill a man you shouldn't be too eager.

Now he notices that the trousers are a little too long for him. He bends down and makes two folds. He regards himself in his new safari suit and remembers the red book that found its way into his hands on some transatlantic flight. A German book, by some contemporary philosopher, who wrote something strange about jumping through a hoop of fire and the moment when some change of costume, pregnant with meaning, takes place. The obscure sentence comes back to him now, and he understands it in his own way.

The dying man stripped of his shirt and trousers is still twitching on the ground, the intervals between one gasping breath and the next growing longer all the time, and the thought crosses Hanina's mind that now he looks like someone dressed for running. If they find the body, dressed in fashionable boxer shorts and brand-name sport shoes, the pathological examination will confirm the assumption that the innocent-looking man set on a desert run and died of a massive heart attack, accompanied by a collapse of all the systems of his body. Which is actually the truth, he sums up to himself.

The screech of a bird makes him raise his eyes to the sky. High above them a black bird with a huge wing span and a bald neck circles. Some kind of black hawk. When the living man leaves the dead man lying on the ground the bird will land close to the body, inspect it carefully to make sure it isn't a trap, and go to work. Other raptors seeing him land will come down after him, and even before the corpse begins to go cold, there will be six or seven birds of prey here, tearing the flesh which was pampered and nourished by the choicest foods and wines, and is presumably as sweet and tender as the calves fed on beer in the Japanese city of Kobe famous for its meat—and while the vultures are still busy tearing off strips of flesh the wolves and coyotes and buzzards and all the other sanitary workers of nature will appear and wait their turn, and one after the other they will pick clean the leavings of those who went before, and in two or three days' time the bare bones will gleam in the sun, and only the expensive boxer shorts by Hugo Boss and the fine shoes by Gucci will bear witness to the fact that what was once a man of superior taste is lying here in the desert.

63

He turns to go back, dressed in the man's expensive clothes. The wind, carrying grains of sand like a fine fur over the surface of the desert, increases in strength and brings heavy clouds from beyond the horizon. The first flash of lightning splits the darkening distance, and seconds later there is an explosion of dull, heavy thunder. Hanina reaches the car just as the first big, heavy drops begin to fall, and suddenly a deluge pours down from the sky.

In the trouser pocket he finds a bunch of keys and recognizes the head of an ignition immobilizer. He places it in its housing next to the steering wheel, starts the clumsy, powerful car and drives into the curtains of rain. He drives for about an hour on empty godforsaken roads and arrives at a roadside inn, the lower half of whose walls are made of stone, and the upper half of wood. He drives into a big, deserted parking lot in front of the inn, which at first glance seems to be abandoned. He goes up to the door and tries the handle. The door opens, and he enters a deserted hall. He sits down at a table and stretches his limbs. The sound of clogs comes from behind the door next to the bar, and a buxom, sloppily dressed young woman appears.

Hello, she drawls in a lazy voice, can I help you?

I need a drink, he says.

You can get a drink, she says, but the kitchen's closed.

What kind of whiskey do you have, he asks.

I don't know, she apologizes, I'm not a professional bartender. I'm a student. I came here on my vacation, to make a bit of money. If you're in luck there may be a bottle left—if the cook hasn't polished it all off.

Bring me what you've got, he says.

She goes to the bar at the end of the hall, bends under the counter, and while she's busy opening and shutting cupboard doors, he takes the cell phone and makes a call.

64

I don't like talking to answering machines either, Bridget's recorded voice says, so make it short.

Hi, bye, he says and hangs up.

He dials another number. Six rings, and the answering machine comes on.

I'm at sea till the end of the week. If there's no alternative, leave a message.

There's an alternative, he says and hangs up.

He punches in another number, and is answered by a recorded message again:

I'm in Eilat. Everything's great, he hears the happiness in Yadanuga's recorded voice.

Friend, he says, the Belgian pathologist was a double agent. You can wipe your ass with his report.

He punches in a final number.

Hi, this is Winnie. Leave your number and I'll get back to you as soon as I can.

You're a free person, he says. Do what you want with it.

When he raises his eyes, she's standing in front of him with a bottle of nine-year-old Knob Creek Kentucky Straight Bourbon in her hand. She puts the bottle and a glass down on the table and apologizes:

I hope this is good enough for you. Our cook had an accident. That's why the kitchen's closed. But if you like I can make you an omelet.

Thanks, he says, whiskey's fine.

April, 2004

Translated by Dalya Bilu